TECH MAGE

MAGITECH CHRONICLES BOOK 1

CHRIS FOX

CHRIS FOX WRITES LLC.

ISBN: 1976382831
ISBN-13: 978-1976382833

For Margaret Weis & Tracy Hickman.
You inspired so many of us.

Want to know when **Void Wyrm: Magitech Chronicles Book 2** goes live?

Sign up to the mailing list!

Check out MagitechChronicles.com for book releases, lore, artwork, and more!

PROLOGUE

Voria hopped from the ramp before the transport had completed its landing. She clung tightly to her jacket as the sudden wind buffeted her. Voria didn't let it deter her, leaning into the gale as she crossed the landing pad. Like everything in the Tender's palace, the landing pad was cut from shayawood, taken from the corpse of the goddess herself.

That wood shone in the sun, whorls of brown and red, drinking in the sunlight. Voria had never been this close to the palace, and had never seen so much shayawood. It had been designed to awe, and it succeeded.

The view only reinforced that awe. The palace floated in the sky over the world of Shaya and afforded a magnificent view of the goddess herself. Her body stabbed into the sky, the immense redwood branches scraping the upper atmosphere. A multitude of tiny starships flitted back and forth between them like flocks of tiny birds.

Were a single limb to break, it would doom the cities clustered at the base of the mighty tree. That was the dilemma of Shaya. The goddess's lingering energies created a breathable atmosphere around her body, but if you left that radius the rest of the moon was barren and inhospitable. They needed her body to survive, but that body could also destroy them.

Voria wove a path through the wind, snaking her way to a pair of wide palace doors. They were flanked by a pair of war mages, each encased in golden Mark VIII spellarmor. They cradled menacing black spellrifles, the barrels lined with spell amplification sigils. Voria could make out nothing of their faces behind the mirrored faceplates.

To her surprise, both war mages snapped to attention when she approached.

"Major," boomed a male voice from the mage on the right. "The Tender is expecting you. She's made the... unusual request that you be allowed to carry your weapons, and that you not be searched."

"What is it you think I'd be hiding, exactly? All I'm carrying is a spellpistol. If the Tender wants to wipe me from existence, no spell I'm going to cast will make any difference," Voria countered. She waved at the doors. "Let's get this over with. I have a war to fight, and I don't have time for politics."

The guards stepped aside, snapping back to attention. Voria eyed them suspiciously as she passed, trying to understand the reason for their respectful behavior. The Confederate Military was a joke to Shayan nobility. War mages did not salute officers, rank non-withstanding. Even her training as a true mage wouldn't warrant that kind of respect.

She entered a spacious greeting room lined with hovercouches. A blue one floated in her direction, nudging her hip in invitation. Voria shoved it away, and continued toward the room's only occupant. The Tender stood next to a golden railing, shayawood vines snaking around it. Shaya's branches were visible behind her, though the woman herself commanded attention.

Her hair shone in the sun, capturing all the colors of autumn. Reds and yellows and golds all danced through her hair, changing as the light shifted. It poured down her back in a molten river, contrasting beautifully with the Tender's golden ceremonial armor.

Voria had often been called pretty, but she knew she was a frumpy matron next to the Tender. Though, in Voria's defense, she didn't have the blood of a goddess to magically enhance her beauty.

"Welcome, daughter," the Tender said, beaming a smile as she strode gracefully from the railing. "Thank you for coming so quickly."

"Just because you slept with my father doesn't make you my mother," Voria countered flatly. She schooled her features, attempting to hide the pleasure she took from needling this woman.

The Tender raised a delicate eyebrow, stopping a meter away. She frowned disapprovingly, and even that was done beautifully. "I meant figuratively, daughter."

"Why did you call me here?" Voria demanded. She'd fluster this woman if it killed her.

"Because this, all of this, will be wiped away unless you prevent it." The Tender stretched an arm to indicate Shaya and the cities below her. She smiled warmly, as if she'd just related a bit of political gossip. "Would you like some lifewine? Or an infused apple?"

The Tender crooked a finger, and a crystal ewer floated over to Voria. Golden liquid swirled within, and Voria could feel the power pulsing from it. It was, for her people at least, literal life. But drinking it would cause her eyes to glow, revealing her true nature for hours.

"No, thank you." Voria stepped away from the ewer and frowned at the Tender. "Certainly your time must be valuable. You've dropped a melodramatic statement about Shaya being destroyed. Please tell me that's just hyperbole."

"I am being quite literal, I'm afraid. If you do not fulfill your role in the struggle against Krox, then all of this will be wiped away," the Tender explained. She sighed...prettily. "Please, come with me."

"Fine." Voria crossed her arms, eyeing the Tender as the woman led her from the railing.

The chamber curved around the outside of the palace for nearly a hundred meters, finally ending at a pair of tall double doors. Unlike most of the palace, these were not shayawood. They were covered in a multicolored mural depicting Shaya herself.

Voria leaned closer, realizing that the door was covered in thousands of tiny scales. Dragon scales, each of incalculable worth. They glowed with their own inner fire and their combined magic brought the mural to life. Branches swayed as an invisible wind rippled over the doors.

The Tender placed a palm on each door, then pushed gently inward. The doors opened of their own accord, sliding away to reveal a dark chamber. Voria followed the Tender inside and waited impatiently for her eyes to adjust.

The doors slammed shut behind them, and a bonfire sprang into existence near the center of the room. The flames were pure blue, edged in white. Their sudden light illuminated sigils emblazoned on the floor in a circle around the flame. A ritual circle, possibly the most powerful that Voria had ever witnessed.

"What am I seeing?" Voria asked, abandoning all attempts to fluster the Tender. She'd fought in the Confederate Marines for four decades, and had never seen magic on this scale before. The immensity of the power humbled her.

"This is the Mirror of Shaya. It is an eldimagus for finding and interpreting auguries. You are familiar with auguries?" the Tender asked, walking gracefully to stand just outside the magical circle. The flame brightened at her approach, like a pet preening for an owner.

"Conceptually. They're visions of a possible future, dreamed by a dead god," Voria ventured. Divination wasn't one of her strong suits, though she was proficient enough with the basics.

"Some auguries are," the Tender corrected gently. "Some were created by living gods, before the moment of their death. These auguries are of immense power, designed to shape the future for hundreds or even thousands of millennia. I've spent the last several years studying just such an augury."

"And you feel that has something to do with me?" Voria raised an eyebrow.

"I'll allow you to judge for yourself." The Tender smiled mischievously, then turned to the ritual circle. She sketched the scarlet sigil for *fire*, and a pinkish one for *dream*.

The mirror flared and immense magical strength gathered within the light. It resolved into an image, so lifelike that Voria recoiled. A vast force hovered in the void, its body comprised of stars, its eyes supernovas. The creature was a living galaxy, a god that made every god or goddess Voria had encountered seem a tiny speck.

"What is that thing?" she whispered, unable to drag her gaze from the vision.

"That is Krox," the Tender answered. She rested a hand on Voria's arm, and warmth pulsed into her. It eased the fear the image had evoked, though not the horror that something so alien could exist. "The forces you fight, what you call 'the Krox', are his children. And they are united in a singular purpose, the resurrection of their dark father. This augury is a desperate cry from the past. It's meant to give us the tools necessary to stop his return. If we fail in this, the cost is incalculable."

Voria studied the flames, silently digesting what the Tender had just said. After several moments another image flickered into view. An enormous skull floated in orbit over a barren world. Long, dark horns spiraled from the temples, and purplish flames danced in the eye sockets and mouth.

"That's the Skull of Xal," Voria ventured, recognizing the Catalyst.

The face of a young man superimposed itself over the the flames, covering the image of the skull. The hard eyes and strong jaw made him look older than he probably was. He held a sword loosely in one hand and dark lightning crackled from his hand into the blade.

"What am I seeing?" Voria asked. She recognized the spell, basic void lightning. But she had no idea why she was seeing it.

"This man will be instrumental in helping you triumph in your impending struggle," the Tender offered. The light of the flames reflected off her eyes as she studied the images still appearing. "He can be found at the Skull of Xal, along with something else vital to the coming battle."

"You mentioned a coming battle twice. That makes me think you've got the wrong person." Voria eyed the double doors, but didn't attempt to leave. "The *Wyrm Hunter* is low on munitions. We're down to a handful of tech mages, and no other true mage besides myself. We have no potions, and the Marines sent from Ternus have no battle experience. The worst part? We're down to six support crew. Six people, to keep an entire battleship flying. Trust me. Whatever battle this augury thinks I'm a part of, it's got the wrong person. *Hunter* should be in space dock, not leading a charge."

"I understand your reluctance, but I assure you that you are the person this augury is meant for." The Tender's rebuke was gentle, but still a rebuke.

Voria licked her lips, forcing herself to be silent as she watched the augury. It now showed a familiar man, one of her tech mages. "That's Specialist Bord."

The Tender said nothing, watching intently as the images continued. The view zoomed out to show Bord's surroundings. He stood next to a golden urn the size of a tank. The surface was covered in sigils, and a sickly grey glow came from the top.

"I do not know how, but this 'Bord' will be instrumental as well, in a different way. You will need both the men displayed in order to stop her," the Tender's voice whispered.

"Her?" Voria asked, blinking.

The augury shifted again. This time the flames showed a gargantuan dragon, floating in orbit over a blue-white world. Its leathery wings stretched out to either side and its head reared back. The dragon breathed a cone of white mist that billowed out around a Ternus space station.

"Nebiat," Voria snarled. Her eyes narrowed as she studied the ancient dragon, a full Void Wyrm. The dark scales and spiked tail were unmistakable. She ground her teeth, acid rising in her stomach. She'd do anything to kill that Wyrm. Anything.

"I thought you'd recognize her. Whoever created this augury believes you are the one person strong enough to stop her." The Tender stretched out a hand and rested it on

Voria's jacket. Pleasant warmth flowed into her. Voria wished she'd stop doing that. "I know that you lack the resources you need. But I also know that you are needed. If you will not do this, then the Krox will burn another world. You can stop that, Voria, though the personal cost will be high."

"Isn't it always?" Voria straightened her jacket, already turning to the door. "I'll find a way to stop Nebiat, but that will be a whole lot easier with Inuran weaponry. They're hunting for Kazon. If I can find him before anyone else, the Consortium will provide me with enough material to pursue your augury. Help me find him, and I'll help you fulfill it."

"I already have." The Tender turned back to the flames as the augury began to repeat. "Study the augury carefully, Major. There are many layers to be delved, including Kazon's whereabouts. Pursuing the augury will lead you to him."

1

TECH DEMONS

Aran lurched awake as the transport entered free fall. Gravity pulled him upward, jerking him to the limits allowed by his restraints. The ship shook violently, the thin lights flickering for several moments before returning to a steady illumination.

"Wake up," a female voice bellowed. The speaker moved to stand in front of Aran, and he realized groggily that he was surrounded by other men and women in restraints.

The chrome harnesses pinned their wrists between their legs, preventing them from standing or defending themselves. Glowing blue manacles attached his wrists to the harness, and he could feel their heat even through the armored gauntlets. He wore some sort of environmental armor, the metal scarred and pitted from long use.

"Good, the sleep spell is wearing off." The speaker wore a suit of form-fitting body armor, much higher quality than Aran's. Her helmet was tucked under one arm and the other hand wrested on a pistol belted at her side. A river of dark hair spilled down both shoulders. "You're probably feeling some grogginess. That's the after effects of the mind-wipe.

Each of you have been imprinted with a name. That will be the *only* thing you can remember. We've given it to you, because otherwise slaves tend to have psychotic breaks."

Aran probed mentally, reaching for anything. He couldn't remember how he'd gotten here, or what he'd had for breakfast. Or where he'd been born. There was a...haze over the part of his mind where those things should be. His name was, quite literally, the only thing he could remember.

A beefy man on Aran's right struggled violently against his bonds. "Listen little girl, you'd better let me out of this chair, or I'll fu—."

The woman withdrew her pistol and aimed it at the beefy man. White sigils flared to life up and down the barrel, and dark energy built inside the weapon.

The weapon hummed, discharging a bolt of white-hot flame toward his chest. It cored him through the heart, filling the chamber with the scent of cooked meat. His body twitched once and then he died silently.

"Nara, you began the demonstration without me," called an amused male voice. It came from out of Aran's field of view, but the booted footsteps approached until Aran got a glimpse of the speaker. "You know how much I hate missing it. This is my favorite part."

A tall, slender man walked over to the woman who'd executed the beefy man. He wore jet-black environmental armor, and had a stylized dragon helm clutched under his arm. One of his eyes had been replaced with a glittering ruby, and his bald skull was oiled to a mirrored sheen. His right gauntlet was larger than his left, and studded with glowing rubies and sapphires.

Aran could sense...something coming from the gauntlet. A familiar resonance that danced elusively out of reach.

A cluster of armored figures entered the room behind

the one-eyed man. They fanned out, taking up relaxed positions along the far wall. Each guard carried a rifle similar to the pistol the woman had fired. Blue-white sigils lined the barrels, though they appeared inactive at the moment.

"I'm sorry, Master Yorrak," the woman he'd called Nara finally replied. She gave a deep bow, which she held for several seconds. Finally she straightened. "This prisoner... volunteered. And I know that we are pressed for time. I thought it prudent to educate this batch quickly."

"Efficient as always. I'll handle the rest of the orientation." Yorrak patted her cheek patronizingly, then turned toward the slaves. Nara shot him a hateful glare, but he seemed oblivious. "Good morning, slaves. My name is Yorrak, true mage and pilot of this vessel. I'm going to make this very simple. In a moment we'll be landing. When we do, your restraints will be removed. There is a rack of rifles near the door. Take one, and step outside. Nara and her squad will lead you beyond that. Obey her orders without question, or meet the same fate as our late friend here." Yorrak moved to the corpse, prodding it with a finger.

"Are there any questions?" he asked, rounding on them.

"Where are we?" Aran rasped. His throat burned, and he blinked sweat from his eyes.

"The Skull of Xal, one of the more remote, and most powerful, Catalysts in this sector," Yorrak proclaimed, thrusting his arms dramatically into the air. "You're about to be granted a wonderful opportunity. If you survive, you will become a tech mage. Those of you who apply yourselves might even rise to the rank of true mage, one day. That will increase your relative value, and I treat my mages very well. Now, I'll leave you in Nara's capable hands. I'll pick up any survivors in the second ocular cavity. You have two hours. Oh and one more thing. If

Nara isn't with you when you exit the Catalyst, I'll disintegrate the lot of you."

Yorrak strode past Aran, eyeing the slaves gleefully as he exited. What a sadistic bastard. Aran caught a brief glimpse of the hallway before the door hissed shut behind him, but saw nothing that helped his current situation. The transport, if it was a transport, shuddered violently for several moments, then finally stabilized.

"If you listen to me, you have a very high chance of survival," Nara said, drawing their collective attention. She stepped into the light, affording his first real look at her. She had liquid brown eyes, and a light dusting of freckles across her entire face. She was pretty enough that Aran understood why she'd been picked to lead them. The whole girl next door thing made them that much more likely to trust her. "In a moment I'm going to release your restraints. You'll arm yourself from the rack, and then move outside. Some of you might be tempted to attack us. Before you do, consider your options. It's in both our best interests for you to survive. If you die, Yorrak has less slaves. You don't want to die, and we don't want you dead."

Her argument made sense, though Aran detested the idea of working with his captors. He didn't know anything about them, or about himself really. Was he a hardened criminal? Or just some idiot in the wrong place, at the wrong time? It was just...gone. All of it. Only his name remained, and even that might not be real.

The restraints whirred, and the harness released him. The manacles were still around his wrists, but the chain linking them together had disappeared. Aran rose to his feet and the other prisoners did the same, each looking warily at the others. It seemed an effective tactic on the part of their captors. Since none of them knew each other, they weren't likely to cooperate. That made mutiny a much lower risk.

Aran moved to the rack along the side of the wall, picking up the first rifle. It had a heavy stock, and a long, ugly barrel. The metal was scored and scratched, though the action worked smoothly. He scanned the base of the rack, bending to scoop up two more magazines. He had no idea what he'd need the weapon for, but more rounds was rarely a bad thing.

Other slaves moved to take weapons, the closest a tall man with a thick, black beard. He eyed Aran warily, moving to the wall two meters away.

Nara walked to the rear of the room and slapped a large red button. A klaxon sounded, and a ramp slowly lowered. A chill wind howled up the ramp, dropping the temperature instantly.

"Outside, all of you. Now!" Nara's words stirred the slaves into action, and they began filing down the ramp. Aran moved in the middle of the pack, and found himself next to the bearded man.

"Watch my back?" he asked, eyeing the bearded man sidelong. His arms were corded with muscle, and his eyes glittered with intelligence.

"Do the same for me?" the man answered, eyeing Aran in a similar way.

"Done." Aran pivoted slightly as he walked down the ramp, angling his firing arc to slightly overlap with the bearded man. The man echoed the motion. "What name did they give you?"

"Kaz. How about you?"

"Aran." The ramp deposited them onto a bleached white hill. A hellish purple glow came from somewhere beyond the ridge ahead of them, as bright as any sun. Aran's teeth began to chatter, and his breath misted heavily in the air.

"The cold isn't life threatening, if you keep moving," Nara called. Her guards fanned out around her, covering the slaves with their strange rifles. Something about the weapons tickled at the back of his mind, but the haze muddied the sense of familiarity. "Form two groups, one on either side of the ramp."

The guards broke into groups, pushing slaves into two lines. Aran moved quickly to the one on the right, and the bearded man followed.

"Do you have any idea where we are?" Kaz asked. Aran followed his gaze, taking in their surroundings.

A high ridge prevented him from seeing beyond the closest hills. The rock reminded him uncomfortably of bone, its porous surface just the right shade of pale white.

The purplish glow flared suddenly and Aran raised a hand to shield his eyes. Harsh, guttural voices boomed in the distance, and he heard the rhythmic pounding of metal on stone.

"Those," Nara began with a yell, "are tech demons. This is their territory, and they will defend it with their lives. Your job is to kill them, without dying yourself. Follow my orders, and we'll all get out of this safely."

A brutish creature leapt into view at the top of the ridge. Twin horns spiraled out from a thick forehead and it clenched and unclenched wickedly curved claws. It stared down at them with flaming eyes, the same hue as the glow behind it. The creature wore dark armor, not unlike the armor Nara and her guards had.

"Fire!" Nara roared.

2

USED

Aran reacted to Nara's command, snapping the rifle to his shoulder and sighting down the barrel. He'd guess the demon to be about seventy-five meters away, but it was hard to judge distance without knowing how large the thing was.

The rifle kicked into his shoulder, firing a three round burst that echoed off the rocks around them. The rounds peppered the demon's left side but only pinged off armor. Kaz snapped up his rifle as well, but the shots went wide. Other slaves fired, the chattering of weapons fire lighting up the area around them as they added to the thick stench of gunpowder.

All their collective fury accomplished nothing. The rounds, even those that hit the demon directly, simply ricocheted off. The demon's face split into a wide grin, revealing a sea of narrow fangs. It leapt from its perch, bat-like wings flaring behind it as it sailed in their direction.

Only then did Aran realize the creature carried a rifle too. The weapon was heavier than their own rifles, and the fat barrel was ringed with red sigils, like the rifles their captors used.

"That thing is packing a spellcannon. Tech mages, end him!" Nara barked, stabbing a finger at the descending demon.

Too late. The creature raised the cannon, and the sigils along the barrel flared to brilliant life. The cannon kicked back, and fired a blob of darkness. The blob expanded outwards, bursting into thousands of fragments. The fragments rained down on the other group of slaves, and their armor began to smoke and hiss.

They frantically tore at the armor, but within moments the hungry magic had eaten through...first metal and then flesh. One by one they slumped to the bleached stone, groaning out their last.

The guards around Nara, the ones she'd called tech mages, opened up with their spellrifles. Blue and white sigils flared, and bolts of superheated flame peppered the demon. The bolts superheated the armor wherever they hit, painting it an angry red. The fire bolts met with more success against the demon itself, and it shrieked as a large chunk of its neck burned away.

"This way," Aran roared, sprinting low to the left, into the demon's blind spot. He dropped to one knee behind a fold of rock and sighted down the barrel at the demon. He kept his finger off the trigger, though.

Kaz slid down next to him. "You have a plan?"

"Yeah, let those bastards deal with it. They're using us as fodder. There's no way we can hurt that thing with the crap rifles they gave us." Aran plastered himself against the rock, its craggy surface bitterly cold even through his armor.

Nara strode from her ranks raising two fingers. She began sketching in the air, and wherever her finger passed a residue of multicolored light was left behind. The light formed sigils, which swam in and out of Aran's vision. The more he focused on any particular one, the more blurry it became.

The sigils began to swirl in interlocking patterns of pale grey, and a dark, ocean blue. They were drawn together with a sudden thunderclap, then exploded outward in a wide fan. Fist sized balls of swirling energy shot toward several of the surviving slaves, each ball slamming into their backs. The energy passed through the armor, disappearing.

Each person hit by a ball began to grow, their armor growing with them. Over the next few heartbeats they doubled in size, and now stood shoulder to shoulder with the demon.

It did not seem impressed.

The demon leapt forward and wrapped its tail around one of the giant slaves. It tugged her from her feet, dragging her across the rough stone. The demon yanked the slave into the air, just in time to use her as a shield against another volley of fire bolts from Nara's tech mages. They slammed into the poor woman, who screeched in shock and pain, until the final fire bolt ended her cries.

"Those things they're firing, spells I guess," Aran yelled over his shoulder to Kaz, "They're the only thing that's hurt that demon so far." He cradled his rifle, trying to decide what to do.

"Then unless you've got a way to cast a spell we have to sit this out and hope," Kaz called back. "We can't do anything to that thing."

One of the tech mages slung his rifle over his shoulder and drew a slender sword. He sprinted wide around the demon, clearly hunting for an opening. White flame boiled up out of his palm and quickly coated the entire blade.

The tech mage darted forward and lunged upward at the much larger demon. The blade slid between two armored plates, biting deep into the small of the demon's back. The flames swept up the blade and into the wound, which drew a roar from the demon.

The creature rounded on the tech mage and back-handed him with an enormous fist. The blow knocked the tech mage into the air, and his blade spun away across the stone. Before the tech mage could recover, the demon fired his spellcannon and a bolt of blackness took the mage in the chest. There was no scream. No final death throws. The body fell limply to the ground and did not rise.

"I'm going to try for the blade," Aran called to Kaz. The bearded man shot him an incredulous look. "Hey, after it kills them, it's going to kill us."

Aran sprinted fast and low across the stone, the sudden movement removing the edge of the numbing chill. He bent low and scooped up the sword the tech mage had dropped and then dove behind another outcrop.

The hilt was warm to the touch and fit his hand perfectly. The blade shone an unremarkable silver, and the weapon was heavier than he was used to. Used to? He couldn't summon a specific memory, but felt certain he'd held a weapon like this, and recently.

The weapon called to something inside Aran, the same thing that had resonated with Yorrak's gauntlet back on the ship. Magic, he realized. He didn't understand how, but there was a power inside him, calling out to be channeled through the spellblade. That's what the weapon was.

"Are you mad?" Kaz roared, skidding into cover next to him.

"Maybe." Aran poked his head out of cover and assessed the situation. The remaining tech mages had scattered, and were harrying the demon from different angles. One narrowly dodged another black bolt, but was too slow to dodge the next. His right leg ceased to exist, all the way up to the thigh.

The surviving slaves had all sought cover, except for the giant ones who had nowhere to hide. Only three remained, and they made a concentrated push at the demon. It spun at the last second, balling its clawed hand into a fist and slamming it into the closest slave. That slave's jaw exploded, and he toppled to the stone with a muffled cry.

The next slave got his arms around the demon, briefly pinning it. The last giant slave jammed his rifle into the demon's mouth and pulled the trigger. The demon twitched violently, its head jerking back and forth as the slave emptied the magazine.

Aran lurched into a run, his gaze fixed on the demon. The energy in his chest surged outward, down his arm and into his hand. Electricity poured into the weapon, snapping and crackling around the blade as he made his approach.

The demon broke free from the slave's grasp and plunged two claws through the man's eye socket. It hurled the dying slave into its companion, knocking the last giant slave to the stone.

Aran circled behind the rampaging demon, keeping within its blind spot. He waited for it to pass his position, then sprinted the last few meters, ramming his sword into the wound the tech mage had already created. The armor was scored and blackened, offering little protection. The spellblade easily pierced the demon's flesh and plunged deep into the wound.

Electricity discharged, and the demon went rigid for several seconds. A trio of fire bolts shot into the demon's head, the scent of burned flesh billowing outward as life left the demon's smoldering gaze. Finally, the body toppled.

"Well done," Nara called as she rose from cover. She gestured at her three surviving tech mages. "Get the surviving slaves moving. That thing was a scout, and its death will alert the others. We need to reach the Catalyst before they mobilize."

3

ALLIES

"You there. Aran. Come here." Nara's voice held a definite edge of command, and Aran knew there was no way out of answering.

He trotted over, the spellblade still clutched in his left hand. He raised the other in a tight salute. Now where the depths had that come from? He had no memory of saluting anyone, much less this woman.

"You did excellent work with that spellblade. Clearly you are already a tech mage. Can you handle a spellrifle?" She studied him with those intense brown eyes, and he very much believed that his fate depended on the answer.

He briefly considered lying and accepting a rifle, but figured that having her find out he'd lied would be even worse than admitting the truth. "I don't know, sir. The thing I did with the spellblade was...well instinctual, I guess."

"I want you to take charge of the rest of the slaves," she commanded, pointing at the rest of the slaves with her spellpistol. "Move ahead of us, up that ridge. If we get attacked, get your people into cover. Try to distract them while my people deal with them."

"Sir, we just lost two tech mages and a half dozen slaves to a single one of those things," Aran pointed out. "If we get attacked by a group—."

"Don't mistake your position here, slave." Nara's eyes went cold. "Is this going to be dangerous? Absolutely. But keep your wits about you, and some of these people at least, will survive. How many really depends on how smart you are about deploying them. You want to save some lives? Step up."

Aran stifled the urge to take a swing at her with the spellblade. He was fast, but there was no way he could close the gap before she got a spell off. Besides, she was right. He could hate her as much as he liked, but if he wanted to live, if he wanted any of these people to live, then they needed to get through here as quickly as possible.

"Yes, sir." Aran turned on his heel and trotted back over to the other slaves. "Kaz, you're on point. Double time it up that ridge and let us know what you see at the top."

The bearded man nodded, then sprinted up the ridge. The other slaves followed and Aran brought up the rear. He glanced over his shoulder, unsurprised to see Nara and her surviving tech mages hanging a good fifty meters back. No sense being too close to the cannon fodder.

He trotted up the ridge-line, surprised by how easy it was. This place had lighter gravity than he was used to, a small blessing at least. Aran paused at the top of the ridge, looking back at the ship they'd emerged from. He was far enough away now to get a good look at her.

The starship was about a hundred meters long, a boomerang shaped cruiser. Blue spell sigils lined the hull, but many were cracked, and more than a few had sputtered out entirely. The ship itself seemed to be in good repair, though off color metal patches dotted different parts of the hull.

The ship lifted off and zoomed slowly out of sight, leaving an unbroken starfield in its wake. Wherever he was, it appeared they were directly exposed to space. So how was he breathing?

Yorrak had said 'other ocular cavity'. Was this the eye socket of some sort of moon-sized skull? That would mean this wasn't bleached stone. It was bone.

"Keep moving!" One of the tech mages boomed as he trotted up the ridge toward Aran.

Aran did as ordered, turning back toward the rest of the slaves. Kaz was still in the lead, picking a path across the bone field, painted violet by the smoldering orb in the distance. He raised a hand to shield his eyes from the painful brilliance. It was like staring directly into a sun, but somehow made worse because of the violent cold.

"Order your men to take up defensive positions along those outcrops," Nara ordered, pointing at a series of bone spurs that jutted out of field.

Aran trotted forward, dropping into cover behind the closest outcrop. It only came to his shoulder. "You heard the lady. Get into position behind this terrible cover, with weapons that won't do shit to an enemy that we can barely see."

Nara stalked several meters closer. "I could execute you right now, if you prefer." Her tone suggested it wasn't a bluff, and he found confirmation when he turned in her direction. Her spellpistol was aimed directly at him, her face hidden behind helmet.

"Uh, I'm good. Bad cover is better than no cover." Aran raised his hands and offered an apologetic smile.

Nara turned coldly away, and began leading her tech

mages along a ridge that sloped up into the darkness. Their path took them toward the light, but in a more winding route. It also took them away from the defensive position she'd asked him to establish. Aran shaded his eyes, but couldn't make out much as their forms became nothing more than silhouettes.

"What are they after, do you think?" Kaz asked from the next outcrop.

"I don't know, but whatever it is I'm betting it's a whole lot safer than sticking around here." Aran rolled to his feet, but stayed low. The rhythmic pounding was getting closer, and he could make out shapes now, against the blinding purple sun.

Their silhouettes were monstrous, approaching with alarming speed. He judged their approach, coming to the only possible conclusion. "They're going to overrun our position almost instantly. If we stay, we die."

"What are you proposing?" Kaz asked as he rose slowly to his feet.

"Run!" Aran turned and ran full tilt after Nara and her tech mages. He felt a moment's pity for the rest of the slaves, but staying here and dying wouldn't save them.

Kaz panted a few meters behind him, keeping pace as Aran picked a path through the bony ridges. In the distance he caught the flash of a fire bolt, but by the time they made it around the corner there was no sign of whoever had fired it.

Before them lay an unbroken wall of purple flame, the blinding sun that they'd glimpsed from the first ridge. Intense cold radiated from the flames, but there was more to it than that. There was a power there, a sense of infinite age, and timeless wisdom. He had no idea what he was looking at, but whatever it was— it was greater than any human mind.

Something scrabbled across the bone behind him, and Aran spun to see a demon charging. Instead of a spellcannon, this demon carried a truly massive hammer, clutched effortlessly in one clawed hand. The creature roared and charged Kaz.

The bearded man roared back, charging to meet his much larger foe. The demon brought the hammer down, but Kaz dodged out of the way at the very last moment. The hammer impacted and shards of bone shot out in all directions, pinging off their armor.

Aran glanced at the blinding purple light where Nara and her friends had disappeared, realizing he could make it in before the demon could deal with him. For a moment he was frozen. Was he the kind of person that would abandon the closest thing he had to a friend?

Screw that. He circled around the demon, waiting for an opening. "I'm going to paralyze it, like I did the last one. See if you can get that hammer away from it."

Aran reached tentatively for the power he'd felt before. The magic rose easily at his call, as if it wanted to be used. There was a separateness to it. The magic was inside him, but it was not him. It responded to his command though, and right now that mattered a lot more than figuring out where it came from.

The lightning leapt down his arm and into the blade, reaching the tip as Aran began his charge. He sprinted fast and low, leaning into the blow as he planted his blade into the back of the demon's knee. The enchanted steel failed to pierce the demon's armor, but that had never been the intent. Electricity crackled through the metal, and the demon twitched silently, struggling to regain control of its body.

Kaz stepped forward and yanked the hammer from the creature's grasp. He took a deep breath, then brought the weapon down in a tremendous blow. It crushed the creature's skull, splattering them with black ichor.

Behind them, the final screams faded to silence. Aran turned to see a half dozen demons moving past the corpses of the slaves— in their direction.

"Looks like we've got no choice but to brave the light." Kaz offered a hand. Aran shook it. "Good luck, brother."

"Good luck, brother." Aran turned, took a deep breath, then leapt into the light.

4

ENLIGHTENMENT

Aran had no words to describe what came next. A vast, unknowable consciousness lay before him—an ocean of power and memory, compared to his single drop. He fell into the ocean, became that consciousness. The universe stretched out before him, vast yet somehow perceivable with thousands of senses, all at once.

He understood how the worlds had been created, how the stars were given form. He watched the making of all things, from the perspective of a god who'd not only witnessed but participated. Xal was not the eldest of gods, but he was among them.

Understanding stretched beyond the comprehension of time. Aran saw the strands of the universe, how they were woven into existence using magic. He understood the eight Aspects, and the Greater Paths that could be accessed by combining them. The complexities of true magic, as Nara had used, became simple.

This power suffused him, endless, like space itself. If he wished, he could create a new species, or snuff one out with equal ease. Dimly, he was aware he had a body, aware of his petty temporal problems. They were inconsequential when compared with the vast infinity of Xal.

Yet, in his sudden understanding, he also saw Xal's undoing: a ghostly memory of many younger gods, all united in their purpose. They flooded the system, using their magic to prevent Xal from escaping into the Umbral Depths.

The memory seized Aran. He was there. He *was* Xal.

"You have come to come to destroy me," Xal said, turning sadly to face the assembled host.

"Your children are evil," called a goddess surrounded by armor of primal ice. "They have laid waste to many worlds, and Krox has warned us they will come for us next. We will not allow it. You might be stronger than any of us individually, but together we will destroy you."

"And who spun you this tale? Krox?" Xal shook his mighty head sadly. "Do you know nothing of his ways? Krox, the first manipulator? He is using you to attack me, so you will weaken yourselves. If we battle today, many of us will fall. The survivors will be weaker for it, and easier for Krox to pick off one by one. After today, there will be none strong enough to oppose him."

Xal examined all possibilities, trillions upon trillions. There was no possibility of his own survival. But the war between him and Krox would not end with their deaths. It would outlive them, unfolding until the last sun went cold.

And there was something he could do to ensure he won that war.

The smaller gods surrounded Xal, who made no move to defend himself. Instead, he allowed his foes to tear him apart, knowing that one day those same gods would dismember Krox. If he killed any of them, that possibility diminished greatly.

Aran watched Xal die. No, *die* was not the right word. A god could not be killed, not truly. They could only be shattered, with the pieces of their bodies forever seeking to reunite. Aran understood why the head of Xal had been severed.

The younger gods scattered the other pieces across the galaxy, ensuring it would be nearly impossible for Xal to resurrect. This filled Aran with rage, and loss, and pain—Xal's emotions, still echoing through Aran's dreaming mind.

Aran focused on the secrets of the universe, struggling to hold onto them. Briefly, he understood the illusion of time. He lingered with the knower of secrets, listening to his endless whispers. He peered into the Umbral Depths, and saw the things that dwelt there.

He noticed the great, and the small. Something tiny drew his attention—a speck of light he'd only just noticed. It lay in his hand, so small he'd missed it in the blinding brightness of Xal's majesty. Dimly, Aran realized it was the spellblade he'd picked up.

That spellblade was a living thing, waiting to be shaped. So he shaped it. It came instinctively, power and knowledge borrowed somehow from the god's mind.

He poured Xal's power into the blade, altering its shape to be more pleasing. Aran infused it with void, and the blade darkened even as it grew lighter in his hand. The intelligence within the blade grew more aware, more capable of complex thought. Aran forged a bond between them, connecting him to the new intelligence as a child is connected to parent. The weapon couldn't yet think, but there was a dim awareness there, watching.

The need to create did not diminish, and he burned to use the understanding Xal shared with him. He realized that the spell that had wiped his mind could be removed, and his identity restored. Such a thing was possible, though not trivial. Yet Aran couldn't quite grasp the spell. To do that, he needed more of Xal.

He plunged deeper into the god's mind, seeking the power that would allow him to become whole. It must be here, somewhere. An urgent buzzing began in the distance, but he ignored it, swimming toward the wonderful power.

The pain grew blinding, yet it brought with it knowledge. The pain was worth the price, if it would restore his mind.

The buzzing grew more intense, and a sharp prick shot through his palm. Aran looked down and realized that he was holding the spellblade. It was the source of the buzzing, and as he studied it Aran understood.

"You're warning me." Pain built behind Aran's temples as he stared deeper into Xal's mind. The sword vibrated in his hand, breaking the siren call.

Icy fear brought clarity. Xal's vastness was tempting, but Aran needed to flee before it reduced his mind to cosmic dust. Thrashing frantically, struggling away from the power, Aran forced himself to look away from the universe, snapped his eyes shut and tried to focus. Relief pulsed from the spellblade.

Then, as suddenly as the experience had begun, it was over. Aran tumbled away from the majesty and power, secrets slipping from his mind like oxygen from a hull breach. He shivered, cold and barren in the wake of all that power. Only a tiny ember remained, smoldering coldly in his chest. That piece was woven into him, a part of him even as he was now a part of Xal.

Aran caught himself against a bony ridge, trembling and weak, and rose back to his feet. He glanced back the way he'd come—at the purple sun—still as brilliant as ever, but he no longer squinted. He no longer felt the chill. This place was home now; it was part of him, as he was part of it.

The blade clutched in his right hand had changed. Instead of the slender short-sword, Aran now held an officer's saber, sleek and deadly. The weapon fit his hand as if molded to it, like an extension of his body. It waited, ready to be used.

"I told you," Nara's voice said, sounding muffled and far away. "He made it through, and he made it through first."

Aran turned toward her, blinking. She stood with a cluster of people, the three tech mages, and four more people in conventional body armor. All had weapons, either spellpistols or spellblades. Their posture wasn't threatening, but neither was it friendly.

Behind them sat the boomerang shaped starship, its ramp already extending.

He glanced at Nara and her companions, then at the ship. Even if he could reach it, what then? There was no obvious means of escape. That didn't mean he was giving up, though. Sooner or later these people were going to let their guard down, and when they did he'd be ready.

5

BETRAYAL

Rage flashed through Aran but burned out quickly, denied the oxygen it needed to burn. Anger left him vulnerable, even easier to manipulate than he already had been. He composed himself, straightening. If he were going to die, he'd do it on his feet. Fighting.

Nara and her compatriots were laughing and joking.

"You used us as bait, didn't you?" he demanded, as emotionlessly as he could manage. Scorn leaked into his tone anyway.

"Of course we did. You didn't think we'd risk our own lives against tech demons, did you?" Nara mocked, rolling her eyes. The girl-next-door mask vanished, replaced by a cold mercenary manner. "Don't take it so personally. Maybe think of it as an initiation. Becoming a tech mage is dangerous business. The demons here are both powerful and territorial. If we'd tried to do this on our own, none of us would have survived."

"So you came here for magic, and spent our lives to get it."

"...And you're pissed off about it. I get that." Nara slowly folded her arms. Aran tensed, but didn't react. If he attacked her, her companions would cut him down, and she clearly knew it. "Don't be so dour. You're alive, and you're more powerful now than when we picked you up. Much more powerful. This isn't just any Catalyst. This is a Void Catalyst. That means you have access to void magic, and through it, gravity magic."

"Wow, that's really great... but I don't give a shit. Where did you pick me up? And who was I?" Aran demanded, studying Nara. Hot shame gurgled through his gut. He couldn't believe how gullible he'd been. How many similar groups of mind-wiped slaves had these people led to their deaths? And, more importantly, what happened to survivors like him?

"We have bigger problems right now. You've got a decision to make." Nara nodded at the ship.

Behind her, Aran could see a group approaching, walking slowly in their direction. Four more guards escorted Yorrak—coming to inspect his new 'cargo', no doubt.

"I know you blame me for this." Nara pursed her lips. "Are you sure that's fair? I'm not in charge, Yorrak is. He's the one who kidnapped you and the others, just like he kidnapped me. He tossed you into a Catalyst, not me. Trust me when I say you've never met a more terrible person. Whatever you think of me, I promise he's infinitely worse."

She had a point. Aran knew she was merely deflecting blame, but he glared at Yorrak anyway. Ultimately, the true mage was the greater of two evils. Overcoming Nara would accomplish nothing if he couldn't also deal with Yorrak.

Aran whirled instinctively as something clattered to the stone behind him. The bearded man plunged out of the purple sun, landing in a crouch. Kaz's broad shoulders tensed as he rose to his feet. He held the hammer he'd taken from the demon, but, like Aran's sword, it had been reshaped to fit the wielder. Now the head was ringed with half-meter long spikes.

The bearded man's chest heaved, and his lip curled upward as he glared around him. "Which of you bastards is responsible for enslaving us?"

"He is," Nara said, pointing at Yorrak's approaching figure.

Kaz tensed, ready to charge the true mage.

Aran raised a hand to stop him. "Not yet," he hissed, taking a step closer.

The bearded man's eyes were wild, but after a long moment of indecision he finally nodded. His voice boomed around them, easily loud enough for Yorrak and his approaching goons to hear. "I'll wait, for now. But make no mistake: I'm going to kill that mage."

Aran sighed. So much for that plan.

"Yes, yes, I'm utterly terrified," Yorrak called back, striding arrogantly up. One of the guards was holding Yorrak's helmet, but the other three held their rifles at the ready. "Two survivors, more than I expected." He turned to Nara. "You've done well. Ready my bed, and have a glass of mulled wine waiting."

He waved dismissively at Nara, missing her murderous gaze. Her hand slid to her spellpistol.

"Now," Aran whispered to the bearded man, realizing they had a sliver of opportunity.

The bearded man roared, sprinting toward Yorrak. The mage blinked in surprise, waving at his guards. Aran took a step in their direction, but Nara's spellpistol was in her hand before he could attack. A cloud of white dotted with soft pink motes settled over all four guards, and they slumped to the ground—dead or asleep, it didn't matter. They were out of the fight, just like that.

Aran circled wide, moving into Yorrak's blind spot. Kaz charged again, but at the last second he popped out of existence, reappearing a moment later directly behind Yorrak. Aran recognized the spell as void magic, remembering it dimly from his time in Xal's mind.

The bearded man slammed his hammer into Yorrak, driving a spike through Yorrak's armor. It punched through his shoulder in a spray of blood. Yorrak staggered back with a cry and struggled desperately to maintain his balance. Aran maneuvered behind him, looking for an opening. He was vaguely aware of Nara and her companions, who were quickly and efficiently slitting the sleeping guards' throats.

Yorrak stabbed a finger at the bearded man, hastily sketching a trio of sigils. A wave of dark blue light washed over the bearded man, clinging to every part of his body. Aran watched in horror as the slave began to shrink. His bushy beard spread across his entire body, and within seconds the man was gone. In his place squirmed a tiny and quite harmless... hedgehog?

For several moments Aran rocked back and forth, trying to decide what to do. Every instinct screamed that he needed to flee before Yorrak did the same to him. But fleeing would only guarantee he lost.

Aran tightened his grip around his spellblade, gliding toward Yorrak. He reached for the lightning he'd used on the demons, and the magic responded. This time, though, the power felt...different. More layered.

Purple lightning crackled from his palm, surging down the blade. Aran eyed it in wonder, realizing it must be a mingling of the power he'd already possessed, and this new void magic that he'd acquired.

He rammed the blade into Yorrak's back, right above the fourth vertebra. The sword bit eagerly into the mage, its recent catalization making it hungry to be used. The blade *wanted* to kill.

The violet energy rippled through the mage's body, and he twitched and thrashed. Smoke rose from his eye sockets and mouth as the void lightning completed its work. The charred stench of human flesh billowed out from his armor.

Aran blinked, struggling to grasp the power of what he'd done.

"That was truly impressive," Nara said, with a low whistle. He looked up to find her aiming her spellpistol in his direction. "There's no way our mutiny would have succeeded without you. You're going to make a wonderful apprentice, assuming you're smart enough to drop that sword and come with us."

Behind her, all four of her companions were pilfering armor and weaponry from the dead guards. There was no way Aran was going to overcome them all. He didn't trust Nara, but he didn't have a better choice. He dropped his sword.

Nara waved her spellpistol at her closest supporter. "Go pick that up, and grab the spellhammer the other slave dropped. We'll give the sword back to Aran when we're sure he's not going to do anything stupid. Let's go."

They started back for the ship, two of them dragging Yorrak's still-smoking body. Aran wasn't surprised. The mage's armor, the ruby in his eye socket, and his gauntlet were all of nearly incalculable worth—certainly more than he was.

Aran sighed, bending to scoop up the hedgehog. It peered up at him suspiciously, growling.

"Hey man, don't blame me." He tucked the wriggling hedgehog into his pouch, and started for the ramp leading back into the starship.

6

SHIP

"Move," one of the tech mages growled, shoving Aran from behind.

Aran stumbled forward, catching himself against the rusting railing. All the rage, all the impotent frustration, the inability to control his circumstances, Aran channeled it all. His elbow shot back, smashing the man's nose; he scythed out a leg, shattering his captor's knee. His armor might stop a round, but the joints offered little protection.

The thug cried out, seizing his broken leg in both hands as he tumbled to the catwalk. Aran glanced over the side of the railing, judging a leap back into the cargo hold they'd deployed from. He was about to jump when he caught a bright flash out of the corner of his eye and turned to see Nara discharging her spellpistol. The pale grey bolt took him in the chest, and ripples of energy crackled over his entire body. Wherever the energy passed, he went numb.

"That's better," Nara said pleasantly. She approached, stopping in front of him. "The paralysis will last several minutes—assuming we let you live that long."

Aran thrashed inside the confines of his own mind, struggling desperately to force his body to move. It refused. He couldn't so much as twitch his fingers, putting him completely at Nara's mercy. It was somehow even more horrid than the lack of an identity. Not only could he not remember who he was...he couldn't even control his own body.

He let out a low keening wail, all his traitorous body would allow. In that moment, he'd gladly trade his life for Nara's. If only he could move.

"Oh, we're definitely not letting him live," snapped the man whose leg Aran had broken. "We're going to jettison him as soon as we leave this infernal place."

"Don't be hasty, Vash," Nara said. "He could be worth a lot of coin, maybe enough to overhaul the ship."

The other three captors seemed undecided.

Nara turned from Aran, addressing her crew. "We have the ship, but we don't have the funds to run it."

"Yorrak was rich," a short, severe woman protested. "If we can find his stash, we might have enough credits to retire."

"I kept the man's bed, remember?" Nara snapped, her eyes blazing. "Yorrak was *not* rich. Trust me, he liked his toys far too much to stash much in the way of currency. There's money, but likely no more than a handful of dragon scales. No, right now Aran here is our prime currency. We can sell him and the weapons we took from Yorrak."

The hedgehog growled, wriggling inside Aran's makeshift belt pouch. Nara glanced down at it suspiciously, then back up at Aran. She smiled. "You saved the poor fool Yorrak 'morphed. You may as well put him out of his misery. Finding a true mage powerful enough to dispel it will be expensive, and as you've heard we're not exactly flush with resources." She waved her hand and the numbness dissolved.

Aran blinked at her. "You're releasing me?"

"You're releasing him?" Vash asked, still cradling his leg. "After what he did to me?"

"You started the fight, you fool," Nara snapped, scowling down at him. "If you poke a Wyrm, expect it to eat your vessel."

"What about my leg?" Vash growled, staring hatefully at Aran.

"Yorrak kept a stash of life ointment," Nara offered. "I know where. We can use that to get you walking, and maybe the limp will remind you to be smarter." Two of the other crew laughed at that. Vash was on the verge of saying something, but Nara stared him down. "Legga, Firk, carry him to the infirmary."

"What about him?" The severe woman nodded pointedly in Aran's direction. "It will be just the two of us on the bridge. Are you sure keeping him loose is a good idea?"

Aran decided to call her Scowly.

"Oh, we'll be fine," Nara said, directing a predatory grin at Aran. "The spell I used earlier is still active. If he misbehaves, I'll simply paralyze him again. I can jerk him about like a puppet."

"All right," Scowly said, warily. She started up the catwalk, then disappeared through a small hatch.

Nara gestured at Aran to do the same, so he followed. She walked several paces behind him, her hand within easy reach of her sidearm. Aran didn't recognize the sigils on the barrel, but he'd already seen her dish out some serious spells. He didn't need any further encouragement.

He threaded up the catwalk, ducking through the hatch into a room that strummed a chord in his subconscious.

This was a battle bridge. He knew that instinctively, though he'd never been in this room before, at least so far as he knew.

A wide scry-screen hung on the far wall, opposite where the pilots were supposed to stand. At the moment it showed an empty star field. He looked back at Nara to find her staring quizzically at him.

"You recognize this place?" Nara asked. She raised an eyebrow. "A mind wipe often leaves traces, but its hard predicting which bits will remain."

"That's a matrix. You use that to control the ship," Aran said, nodding toward three concentric rings spinning slowly around each other. They were large enough for a person to stand inside them, and each ring was covered with dozens of faintly glowing sigils.

The smallest ring was gold, the next silver, and the largest appeared to be bronze. Each had the same repeating sigils, but they were so much gibberish. He could feel the power emanating from them, though. A simple steel stabilizing ring stood at about waist height, with a break in the side to allow a pilot to enter.

"Our matrix also allows me to control our weapons. Normally I would have a defensive matrix as well, but the sigils that control it burned out."

"Won't that mean we're defenseless if we have to fight?" Aran moved to inspect the matrix, stretching out a hand. A subsonic hum came from the device, and the sigil nearest his hand brightened.

"We just have to get in the first shot," Nara said, shrugging. She stepped into the rings, which somehow avoided striking her as she entered. They flared around her, creating a nimbus of multicolored light. "I doubt we'll run into any trouble. We're way outside the Confederacy. Only slavers bother to make the trip out here."

Aran nodded, turning his attention back to the scry-screen on the far wall. They were moving toward a planet, in a wide orbit. The ship shuddered, and they picked up speed.

"You're making for the umbral shadow." Aran cocked his head. He wasn't sure exactly what that meant, only that it was significant.

"That's right," Nara prodded, smiling savagely through the rings. "I waited, and waited. I've had the power to kill Yorrak for some time, but there was always a piece missing. I've always needed him to power the matrix."

"Gravity magic," Aran said, remembering what she'd said outside the ship. "You needed it to pilot the ship?"

The sound of the universe tearing knocked Aran to one knee. He clutched at his head and stared wildly at the scry-screen as something terrible lit the blackness outside the ship. A sudden break split the space outside the ship, brittle cracks snaking out around it—a sinkhole in reality. Within those terrible depths lay a hellish glow, somehow worse than the fires of Xal.

Something in those depths called to him, to the part of Aran that was Xal. Something kindred. He shuddered, but the emotion was short lived.

"Damn it," Nara snapped. "A vessel is coming through the Fissure." She touched a red sigil, then a pink. The scry-screen shimmered, the point of view zooming toward the tiny ship. As the vessel grew, Nara began to mutter under her breath. "Oh-no-oh-no-oh-no," she whispered, her eyes going wide. "That's a Confederate warship."

The blocky grey battleship's hull sloped forward like a bird of prey in flight; it was matte black and almost disappeared against the void. A truly terrifying spellcannon jutted from the prow, aimed in their direction. Size was difficult to judge, but he guessed the battleship to be perhaps four hundred meters from bow to stern.

Scowly stalked up to Nara. "What the depths are they doing out here?" she demanded. "You've got to get us out of here. They'll mind-wipe us, and drop us into their damned Marines. We've got to run."

"Don't you think I know that?" Nara snapped. She turned back to piloting.

Aran smiled. He had no idea who this Confederacy was, but he doubted they'd look too kindly on illegal slavers. *The enemy of his enemy*, and all that.

Besides, how much worse could things really get?

7

VORIA

Voria released the breath she'd been holding, relaxing slightly as a crack split the space in front of her vessel. Purple fires lurked along the edges of the Fissure, veining across the sky as the cracks widened and expanded.

Wyrm Hunter sailed silently through the Fissure and returned to normal space. The Fissure snapped shut in its wake, leaving unbroken space around them. Tension eased across the bridge, with everyone relieved to be outside the claustrophobic darkness of the Umbral Depths.

They'd entered a system with a single world orbiting a massive orange sun. The world was of no interest, but the Catalyst orbiting it was another matter.

"Why have we come here, Major?" Captain Thalas growled like a dog barring its teeth. The sour-faced Shayan bore the otherworldly beauty that was the hallmark of their people, but that did little to soften the sting of the man's overweening arrogance.

Thalas stood several meters away from her, inside the ship's defensive matrix, a trio of slowly rotating rings identical to the command matrix she stood in. Each ring was emblazoned with sigils linked to the eight aspects of magic. The sigils were dim now, giving off only a faint glow, but that would change if *Wyrm Hunter* engaged in battle.

"We've come," Voria said, "because I received an augury telling me to be here today. This is where we'll find Kazon." She studied the floating skull. Demonic horns curled into the darkness, and the cold flames in the eyes gave the dead god the appearance of life. It hovered over a barren blue world. "We don't know if that place has a Guardian, but the primals will be nasty enough. Demons, I'd wager. Just as well we aren't docking. Sergeant Crewes, can you give us a better view of the vessel?"

The scry-screen rippled, the scene shifting from a view of the entire system to a tiny swatch of space. That swatch was dominated by a small cruiser, many of the sigils on its battered hull dark or dying.

"Uh, she's unregistered, sir," Crewes rumbled.

The sergeant was a dark-skinned bear of a man stuffed into Marine body armor. Under normal circumstances, Crewes would never be on the bridge, but he was the only surviving member of her battalion who could channel fire magic. That ability gave him access to divination, which meant her ship wasn't flying blind, so she used him where needed.

Crewes spoke again. "Looks like they're firing, sir. Offensive spell. Void-based."

"That makes sense," Voria said, calmly, "given the Catalyst they're leaving. I'll handle it."

The cruiser wasn't a real threat, even if it was backed by a talented mage—not against a full battleship like *Wyrm Hunter*. Voria cleared her mind and watched the vessel through the scry-screen.

Power gathered within her breast, and she cocked her head, listening to something past the edge of hearing. She rested her right hand briefly on the spinning silver ring, grounding herself to the sigil for *void*. Then she added its opposite, the sigil for *life*. She repeated the process on the gold ring, then the bronze.

A bolt of crackling negative energy shot from the smaller vessel, whipping toward the *Hunter*. Voria studied the spell for a long moment, then touched a final sigil. She pulled deeply from the core of power in her chest, feeding it into the sigils she'd ignited.

Those energies were amplified, flowing through the base of the matrix and into the hull. The matrix carried it to the spellcannon, which launched a burst of grey light into space. The counterspell caught the enemy void bolt, and both spells dissipated.

Counterspells were an effective way to gauge an enemy, because a counterspell could generally unravel a stronger spell. That meant it would cost the enemy caster more energy to assault than it cost her to defend. If this became a game of attrition, it was one she could confidently win. Every spell her opponent cast taught her a little more about them.

Voria's sucked in a deep breath, wiping sweat from her cheek. She watched as the cruiser grew larger. How would the enemy mage react? What tricks did they know?

The enemy ship shimmered from sight, fading into the black. Illusionist, then.

"She's cast an invisibility spell. Crewes, deploy clinging flames," she ordered, guiding the *Hunter* in a wide arc as she circled the planet's umbral shadow. That would be her enemy's target. If they escaped into the Umbral Depths, there'd be no catching them.

"Firing, sir," Crewes growled through gritted teeth. He touched a fire sigil, then a dream sigil. A sheen of sweat broke out on his dark skin as a nimbus of fiery energy grew around the matrix. It flowed from Crewes into the metal around him, then down into the ship itself.

The spell shot from the spellcannon, exploding into a wide cone of scarlet flame that blanketed the area of space where their enemy had disappeared. Most of the fire quickly sputtered out, but some of the flames clung to an object, exposing the fiery outline of the enemy cruiser.

Space shimmered, then the enemy vessel flickered back into view.

"Nice work, Sergeant." Voria moved her hands to *earth* and *spirit*, channeling a binding spell. The matrix ripped a large chunk of power from her chest, sucking it into the ship. She sagged a bit from the effort, lightheaded as the torrent of power poured into the matrix. A glittering net of pale white energy hurled toward the enemy ship, which desperately attempted to evade.

Had the vessel been fully repaired and outfitted, it might have dodged the attack. Instead, the net crawled over the ship like a living thing, bonding to the sigils on the hull. Those sigils flared brightly wherever the net touched, then faded to a muted white, barely giving off any illumination at all. The ship's engines sputtered, then died. She was drifting.

"Vessel successfully neutralized, sir," Crewes boomed, snapping to attention when she glanced in his direction.

"At ease, Sergeant," she commanded, resting against the support ring. The battle had been short, but taxing. "Captain, now that they're immobilized, I want you to lead a team over there to secure the vessel. Non-lethal force only. If you find Kazon, send word immediately."

"And if we don't find the target, Major?" Thalas demanded. It wasn't quite a direct challenge, but it was as close as a Shayan noble was willing to risk when speaking to a superior officer.

"Then this entire trip will have been wasted. We find Kazon, and bring him back to the Inurans." Voria kept her tone firm, stowing her doubts. There was every likelihood Kazon was already dead, and if that were the case, they'd come all this way for nothing.

8

WORSE

Aran winced as something slammed against the hull of the ship. The lights on the bridge dimmed, and the spelldrive died with a groan.

Nara tumbled into the side of the command matrix, barely catching herself. Arcs of golden energy shot out around her, aftereffects from whatever spell the Confederate battleship had fired. The energy dissipated, leaving wisps of smoke in its wake. Nara's eyes drooped, and she stumbled out of the matrix.

She wove drunkenly in his direction. "Listen, I know you don't trust me. But right now we need each other." She shook her head, some of the color coming back to her face.

"Really?" Aran asked, grinning. He folded his arms, enjoying the moment. "From where I'm standing you're about to be boarded by the local navy. Me? I've been kidnapped. You? You're a slaver. I like my chances."

"Do you?" Nara barked out a short laugh. "You don't know the Confederates, not like I do. They won't pat you on the head and put you back where we found you. They'll trump up a charge, a reason to arrest you. Then they'll mind-wipe the lot of us and drop us into the Confederate Marines."

Aran studied her, trying to determine if she was lying. He knew she was capable of deception, but her fear didn't seem feigned. Either she were even better at this than he'd assumed, or these Confederates were as bad as she was.

"Let's say I believe you. What is it you think I could do to help?" Aran asked. "I'm unarmed, remember?"

"Point taken. Give him his weapon back." She nodded to Scowly, who grudgingly offered Aran his spellblade.

Aran hefted the weapon, which thrummed with eagerness. "I still don't know what you expect me to do. That ship is large enough to have a full company of Marines, assuming they don't just disintegrate us. If they want to take us down, they will."

"I realize our odds aren't good," Nara said, "but we still have a chance. I expect you to stand with us. I expect you to—"

A deep boom came from the cargo bay. There was a quick whoosh of escaping atmosphere, then relative silence.

"They've sealed their docking tube." The words came from Aran's mouth, but had come of their own accord. He'd never seen a docking tube, and certainly couldn't recognize one from sound. It alarmed him that parts of his mind were functional still, but that he couldn't access them in a meaningful way.

Aran gave his spellblade an experimental twirl, pleased with the weight. The weapon was lighter now, and speed often mattered more than force when delivering a spell. "If they're following standard procedure, they'll send a company of tech mages. They'll be wearing spellarmor, so conventional arms will be useless."

"How do you know that?" Scowly demanded, shaking

her head. She turned to Nara. "I don't like this, not one bit. No one resists a mind-wipe, not to that degree. How does he still know stuff?"

"I don't know," Aran snapped. "What I do know is these Confederates are approaching, right now. There's only one choke point between them and us. We hold that point, or we lose. It's that simple."

"He's right," Nara said, a quaver of weariness in her voice. "Hepha, take up a position behind the console."

Nara hurried to the matrix, stepping behind the rotating rings. Smart play. The invading Marines weren't likely to risk firing a spell at the matrix, and a conventional round would be deflected by the rings.

Aran surveyed the room, finally deciding on a position right inside the doorway. He stood to the right, ready to assault the first person through. Then he hesitated. What if Nara was playing him again? What if the Marines were the good guys, and would simply free him while imprisoning her?

Scowly—Hepha—seemed to share Nara's fear, but then she was also a slaver. Even if they were the good guys, would that save him? How could he prove his story? Would they believe he was merely a slave, or assume he was just another slaver protesting his innocence?

Heavy footsteps pounded on the catwalk outside, approaching quickly. Aran tensed and reached for the well of energy inside him. As he'd done with Yorrak, Aran summoned crackling purple lightning; the spell flowed from his hand and up the blade.

A bulky, armored figure flashed into view, and Aran struck. He rammed the blade toward his opponent's chest; the figure met the sword with a shimmering blue-white spellshield. The purple lightning flowed harmlessly around it, dissipating into wisps.

The armor brushed a memory somewhere deep in Aran's subconscious. He recognized the sleek grey curves and the shoulder mounted grav thrusters; the rifle's short, thick stock was familiar. Spell amplification sigils orbited the end of the barrel, feeding magical energy into the weapon.

His opponent raised the rifle, and Aran reacted instinctively, shooting out a hand and tapping the well of energy again. That well had diminished, and it receded further as he summoned the spell. The power fueling it was different than Xal—less destructive, and more elemental.

A blue-white glow built within the barrel as the weapon prepared to discharge a spell—a lightning bolt, Aran guessed. His heart thudded as the enemy's rifle came level with his face.

Tendrils of wind shot from Aran's palm. They wrapped around the rifle, jerking the barrel up. A bolt of jagged blue lightning crackled harmlessly over Aran's shoulder and flowed into the pitted steel bulkhead above.

Aran yanked his arm back, and the tendrils ripped the rifle from the armored hand and into his own. He snapped the rifle to his shoulder and stroked the trigger. The weapon reached forcibly into Aran's well, tearing out a chunk of raw power. It didn't seem to distinguish, drinking equally from Xal and from the part Aran that had summoned the lightning against the demons.

A dark purple bolt shot from the barrel, slamming into the armored figure. The enemy lurched back and crashed into the wall behind him. Aran tried to follow up, but another armored figure plunged into the room. This one was taller and broader, its armored shoulders sending up sprays of sparks as they scraped the ceiling.

"Drop it, zero," a voice boomed from the armor. A spell-cannon with a barrel wider than Aran's face swung into position.

"Okay." Aran dropped the rifle, then became very still.

Two more suits of spellarmor sprinted into the room, the first distinguished by an enormous metal hammer that looked like it could splatter him all over the deck. The other armor was smaller, and carried a pair of spellgauntlets, similar to what Yorrak had used.

"I think he's goin' to wet himself," a female voice piped up from the armor carrying the hammer. Aran didn't recognize the lilting accent. "In fact, I think he might've already done it."

"Oh, thank Shaya, it's the Confederate Marines," Nara called, stepping out from behind the matrix. She'd somehow found time to remove her spellarmor, stripping down to a plain black jumpsuit. There was no sign of her spellpistol, and her hair was rumpled. She'd even added a tear down the middle of her suit, exposing a hint of cleavage. "Please, don't let them hurt me any more. I just want to go home." A single tear slid down her cheek. It was masterfully done.

"Wow, you are even better than I thought," Aran muttered, both impressed and irked at having been played. "Well played."

"You traitorous bitch," Hepha roared, rising from cover and aiming her spellpistol at Nara.

She made it two steps before the spellcannon covering Aran moved to track her. A subsonic whine made him wince, then the cannon fired a large glob of magma. Hepha's brief scream was cut off as her smoking corpse tumbled to the rusting deck.

The stench of burnt meat billowed out, and Aran looked away—right into the face of the armored foe he'd stripped the rifle from. He couldn't see the man's—or woman's—face under the mirrored helmet, but imagined they were pretty pissed about losing their weapon. That person also seemed to be the one in charge, based on the body language of the others.

"Sergeant Crewes," in charge guy said, his voice crisply accented. Different from the lilting accent, "escort these two pirates to the brig, then inform the major we have prisoners. Have Corporal Kezia and Specialist Bord keep searching the vessel. It's possible they've got a bolthole somewhere. If Kazon is here, I want him found."

"Sir, if the target were here, they'd have kept him on the bridge," boomed the man who'd roasted Scowly—Sergeant Crewes, Aran assumed. His armor was larger than the rest, and he was the only one carrying a spellcannon.

"I may not agree with the major's use of Confederate resources," the crisply accented man groused, "but that does not mean we disobey orders. We search this vessel, top to bottom. Find Kazon. If you can't, I want you to be able to say with certainty that he isn't aboard."

Aran had the feeling he'd picked the wrong guy to disarm.

"Move. Now." In charge guy shoved Aran hard, and Aran staggered to the doorway then recovered, walking quickly back toward the cargo hold. Nara trailed after, still pleading her innocence.

And here he'd thought things couldn't get any worse.

9

COMPLICATIONS

Voria swept into the brig, resting her spellstave against the wall near the entrance. There were six cells, each ringed with glowing black bars whose void energy was silent and somehow menacing. Only two adjacent cells were occupied, one containing a disheveled woman and the other a calm, hard-eyed man.

Unfortunately, the man wasn't Kazon. She'd been so certain it would be. The Tender herself had promised she'd find him here. It was possible to fake magics, even an augury, but why go to the enormous trouble, or expense? It seemed far more likely she simply hadn't found him yet—or so she hoped.

"There were only two survivors?" she demanded, stopping next to Sergeant Crewes. He still wore his spellarmor, but had removed the helmet, exposing his dark face.

"Only two confirmed, sir," Crewes rumbled. He looked uncomfortable. "I killed a third, as she was threatening another prisoner."

"I'm sure the response was warranted," Voria allowed. "Where is Thalas?"

"The captain is scouring the ship for additional survivors. He's already encountered three others. They fought back, and were neutralized. None matched Kazon's description." Crewes nodded at the disheveled woman. "She claims she was a prisoner of the pirates, and seems cooperative."

"What about the man?" Voria asked, turning her attention back to him.

The hard-eyed man studied her, his gaze calculating. He was tall, just shy of two meters. His broad shoulders spoke of physical training, and she noted callouses on both hands. He was arguably handsome—a strong chin, dark hair framing a pair of clear grey eyes—but not in the delicate way of her own people.

She knew his face intimately. After all, she'd seen it often enough while watching the augury. Voria still had no idea who he was, only that he was critical in the confrontation with the Krox.

"He hasn't said anything yet," Crewes said, then shrugged his armored shoulders. "To be fair, I didn't ask him anything. He was carrying a spellblade, and conventional armor. We added both to the lockup."

"I'm standing right here," the man said, rising and moving to stand near the bars. "If you have a question, I'm happy to answer it." He folded impressively muscled arms, staring at her with complete confidence, as if he were in charge of the situation.

Voria didn't focus on him, choosing instead to study the woman out of the corner of her eye. She appeared innocent enough, and might be what she claimed. In Voria's experience, though, that was unlikely—and even if it were accurate, it didn't change what Voria needed to do.

"I'm looking for a tall man with a thick, black beard,"

Voria said, approaching the first cell. She stopped right outside the bars, looked evenly at the man inside. "Do you know what happened to him?"

"Yes."

Voria stifled her hope. Perhaps the Tender had been right after all. "And? Is he alive?"

The man nodded at Crewes. "He called you *Major*," he said. "I'm guessing that means you're in charge here, right? My name's Aran. I'm happy to cooperate, as soon as you free me."

"I'm afraid that's not how things are going to work," Voria explained. "You'll be tried, and if found guilty you'll be sentenced." She cocked her head, watching Aran closely. "If you cooperate, it may improve your situation."

"All right," Aran said. "I have nothing to hide." He shot a glance at the disheveled woman, and his eyes narrowed. "She, on the other hand, is hiding a great deal. I woke up a few hours ago to find I'd been mind-wiped. This Kazon you're after? He called himself Kaz, but he was the same man. He and I were forced to make a run at the Catalyst out there—the Skull of Xal. That woman, Nara, and some others used us as a distraction to sneak their way to the Catalyst, while demons slaughtered us. When we emerged, she mutinied against the slaver who owned the ship, a true mage named Yorrak. I don't know who I am, much less where I was when she found me. What I do know is I've done nothing wrong, and you have no reason to imprison me."

"Did Kazon survive the Catalyst?" Voria demanded, then moderated her tone. If she showed no empathy, this man would have no reason to work with her. "We'll deal with your situation in a moment. For now, I need to know what happened to Kazon."

"He survived," Aran said, "in a manner of speaking." He reached for a pouch on his belt and Voria tensed, preparing to sketch a sigil if he removed anything threatening. Crewes should have taken that pouch. She'd have to chastise him privately.

Aran withdrew a wriggling black form from inside the pouch. The creature snapped at his finger, growling.

"Is that...a hedgehog?" Voria asked, raising an eyebrow.

"The slaver I mentioned? He 'morphed your friend right before I finished him," Aran explained. "If you've got some way to restore him, then Kazon can corroborate my story. He saw all the same things I did."

"Interesting," Voria said. She sketched a sigil in the air, then added a second. The hedgehog glowed, a soft, velvety green. "It appears you may be telling the truth. You're absolutely certain the man matches Kazon's description? He had a beard, and was very tall?"

"Positive." Aran nodded. "It's him."

She extended a hand through the bars, and Aran set the hedgehog on her palm. She sketched a quick sigil, and the hedgehog yawned, then curled up, snoring softly.

"If this is indeed Kazon, then I owe you a debt, one I'm unfortunately unable to repay right now." Voria heaved a regretful sigh.

"Unable to repay? What in the depths does that mean?" the man snarled, his gaze growing dangerous. He stalked the length of the bars like a caged cat, glaring at Voria.

For a moment, she almost took a step back. "As commanding officer of this vessel," Voria intoned, using her judge's voice, "I hereby convene your trial. Aran, tech mage of Xal, you have come illegally to a dangerous Catalyst, and exposed yourself to its energies. I find you guilty of the crime of theft of magic. Normally the sentence is death, but

I will commute that sentence in exchange for a term of enlistment in the Confederate Marine Corp."

"What?" Aran roared. Voria could feel the power stirring in him, singing its strength. The man had been to several Catalysts, perhaps more. "I just told you I was innocent. I had no choice. It was either brave the Catalyst or die."

"All true," Voria allowed, nodding. "But the fact remains that you committed a crime. The correct thing, from a legal perspective, would have been to die fighting your captors. I realize it isn't fair, Aran. I apologize. I didn't write the law, but I'm sworn to uphold it."

"A law which exists to give you more soldiers," the disheveled woman snarled, finally joining the conversation. She rose suddenly and approached the bars of her cell. Her beauty remained, but she dropped the innocence in favor of dignified grace. "You'll take any excuse to erase our identities, and toss us into the meat grinder you call a military."

"You're not wrong." Voria's lips firmed into a tight line. "This isn't fair to either of you, and I understand that. But it *is* legal. You're both mages now. That makes you powerful weapons, and the Confederacy needs every bit of your power."

"Why?" Aran asked suspiciously. "What's so terrifying that you justify enslaving people and sending them to die?"

"The Krox," Voria answered soberly. "They devour worlds. Last year, we lost Vakera. Two years before that, we lost Starn. Over a half dozen smaller colonies have been overrun in the last month. If their advance is not stopped, then Ternus will be the next to fall. And after that, finally, Shaya itself. The Krox are coming, and if they are not stopped none of us will survive."

"And he's going to stop them somehow?" Aran asked, nodding at the sleeping hedgehog in her palm.

"No," Voria explained, eyeing him frostily. "The Confederacy can't afford the men and material needed to fight this war. We're understaffed, and underfunded. This hedgehog is going to purchase the weapons we'll use to fight."

She turned away from the cell and strode out of the brig. Crewes executed a crisp salute, and she returned it as she passed.

She needed to find a way to dispel the 'morph. This far out, a true mage of sufficient strength would be difficult to locate. There was an option, if she were willing to take it—though Thalas would never let her hear the end of it.

It was time to pay a visit to the Drifters. They charge her dearly, but if anyone could solve her dilemma it would be them.

10

TOLD YOU SO

Aran slowly sat on the metal bench. The bench was the only thing in the cell, other than a rusted toilet that looked like a wonderful way to acquire tetanus. The other cells, including Nara's, were identical.

"I told you," Nara growled through the bars, glaring at him. "I told you they're just going to mind-wipe us, and press us into service."

"So, what, I lose the last twenty-four hours and start over?" Aran asked dryly. "I don't see how my situation is any worse, and I'm still not sure why I should care about yours. You used me, remember? Twice. And you were going to sell me into slavery to fund your crappy little starship. Let's not forget that part."

"No I wasn't," she snapped, pacing back and forth while she furiously combed the fingers of one hand through her hair. "I needed those fools to believe it, but you were the most competent in that entire lot. You and I could have run the ship, and lived like kings. Those others? A means to an end."

"You seriously expect me to believe that?" Aran barked

out a laugh. "I watched you sell out Yorrak, then a few minutes later you sold out Hepha—but somehow *I'm* the special one you weren't going to screw over? How many times have you used that line?"

She stopped pacing, and her face softened. "Dozens. Maybe hundreds. I've only done what I needed to in order to stay alive. You have no idea what I went through, no idea what he made me do. Yorrak terrorized me, for years."

Aran considered her words, but he just couldn't bring himself to believe her. She was too good an actress, and he knew she'd screw him again the first chance she had, for even a momentary advantage.

"I'm sure it was terrible. It still doesn't excuse what you did, or what you were going to do," he countered. "You want me to trust you, even a little bit? How about giving me something to work with? Where did you really pick me up? Who was I? The truth this time."

"What does it matter? They're going to mind-wipe us both. They're probably already coming for us." Nara shot a desultory look toward the entrance to the brig, where Sergeant Crewes still stood at attention. He watched them quietly, seeming to ignore the conversation.

"Then you have no reason not to tell me," Aran pointed out. "I want to know, even if I'll just forget it again."

"Fine," Nara said, shrugging. "Why not? Yorrak had some sort of contract to ambush your vessel. I don't know why, but I think he was paid to kill someone you were transporting. He often took jobs like that. Yorrak always needed money, and he'd make extra by enslaving the crews of the vessels we took."

Aran shook his head. "That's not a lot to go on. Do you know what my name was?"

"No," Nara admitted. Her regret seemed genuine. "I

imprinted you with Aran. I thought it was an amusing little joke."

"Your name backwards?" Aran realized.

"Yeah." She smiled wistfully. "My name is an imprint too."

"Do you think there's any chance of getting out of this?" Aran asked. Not that he thought there was, but Nara was a true mage after all. "A spell maybe?".

"The bars will nullify anything I could cast, and that woman is far, far stronger than I am. You saw how beautiful she was, right?" Nara shook her head enviously. "She's Shayan. They're stiff-necked, and look down on every other race because they don't age the same way. They consider humans, us, beneath them. There's no way we're talking our way out of this, and I don't see a way to escape."

Footsteps sounded outside, and Aran turned to see Major Voria striding back into the room. In her right hand she held a spellstave with three glowing golden teardrops orbiting slowly around the tip. Power radiated from the weapon like heat from a bonfire, but it wasn't what drew his attention.

The woman herself had that. Like Nara, the major was beautiful. But unlike Nara there was something ethereal about Voria, something that separated her from regular humans. Almost superhumanly so. Her face was a perfect oval, her skin a perfectly smooth cream. Her chestnut hair had been wound into a loose bun and even that was artfully done.

"It's time," Voria said. "Sergeant Crewes, please step out of the room, or the spell will affect you too." She waited for Crewes to exit the room, then turned back to Aran. "I truly am sorry for this. I promise if the opportunity to repay you arrives, I'll find a way to do it."

"I'll hold you to that," Aran said, as jovially as he could.

Like it or not, the major had all the power here, and antagonizing her wasn't going to make his new life any easier. It would only call more attention to him, which was the last thing he wanted. Easier to go along with her, then escape when the opportunity arose.

"I'm sure you would if you remembered it." The major raised a delicate finger and began sketching sigils in the air, lines of pale grey and dark brown forming a complex cluster of symbols. The light built as she added a sixth, and finally a seventh, sigil. Light exploded from the staff, washing over the room.

Aran raised his hand to shield his eyes from the brilliance, flinching as the unfamiliar energy washed out of the major. He relaxed when he realized he wasn't the target of the spell. A beam of multicolored brilliance shot into Nara, and she collapsed to her knees.

He opened his mouth to ask Voria what was going on, but his jaw clicked almost immediately shut. Telling Crewes to leave the room wasn't meant to spare him from the spell. It was meant to prevent him from seeing that Voria wasn't wiping his memory.

Voria's gaze flicked in his direction, but she didn't look directly at him. "I'm sorry. This is all I can do for you."

"Thank you." Aran whispered. Losing a few hours time might mean nothing to most people, but when it was all you had...it was everything.

"I—where am I?" Nara asked, a note of panic creeping into her voice.

"It's all right," Voria reassured her. "I know you're confused. You've been pressed into the Confederate Marine Corps. The two of you will be escorted to your new unit, where you will begin training."

"Are we...criminals?" Nara whispered, eyes widening. She clutched her hands to her chest, clearly horrified as she stared at the rip in her uniform. "Did someone attack me?"

"You were criminals, yes." Voria waved a hand, and the bars to the cells disappeared. "Your crimes are forgiven, in exchange for your service. They've been expunged, and so far as I am concerned they never existed at all. This is your chance for a new life. I suggest you take it. Sergeant Crewes."

Aran stepped from the cell as the sergeant re-entered the room. Crewes eyed Aran and Nara balefully, but didn't say anything.

"Sergeant, escort these two to Captain Thalas and have him put them to work," Voria said. She moved to the security desk, and picked up Aran's spellblade, then eyed him searchingly for a long moment. "Before you were mind-wiped, your name was Aran, and this belonged to you."

Voria handed Aran the blade, and he accepted it gratefully. There wasn't much to hold onto right now, and the blade was solid. He could feel the intelligence within, and knew it was somehow happy to be near him again.

"Thank you," Aran said. "But don't think this makes us even."

"Sergeant, get your new privates moving." Voria turned coldly away, striding from the brig.

"Come on, wipes. Move!" Crewes barked, thrusting an armored finger at the doorway.

11

NEBIAT

Nebiat plucked a glass of sparkling wine from the platter, winking mischievously at the servant as she passed her. The woman blinked back with large eyes as Nebiat glided up the crowded path snaking through the mezzanine.

The shops, their fronts decorated in garish reds and yellows, had all been closed for the night to celebrate some local festival. She didn't care. These people would all be dead soon anyway, their corpses used as fodder against the inevitable Confederate response.

That would be the real threat. Ternus itself possessed almost no magic, and while their technological toys were numerous, they weren't terribly effective against her people.

She smiled at a man in his forties, and the man perked up instantly, straightening his jacket and sucking in his ample gut. Nebiat winked at the man's wife, a vinegar-faced simpleton. The woman glared, but did nothing as Nebiat slid past her husband.

The view above drew Nebiat's eye, and she smiled. A

transparent glasteel dome vaulted over the mezzanine, showing a bright blue-green world nestled in the void. Somewhere on that world lay the prize she'd sought for centuries, ever since Drakkon had hidden it away so long ago.

Yet even with the prize so close, Nebiat did not let herself become flustered. This must be handled with patient deliberation, or she risked a mistake—which could not be allowed to happen. The coming days must be handled adroitly, or even she would have reason to fear. Her father would see to that.

Nebiat sauntered up to a pair of lift doors at the base of the largest building in the mezzanine. A pair of guards, one male and one female, flanked those doors. They watched her with relaxed wariness—aware, but convinced she was no threat.

"I'm going up to meet with the governor," Nebiat said, smiling. She touched the male guard's chest. "Then I'm going to bind his will and force him to betray his people. You, your friend there, and everyone else aboard this station will die horribly."

The man's eyes widened, and he reached for a heavy slug throwing pistol. Nebiat's finger twitched, dancing in quick curves. She sketched a simple binding and tossed it at the woman, who gasped as the black sigil sank into her forehead and disappeared. The woman's eyes pulsed black for a moment, then she seized the male guard.

Nebiat took advantage of their struggle to repeat the spell, seizing the male guard's will as well. "Guard these doors. Let no one through."

Nebiat pressed the button to summon the lift, humming to herself as she waited for it to arrive. The doors slid open, and she stepped inside, turning to give a little wave to the guards. They waved back, smiling. The doors closed, and the lift carried her to the top floor.

The doors slid open to reveal a spacious chamber. Every part of it had clearly been built to impress, from the dark wooden bookshelves lining each wall to the view of the dome above the man sitting at the desk.

He had watery green eyes, and hair that had begun the final transition to white. The weathered lines across his face marred what had likely once been quite striking. In its wake, time had left dignity, at least.

"How did you get up here?" the man asked, eyes narrowing as he rose from the desk. He reached for an intercom. "Security, report."

"Yes, sir?" said the male guard from below.

"I ordered you to allow no visitors. Why am I staring at a visitor?"

"It's important you speak with her, sir," the man replied, quite firmly.

The governor's eyebrows knit together in confusion, but the confusion evaporated when he looked up at Nebiat. "You're a mage."

"I'm pleased to see the rumors of your competence aren't exaggerated," Nebiat said, stepping from the lift and moving to the bookshelves. She ran a finger along the spines, taking in the titles. "Quite an eclectic collection, Governor. Books on philosophy. Psychology. Law. Even ancient Terran history. You're a very curious man, it seems. You like to know how things work."

"What do you want?" the governor asked, reaching under his desk. He removed a sidearm, a smaller version of the slug-throwing pistol the guard had used.

"Ultimately?" Nebiat asked, cocking her head. "That's a very difficult question to answer. I want to see the universe reshaped into my grandfather's image, certainly. But after that? Well I don't really know."

She expected a stern warning, or a rebuke, or some other dithering. There was none of that. The governor added a second hand to the pistol, cupping the grip. Then he shot her. Repeatedly. The pistol bucked over and over, filling the office with the acrid smell of gunpowder.

Nebiat could have shielded herself. She could have simply teleported out of the path of the bullets. Either might have intimidated this man, but neither would be as effective as letting the rounds hit. So she stood there, letting bullets ricochet off her into the bookshelf. She waited calmly for the man to finish, then smoothed her dress. There were several holes in the bodice—a tight cluster, right over her heart.

"You're an excellent shot, Governor. It seems you live up to every part of your reputation, so I will treat you with the respect you deserve. No more games." Nebiat raised a hand, and began to delicately sketch a dizzying array of multicolored sigils. They formed a complex binding, the kind of binding most mortal mages would labor a lifetime to master and still fail.

She flung the spell at the governor, much as she'd done to the guards below. He flinched, trying to move as the spell shot directly into his heart. The energy pulsed outward to every chakra. To dominate a person as fully as she needed to dominate this man, the mind alone wasn't enough. She needed his heart. His spirit.

"There, that's much better." Nebiat smiled. "I've left much of your will intact, for now at least. You'll be free to act as you see fit, which could enable you to save the lives of many of your people. Hold on to that, Governor. It's the only way you can fight right now."

"What do you want?" the governor whispered, his expression melting to horror. His whole body trembled.

She turned her gaze back to the bookshelf. A few of the books had been damaged by the bullets, but most were intact. She touched a very old one, simply titled *Terra*. Nebiat sketched a fire sigil and the book burst into flame.

"I want you to address your people on the planet below," Nebiat instructed. "Tell them you have reason to believe the Krox are coming to this world."

"But if I do that, there will be a panic," the governor protested, a bead of sweat trickling down his cheek. "People will flee in droves. There will be chaos."

"That's the point." Nebiat raised an eyebrow. "Oh, and do make sure you send word to Ternus, requesting immediate aid."

Nebiat smiled at the governor's obvious confusion, and she admired the restraint he showed in not asking why she was alerting her enemies to her assault before it even began.

12

KEZ AND BORD

Crewes led Aran and Nara into the largest room Aran had ever seen aboard a starship. It had to be at least a hundred meters across, and half again as wide. The deck was divided into squares, each allocated to a different unit.

Most of those units were conventional Marines in forest-green fatigues. They drilled in platoons of twenty-five men, some running drills while others sparred in a boxing ring. A firing range ran the length of the far wall, but although Aran could see muzzle flares, there was no sound. Magical silence?

"Looks like we got us some fresh meat," came a yell as a platoon trotted by. "Two new techies."

Crewes turned his baleful eye toward the platoon, and they quickened their pace.

"What did he mean by techies?" Nara asked, looking around her in wide-eyed horror.

"Tech mages," Crewes grunted.

"What's that?" Nara prodded, hurrying to walk next to the sergeant.

"Man, you wipes don't know anything—like, literally anything. You're a gods-damned mage. But you ain't had any training." He patted his rifle. "See this? You can use one of these, and the armor I'm wearing. Those zeros? They got zero magical ability. They have to stick to conventional weapons, and conventional weapons suck."

"What's the difference between a tech mage and a true mage?" Aran asked, trotting just behind the sergeant's armored form.

"Training, wipe. That's the difference. True mages cast real spells. We can kinda do the same shit, but we need a spellrifle or spellarmor. Now keep up, rookie," Crewes barked, glaring over his shoulder at Aran. "Not sure why the major let you keep that blade, but don't think it makes you special. You're already on my bad side, and you do *not* want to be on my bad side."

"Do you even have a good side?" Aran muttered. His shoulders slumped when he caught Crewes glaring at him. "You've got really impressive hearing."

"You've got really impressive hearing, *sir*!" Crewes barked, his scowl growing two shades darker. He started clanking forward again, moving with purpose.

Crewes kept a brisk pace, and Aran struggled to keep pace. Crewes wore his armor like a second skin, easily stepping over a low barricade into another section that led toward a largely empty corner of the hangar. No platoons drilled here, though a small squad lounged around a portable table playing cards.

A tiny platinum-blond woman sat on the far side of the table, grinning up at a short olive-skinned man with a rat's nest of dark hair. She was a little too short and a bit too slender to be human, but Aran wasn't sure what race she was. She was pretty, but not like the Major had been. "Face it, you're joost outclassed. Enjoy my maintenance shifts for the next week."

Aran recognized the lilting accent from when they'd been captured. This must be the woman who'd been carrying the hammer.

The olive-skinned man had a mop of curly hair and, though short for a human, was still taller than the blonde. "It's all part of my plan. I'm lulling you into a false sense of security," he shot back, "so when the stakes are higher I can clean you out." His eyes twinkled. "Want to play again? This time, if I win, you make me dinner—*and* breakfast the next morning."

The words had obviously been practiced, and just as obviously used before. The blonde merely rolled her eyes, then rose to greet the newcomers. "Hey there, Sergeant. Looks like you came back with some strays."

She approached Nara first, offering a hand. Nara took it timidly. The blonde only came up to Nara's chest, and Nara wasn't tall.

"Ah, that's the state o' things," she said, giving Nara a friendly smile. "They've joost been wiped, Sarge?"

"Yeah," Crewes confirmed. "And now they're your responsibility, Kez. Take care of our special flower here." He nodded disapprovingly at Aran. "See if you can teach him to use that sword. And find out what they can both do with a spellrifle. Hopefully one of them can actually hit a target. Oh, and see if you can keep Bord from harassing the woman."

"I'll keep him in line." Kez turned to Aran and patted the chair next to her. "Have a seat."

Aran moved to join her, and Nara sat across from the

man Crewes had identified as Bord. Nara still looked scared, but some of the fear had been replaced with curiosity.

"Okay, let's make this official. I'm Corporal Kezia, but mostly I get called Kez. Since it's clear you ain't seen any of my kind before, I'll give you the state o' things. I'm a drifter. We're a race o' short fookers with a terrible reputation. We're cousins to the Shayans, but they don't like admitting it because we're more primal than they are." Kez cocked her head and gave another dimpled smile. "So do either of you have a name, or are we giving you new ones?

"I'm Aran," he offered. It disturbed him how quickly the name came, especially now knowing that Nara had just randomly made it up.

"And what about you, gorgeous?" Bord asked, leering at Nara. "You got a name? I want to make sure I scream the right—"

Kez's tiny fist rocketed out, catching Bord in the gut.

He doubled over, coughing. "Lords, Kez. You're so violent."

"Don't pay Bord any mind," Kez said, winking at Nara. "He'd rut with an asteroid, if it smiled back. He's got a point, though. You got a name there, lovely?"

"I—" Nara looked helplessly around, like Aran had when he'd woken up in the cargo hold. He still didn't trust her, but it was difficult not empathizing with someone so clearly in pain. And he remembered what Nara had said about slaves without imprinted names having psychotic breaks. No one deserved that.

"Her name is Nara," Aran supplied, feeling a small swell of pity.

"You knew me before?" Nara asked, cocking her head in confusion. "That's why I was in the cell next to you."

"Briefly, yes."

"You still remember her?" Kez asked, pursing her lips. "Not sure how the major is going to feel about that. Sounds like the wipe didn't take."

"The major already knows about it." Aran glared defiantly down at the little blond, who blinked up at him in confusion.

"Well you seem a might pissed." She picked up a tin cup and offered it to him. "Here, have a mouthful of this. It'll take the edge off."

"And you said my name is Nara?" Nara interrupted impatiently.

"That's right."

Her eyes narrowed. "And your name is Aran?"

"Yes."

"How stupid do you think I am? Your name spelled backward? Is this a prank?"

Nara glared at Aran. He found himself unsure how to respond. Kez's expression had darkened, and Bord openly frowned at him.

"Answer her question," Bord demanded. His bushy eyebrows knit together in what Aran guessed was meant to be an intimidating way. "You messing with my future wife?"

"Her name really is Nara," he protested. Aran rubbed his temples, wishing he were anywhere else. "We were aboard the ship you just commandeered. I'd been wiped, she hadn't. She's the one who told me my name was Aran." He could see they weren't listening.

"It's okay," Nara said, though she still sounded a bit hurt. "Nara is a fine name."

"Nara it is." Bord grinned, putting a hand on her shoulder. "I'm Bord. As in *boring*. Well *I'm* not boring, but that's how my name is pronounced."

"He is boring," Kez said, clapping Nara on the back.

Neither offered a hand to Aran; somehow he'd come out the bad guy in all this. Not an amazing start to his time as a Marine. "Well, maybe things can't get any w—. What am I thinking? Yes, yes they can."

13

GOING DARK

"Do not do this, Major. Please." Captain Thalas refused to look at her directly, as usual. It was subtle—and constant—disrespect. "Dealing with drifters is highly irregular, possibly even illegal, depending on what crimes these little pikeys are guilty of."

"One of your own officers is a drifter, Captain," Voria said, matter-of-factly. "So if I hear that word pass your lips again, I will remove your ability to make words."

There was no malice to it, but neither was it a bluff. She'd long since grown tired of the antics of bored Shayan noblemen. Their mission in life seemed to be finding a constant state of equilibrium, one where they were always dissatisfied.

Thalas embodied the very worst of that flaw, but added a layer of disdain for every other race.

"Major," he argued, "respectfully, you cannot speak to me this way. My father—"

"Any time you need to reinforce your authority by invoking a parent, you accomplish the opposite." Voria met

Thalas's gaze, forcing him to look at her. "I don't care about your father. Having you here hasn't meant him providing additional funding—or any aid whatsoever. He knows we're undermanned. He knows how close to the edge we're running. He even knows I stick to the fringes of Confederate space, hunting Krox—a pastime he knows will almost certainly be fatal. Yet your father has never once intervened or sought to protect you. So what is it, exactly, you feel his name will get you?"

Thalas paled and his eyes narrowed dangerously. "You are right, of course, Major. I apologize for resorting to such base tactics. Please, let me state my argument more cogently. I realize you think me a simpleton, but I assure you I am not. I know you received a missive, and I strongly suspect it ordered you to report to Marid. I, too, received a missive, Major. The Krox have begun their invasion, and even now the battle rages. And you are meeting with drifters to...to buy beer. Tell me, do you really believe that's the best use of our time? We are needed elsewhere. Sir."

"It shouldn't surprise me that you're aware of the attack," Voria said. "Since you're so well informed, you must be aware of our lack of medical supplies. And munitions."

She touched a void sigil, then reinforced it with another. Power thrummed deep in the ship, and a feedback loop formed between Voria and the primary matrix. She fed energy into the spelldrive, fighting a wave of vertigo as it rumbled to life.

"We're here to rectify that," she said, "because going into battle without those supplies all but guarantees massive casualties. Even with the supplies, we're likely to lose most of the battalion. Now, I am aware of your prejudice against the drifters, but like it or not they are every bit as Shayan as you are. And they possess her magic—even you have to admit that."

Thalas said nothing.

Voria touched a final sigil, triggering the Fissure. A tremendous crack split the black, opening in the exact spot where they'd exited the Umbral Depths. She hated returning to the Depths so soon, bracing herself as she guided the vessel into the Fissure.

Even Thalas grew quiet, paling as he stared up at the scry-screen.

"Send runners through the ship," Voria ordered. "Tell them we're going dark."

She guided the ship through the Fissure and into utter blackness. Only the edges of the Fissure glowed, lighting their path briefly, then it closed and extinguished the only light anywhere.

"Yes, Major," Thalas snapped, the words clipped. He wore his anger like armor, but she could see the fear underneath. He brushed a lock of blond hair from his shoulder, eyeing her haughtily as he departed the battle bridge.

Voria turned her attention back to the scry-screen. Before them lay total darkness, a sea of infinite silence. That sea was not empty, and she had no wish to meet whatever dwelled here. Voria tapped *air*, then *fire*. Finally she added *void*, setting their course. The *Hunter* responded, accelerating into the black.

She tapped a flurry of sigils, touching systems throughout the ship. All around her, lights dimmed as the ship powered down all non-essential systems. Only life support was exempted, and that required the barest amount of life magic. Their void shielding would, in theory, prevent the creatures of the depths from detecting them.

Assuming she'd set the correct course—and she was positive she had—they'd arrive at their destination in two days time. *Two days* in the black, drifting silently through the Umbral Depths, praying to avoid the notice of whatever dwelt here.

14

MARK V

Nara had been running in darkness for a long time, panting as she stared over her shoulder. Something chased her, but she had yet to catch a glimpse of it. Occasionally, laughter echoed through the darkness, high and cruel. A scornful, mocking laugh.

Her laugh.

"Get your worthless Krox-fodder asses out of those bunks, and onto your feet!" The voice boomed from somewhere outside the dream, shattering it.

Nara blinked awake, stumbling to her feet as quickly as she could. She battled exhaustion, positive it couldn't have been more than two hours since she'd collapsed into her bunk. Bord had tried to go easy on her, but spellrifles were not her strong suit.

She wasn't the only one scrambling. Aran had settled into the bunk next to hers, and made it to his feet only a hairsbreadth after her. Sergeant Crewes loomed over them, still wearing that implacable silver armor.

He aimed his spellcannon in their direction. "Yesterday was play time; today we find out what you're made of. Beginning today, you two are, so far as I'm concerned, best friends. You eat together. You sleep together. You pick each other up when the other falls down." A wild look crept into his eyes and he stalked closer, his armored feet booming against the deck. He leaned over them, frowning in disapproval. "Now, I know you're wipes. I know you ain't got shit for skills. But you ain't zeros. You're tech mages; we just gotta teach you how to act like it. That starts with firing a spellrifle, which I'm told both of you did yesterday. Flower boy here ranked pretty good. But you?" Crewes's shadow fell over Nara. "You did abysmally."

Inexplicable fury surged through her, so powerful her mouth moved before she could stop it. "Perhaps if you gave me a real teacher, who actually instructed instead of staring down my shirt, I'd have—"

"Private," Crewed boomed, overwhelming her pitiful words. "Are you telling me the fault lies with the instructor?"

Nara considered that for half a second, glancing at Bord a few bunks over. Bord had done his best, and it hadn't really been his fault she wasn't good with a rifle. The olive-faced little man shot her a timid smile, still wiping sleep from his eyes. He'd instinctively picked up a rifle when he leapt from the bunk. She was shocked to find her spellpistol in her hand as well.

"No," she said, shaking her head. "It isn't Bord's fault. I'm just not good at it. I don't know why."

"I do," Aran muttered, under his breath. There was an edge to the comment, and Nara knew it pointed at their mutual history.

"Then speak up," she snapped, glaring up at him. "I'm already tired of the snide comments, and the eye rolls. I don't know what went down between us. I know you see her, whoever she was, when you look at me. I'm *not* her. I don't remember anything. If you know something, then tell me instead of lording it—"

Crewes shot out both armored hands, faster than Nara would have believed possible. The gauntlet seized her throat, yanking her into the air. Aran struggled beside her, beating at Crewes's other arm in an attempt to free himself. Crewes dragged them both up to his face, his crazy eyes shifting back and forth between them.

"Were you under the impression anyone cares what either of you think? I'm sorry, genuinely sorry. That's my fault. Let me make this clear, like I should have originally: you're going to be dead soon, and you'll probably die bad. Real bad."

Crewes relaxed the pressure on her throat, but didn't set her down.

"Your lives, all our lives, are bought and paid for. It's my job to make sure the Confederacy gets their money's worth." He set them down. "Whatever squabble you have, it's dead now. Debris in the void. Like I said, you're best friends. Is. That. *Clear*?" The last word was deafening.

"Yes," Aran muttered—rather sullenly, in Nara's estimation.

"Yes," she muttered, with much more dignity.

"Good. Yesterday you did a test firing. Easy shit. Today, you're going to do something much more difficult." A maniacal grin joined Crewes's wild eyes. "Today, you're going to get checked out in spellarmor. You're void mages, and that means gravity magic. You're going to learn to fly."

"To what, now?" Nara asked, blinking. "I can barely make the rifle work. What makes you think I'm qualified to make armor fly through space? You're going to lose me, and an expensive suit of—"

"*Move*," Crewes roared, pointing at the barracks door. He dropped them both.

"No. You want me to treat her like a best friend? Okay," Aran interrupted, rubbing his throat. He moved to stand protectively in front of Nara, and while she didn't need the protection it did raise her opinion of the man. Slightly. "I know you're desperate for mages, but you people aren't stupid. Put her somewhere she'll excel, and live. Nara is a true mage. I've seen her cast spells. She isn't just some tech mage. She's had training. A lot of it."

"I don't care if she's Shaya's bloody Guardian," Crewes growled, eyes narrowing. His ire was all focused on Aran now. "Listen, I get it, wipe. You're angry. You're thinking life's unfair, and oh, boy, are you not wrong about that. You're in the Confederate Marines, and it don't get any less fair than that. Get used to it. If you protest again, I'll throw your ass in the brig—after I beat you so bloody you won't be able to make it there under your own power. Am. I. *Clear*?"

"Aran, let's go," Nara offered, touching his arm.

He gave a start, fear flitting across his features before being quickly swallowed by his ever-present mask. She withdrew her hand as if burned. What had she done to him to provoke that kind of reaction?

"*Move*!" Crewes boomed.

Nara ran. Aran fell into step next to her, and they sprinted out of the barracks. Crewes led them toward the suits of spellarmor on the far side of the hangar, where they'd first met Kez and Bord. The rest of the squad followed, shooting amused glances as she and Aran ran.

"Help them get suited up," Crewes ordered, waving his cannon at Bord.

Bord moved to a slender silver suit, beckoning to Nara. "Come take a look. I'll explain the basic features. It isn't as complicated as it looks. This is the Mark V. It's old, but reliable."

Nara slowed, feeling slightly winded by the time she reached the armor. She paused next to it and walked in a single revolution around the armor. It stood two meters tall, an androgynous suit of silver armor with no obvious weaponry.

The armor rotated about half a meter above the ground, bobbing slowly in some sort of unseen field. She could sense the power within, and the power that generated the field keeping it aloft. The armor called out to the part of her that was Xal, its latent magic resonating with the void magic within her.

She touched the metal, surprised to find it warm to the touch. "What is it made of?"

"Mostly feathersteel," Bord explained, moving to the rear of the armor. "They're produced by the Inurans, but we usually refer to them as the Consortium. The Mark V armor is designed for speed and stealth. In a perfect world, you'd be scouts."

"And in an imperfect world?" she asked, positive she didn't want to know the answer. She peered curiously at a trio of clear canisters mounted to the small of the back. "What are these?"

"One question at a time." Bord laughed. It came easily, and relaxed Nara...a hair at least. He reminded her of someone, though of course Nara could no longer remember who. A brother, perhaps. "In an imperfect world, you'll be fighting on the line, alongside heavies like Kez and the sergeant."

"I don't know, I kind of like the sound of having Crewes near us. I bet his face is enough to make whoever these Krox are run." Nara avoided looking at the wall of a man currently staring balefully at Aran. As she watched, Aran raised a hand and delicately sketched a sigil on the chest of the armor. The suit rippled, going translucent. "What did he do?"

Aran stepped into the armor, and his body disappeared. The armor solidified.

Bord gave a low whistle. "Looks like your buddy there is already a pilot. He's just your buddy, right—or a brother, maybe?"

"I don't know what we were," Nara said, absently. Thinking about Aran only raised more irritating questions. She straightened, then turned back to Bord. "You were going to tell me what those canisters are."

"Ah, yeah...those are potion loaders," Bord explained. "They administer potions directly to the pilot. Your suit comes with three, though the sarge has a custom job with a full five slots." His nervousness faded as he talked, and he lit up as he examined the armor. "If we had any supplies, you'd be loaded with at least one healing potion. The other two would be situational. If we were invading a lava world, you might have a potion of flame skin to protect you from the heat."

"We don't have any supplies?" Nara asked tentatively.

"Well, we don't have much of anything," Bord explained. "Potions are rare, and most times we have to fight without them." He shrugged. "It means I have to work a little harder."

"Why you?" Nara asked, moving to stand before the armor. There was no obvious place to trace the sigil, but Aran had done it over the suit's chest.

"I've got life magic. Picked it up from Shaya herself, when I was a fresh-faced Marine. Like six months ago." Bord moved to stand next to Nara, and gently rested his very sweaty palm on her arm. His hand became luminescent, glowing a soft golden white. "I can heal most minor wounds, and treat severe ones. So, it's...uh, kind of my job to put my hands on you." Bord gave her a lopsided grin that aimed for roguish but landed right on top of dork.

Nara shook her head sadly. "You're really bad at this whole *picking up women* thing."

"But I'm frighteningly persistent," Bord said. The glow was fading, and he grinned at her. "We'd better get you suited up before the sarge gives us grief. What you need to do is—"

Nara sketched the sigil for *void* before the chest. She didn't know how she knew the sigil, but it came easily, and power flowed into the air with an audible hum. The armor vibrated, then went translucent as Aran's had.

"I just step inside?" She asked, looking over her shoulder as she backed toward the armor.

"Wow, you are a fast learner," Bord said, giving another low whistle.

The armor tingled as she entered it, lifting her into place, then solidifying around her. It fit her like a second skin, conforming to her entire body. The faceplate flared to life, displaying a paper doll representation of the armor in the lower right corner. Next to it sat three red cylinders that she guessed corresponded to the potion loaders Bord had shown her.

The armor's interior smelled of sweat, and the material made her skin itch. She didn't enjoy the feeling, but being in the armor was still exciting. She liked the idea of flying, even while she was terrified she'd be bad at it.

"Now what?" she asked, grinning. Excitement tingled through her.

"Now," Crewes boomed, clomping over to her. "You

wipes and I are going to go for a little space walk. Stick close, and don't do anything stupid."

"Wait," Aran called, turning his armor to face Crewes. "Aren't we in the Umbral Depths?"

"So?" Crewes asked, staring Aran down as he clamped a helmet down over his face. The stylized skull was somehow less intimidating than the man's dark scowls.

"What does he mean? What are the Umbral Depths?" Nara demanded. The words filled her with clawing terror, though there was nothing tangible she could latch onto.

She didn't know what the depths were, but she knew she was right to be afraid.

15

THE UMBRAL DEPTHS

Aran tensed, his entire body reacting to the words *Umbral Depths*. Even with no specific memory, they evoked dread. So he focused on what he could control.

Like the spellblade, his spellarmor was maddeningly familiar. He knew how it worked, knew how to guide it through a tight turn, and how to avoid enemy fire. He also knew, somehow, that doing any of that in the Umbral Depths would be like lighting a massive flare for anything that lived here.

That terrified him. Not just the knowledge, but the lack of context. How did he know these things? And what else did he know? Did he have the skills to deal with whatever they encountered out there? Could he trust Nara, or even Crewes? Once again, he had nothing but questions. It was getting old. Fast.

"Let's move. Bord, Kez, wait here. I'll hop on the comm if we need anything," Crewes rumbled, walking his armor toward a blue-green membrane that was all that separated them from space.

Aran gritted his teeth, resisting the urge to punch Crewes in the back of his armored head. He willed the armor to follow, and it drifted gracefully in Crewes's wake. His breath was loud in his ears, accompanied by the soft hiss of the environmental regulator.

Nara fell into place next to him, matching his pace. She'd had no trouble donning her armor, and guided it with precision—certainly more than she'd shown with a rifle. They stopped right inside the membrane. Inky blackness lurking beyond.

"Why are they staying here?" Nara asked, crowding closely behind the sergeant. Her suit turned to face Bord and Kez, though Aran couldn't see her face through the faceplate.

"Because they can't fly. That requires void, or fire magic. Air magic will work if we're in an atmosphere," Crewes said. He stepped through the membrane, and into the blackness beyond. "If they fall off the ship, they'll tumble endlessly through the depths. Since you two wipes have gravity magic, you've at least got a chance to make it back. Besides, they've already got experience. You two are greener than that slop they feed us. Now let's get moving."

Crewes leapt through the membrane, his warped form moving to stand outside the ship. After a moment, his voice crackled from a pair of speakers near Aran's ears. "We'll use the comm to communicate, but keep chatter to a minimum."

"You'll be fine out there, there's nothing to be afraid of," Bord said, smiling encouragingly. Then he seemed to doubt his own words, and his face fell. He turned to Kez. "Wait, there's nothing to be afraid of, right? I mean, I've never seen the sarge take a space walk. Not into the Umbral Depths."

"They'll be joost fine," Kez said, waving at them with an utter lack of concern. "There are wards in place that obscure the ship's magical signature from the things that live out here."

"Why is he taking us out there?" Aran asked, the more paranoid part of him wondering if Crewes might want to arrange some sort of accident.

"I don't know, but I'd follow him," Bord cautioned, "and quickly. Sarge isn't patient."

"Yeah, I gathered that," Aran said. He guided the armor through the membrane, and out of the ship.

Nara followed a moment later, and the pair stood facing the ship's long, sloped deck. It stretched into the black, disappearing into the darkness. There were no stars, no nebulas. Nothing but impenetrable black all around them.

Crewes voice came from speakers. "Follow me. Keep your eyes sharp, and don't leave the deck. If you get higher than three meters, you'll be outside the *Hunter's* protective wards."

Aran felt something hot and violent, an unfamiliar magical energy, stir in Crewes. The thruster on the back of Crewes's armor fired, and he drifted slowly along the deck, cutting a path into the darkness. Aran willed his armor to follow, and it obeyed. It took almost no power, barely touching his reserves as he trailed in Crewes's wake.

"Sergeant?" Nara's hesitant voice came from the speakers. "Why did you bring us out here?"

"Because," Crewes rumbled back, "we've got too many jobs, and not enough hands to do them. You wipes need to learn to use that armor, and I ain't got time for funsy drills. We're going to the aft spellcannon. There's a blockage lodged in the barrel. A blockage that showed up after we entered the depths. You two are going to help me remove that blockage."

"How?" Aran hopped over the angled joint where two of

the ship's armored plates met. He forced his spellarmor to remain close to the hull, glancing up uneasily. He couldn't see anything, but there were things lurking in that darkness, he was certain of it.

"With the gods-damned spellrifles you've been training on," Crewes snapped. "Aran, I'm gonna ask this right now. It's only me, you, and your best friend Nara. This is a safe place, so you can be honest. Are you slow? Head injury, maybe? Because that was the most obvious damned question I've ever heard."

"Really? That's the most obvious question? You realize that we *aren't carrying rifles*, right? How do we fire a weapon we don't have?" Aran snapped, following Crewes toward the a truly massive cannon. The dark metal barrel ran along the bottom of the ship then disappeared into the body of the vessel.

The sergeant didn't reply. It was a good thing Aran didn't have a rifle, because he knew exactly who he'd use it on right now.

Long moments passed as they followed the sergeant across the hull. Aran tried to ignore the smothering darkness above. His breath was loud in his ears, and he couldn't shake the sense that something could creep up behind him and he'd never hear it.

Nara finally broke the silence. "Sir, are you sure it's safe out here? I don't think we're alone."

"Of course it ain't safe. You're not a union worker. You are a depths-damned tech mage. No part of your job is safe," Crewes scolded. "Besides, we don't have much choice. Something is blocking the barrel, and if we can't fire the cannon we're defenseless."

"We couldn't wait to fix this until we exited the depths?" Aran asked, unable to resist staring up at the blackness.

"If we had the manpower, maybe," Crewes said. He crawled over the lip of the barrel, disappearing inside. "We've only got a handful of tech mages, and all of us are pulling triple duty. By the time we get to where we're going, I need to have you two wipes ready for combat. We won't have time for recess, like we're doing now."

Aran kept his thoughts about *recess* to himself, climbing over the lip and into the barrel. It stretched before him, the other side so high above it disappeared into darkness.

"How do we clear this without weapons?" Nara asked, echoing Aran's earlier question. "You've got that cannon, but we only have our hands."

"I can't get my brain around how little you wipes know. You've never heard of a void pocket?" Crewes asked, as if it were the single most basic question that had ever been asked of anyone. This despite the fact that he knew they'd been recently wiped and had no chance of knowing what the hells he was talking about.

"The weapons are stored in a sort of pocket dimension," Crewes continued. "You should be able to feel it, above your face and to the right."

Aran stretched out an armored hand. Probing. Much to his surprise he found a cubby, only a foot wide and four feet tall. It existed alongside normal space, invisible to the naked eye. Thinking about it made the cubby go opaque, obscuring the space behind it.

Within that pocket lay a gleaming rifle, the same kind they'd trained with the previous day. Aran picked it up, feeling it connect instantly with the armor. The armor bonded him to the rifle, allowing him to channel spells through it just like he would through his spellblade.

A moment later, a rifle appeared in Nara's hand as well. "You're a quick study."

"Thank you," Nara replied, sounding a little surprised.

"Neither of you has ever, in the history of anything, been described as quick. At anything. Now listen up, wipes. We're going to march down this barrel. I'm going to move up the center. You two will stick to the shadows, and don't do shit unless I tell you to."

"Sir, what kind of debris are we clearing?" Aran asked. The advance the sergeant had ordered sounded more like a tactical advance, with him as bait.

"Who said anything about debris? I said we're out here to clear a blockage." He advanced into the darkness, the light from his thrusters creating a halo around him.

Aran fell back, moving slowly to the right. Nara circled around to the left, raising her rifle awkwardly to her shoulder.

"Not yet," Aran explained quietly. "Keep your arm relaxed until you need it, or your muscles will tense up." He demonstrated how his own rifle was held loosely in his armored hand. Nara mimicked the gesture, then gave a thumbs up.

Crewes increased his thrust, widening the pool of light around him. He zoomed along the inside of the barrel, illustrating how large the battleship must be. Aran's original guess of four hundred meters seemed fairly accurate. The weapon could house a small city block inside the barrel alone.

"Contact," Crewes barked, as shapes descended from the darkness. Bat-like creatures dove at the sergeant. "Pick them off as they come at me."

The creatures moved too quickly to get a proper look, but Aran had the impression of a long tail, and sharp, curved horns. Crewes raised his rifle, unloading on the first creature that dared to close. Its charred form was blasted backward and spun away, untethered by gravity.

Aran snapped his rifle to his shoulder, sighting at the next bat-thing. He saw a face and stroked the trigger. The rifle wrenched power from his chest, flinging a nearly invisible bolt of dark energy at the bat. The creature took the bolt in the face, and half its skull disintegrated. Its body slammed into the barrel, spattering Crewes's armor with black ichor.

One of the creatures curled a tail around Crewes's rifle, attempting to yank it loose. Crewes laughed then yanked the creature toward him, seizing its skull with one armored hand. He crushed it, and more ichor spattered his armor. "Bad move."

Aran sighted, then took down another bat-thing. Beside him, Nara had her rifle raised. She still hadn't fired.

"They're moving too quickly," she protested. The rifle barrel moved as she sought a target.

"Switch to your sidearm, then," Aran suggested, lining up a kill shot on a third bat. He guessed there were a dozen total, but the sergeant's wild cannon shots were thinning that number. "You sacrifice a little range, but, as someone who's been on the receiving end of you with a spellpistol, I think it will be a lot more effective."

Nara flung the rifle back into the void pocket, replacing it with a much smaller spellpistol. It was larger than the one she'd used to subdue him back on Xal, but her armor compensated for the size difference. She cradled the weapon in both hands, seeking a target.

A ring of purplish sigils appeared around the end of the barrel, and the weapon brightened as Nara discharged her spell. Aran didn't recognize the magic, though it was similar to the spell she'd used on the slaves.

The bright purple bolt shot into the sergeant's armor, and a wave of blinding light pulsed outward. Aran's faceplate protected him, but he imagined the bats were probably blinded—assuming they even had eyes.

When the light faded, Aran understood the true purpose of the spell. Four identical versions of Crewes now stood in a rough quartet. The confused bats retreated, circling as they attempted to settle on a target. One finally dove, face contorting in a silent screech as it passed harmlessly through the illusion of Crewes. The creature slammed into the deck, trying to hop back to its feet.

The real Crewes stepped forward, ending the bat with a burst from his cannon.

Aran raised his rifle again and picked off another bat, then another. After several more shots, there was no more movement in the darkness.

"Maybe you wipes aren't a complete waste." Crewes slung his cannon over his shoulder as he guided his armor into the air. "Let's get back inside."

"Sergeant?" Aran asked, thinking if ever there was a time to get away with a question it was now. His anger had faded, giving way to curiosity.

"Yeah?" Crewes rumbled.

"How did you know the bats were here?" he asked. "It made sense to clear them, and I get why you brought Nara and me. We need the experience. What I don't get is how you knew they were out there."

"I've got fire magic, wipe," Crewes explained, though much of the heat had gone from his voice. "That's more than just burning things. The major has been teaching me flame reading. Divination lets me see zeros and stains before they become a problem. Now get your ass back inside. We've got more work to do."

16

NOT MY WAR

Aran collapsed onto the bunk, his cheek resting against the coarse sheet. He groaned, partly at the pain his landing had caused, and partly in relief because he wasn't expected to move any longer.

Killing the bats had been merely a morning warm-up. They'd gone through a full battery of physical training, taken a break for lunch, then spent the afternoon back in the spellarmor. Crewes had forced them to use every bit of their spellpower, until neither could conjure even a single void bolt.

"I have never been this tired," Nara muttered, crashing onto the bunk next to his.

Aran glanced over at her, struck once again by those eyes. It was already growing more difficult to remind himself that this woman had repeatedly screwed him. Part of him wondered if that woman even existed any more. Maybe he should give the new Nara a chance.

"Tomorrow will be worse," Bord said, dropping onto the bunk next to Nara's. "You both did well though. Crewes yelled less than I expected."

Aran pulled himself into a sitting position, resting his back against the wall. His arms shook, after-effects of the mixture of free weights and endless pushups. He had the sense that Bord assumed he was a romantic rival for Nara, but beyond being standoffish, the shorter man hadn't said much to him.

"He's not lying about tomorrow." Kez walked up, kicking Aran's leg out of the way and sitting next to him on his cot. She swirled a tin mug with a dark liquid in it. "This is the last of the beer. Figured after today the both of you'd earned a sip."

She offered the mug to Aran, and he accepted it. The beer was bitter, but the spreading warmth was worth it. Aran passed the mug to Nara, who took it with a nod. She brushed a lock of hair from her cheek, exposing her freckles, and took a mouthful of beer. Her nose crinkled in distaste as she swallowed.

"Crewes can't possibly come up with anything worse than today," Aran muttered. "Please tell me he can't."

"If he can, please just kill me now," Nara mumbled, planting her face in her thin pillow.

"Tomorrow he'll give you individual assignments," Bord explained. "I have a feeling Aran's going to get picked to go to the commissary."

"That doesn't sound bad," Aran said, watching Bord suspiciously. "Especially not after PT. What's the catch?"

"Catch is you need to go through the Marines to reach the commissary," Kez said, laughing. "They're not overly fond of us, and they look for any opportunity to show it. Making a run for supplies is a sure way to get an ass kicking. It's joost the state o' things."

"Why do the Marines hate us?" Nara asked, sitting up.

"Because we get fancy spellarmor, and spellrifles, and

potions. But mostly because the Captain is an ass." Kez finished her beer and set the cup on the floor under Aran's bunk. "Thalas sees these people as fodder. They're joost numbers, and they know that. Tech mages are strategic assets, which means that to Thalas we're worth more. The Marines assume that all tech mages are like that fooker."

"I can't really blame them for that," Aran allowed. He was already fairly certain who was going to get picked to go on this little milk run.

"Yeah, especially if you'd been at Starn," Bord said, staring down at his lap. "We lost nine in ten Marines, and about half the tech mages bought it." He looked up quickly, then back down again. "There were a lot of gaps. The major called for volunteers to become tech mages. She sent two dozen of us into the light. Those of us who survived made it out with some sort of magic. We rushed straight into battle against the Krox, and they tore most of us apart. Kez and I were lucky enough to survive."

"And it *was* luck," Kez said, her pretty mouth turning down into a frown. She brushed golden hair from her face, eyeing Aran soberly. "Watched the fellow next to me get torn apart by a Krox enforcer. Then I watched that man's corpse get back up and start killin' his own friends. They broke us. If the major hadn't pulled out some incredible casting, we'd all have died. As it was, we barely escaped. We haven't been a full unit since. Those of us who survived know our survival is temporary. You've already met the lot of us. Crewes, me, Bord, and Captain Tight Ass. Four tech mages, in a company that's supposed to have twelve to twenty. The next time we fight the Krox, we're all going to die. There joost aren't enough of us left to win."

"So why are we fighting, then?" Nara's eyes went wide,

and she looked ready to bolt. "Is there any chance we can sneak away? I don't want to die, especially not pointlessly."

"Sorry, you're stuck with us. There's no way out." Bord laughed as if she'd made a joke. Nara's expression said she hadn't. "I don't know where the major is taking us, but she probably won't let any of us off the ship. She'll do whatever she needs to do, then she'll take us back into the depths. When we emerge again, it will probably be in whatever system the Krox are invading. Then the fighting starts."

Aran wasn't sure how to reply. There didn't seem to be a way to escape, but that didn't mean he couldn't keep looking. He caught Nara's gaze, and found understanding there. If the opportunity came, he was fairly certain she'd work with him to get away.

He didn't even know what a Krox was. They damned well were not going to die in someone else's war—not if they could find a way out.

17

SIDE QUEST

"Get out of bed, wipe!" Crewes roared, his voice yanking Aran to his feet. Aran did—faster this time, snapping to attention at the foot of his bunk. Crewes clasped armored hands behind his back, staring at Aran with distaste. "I've got a little chore for you, wipe. Rumor is we're going to see action soon, and I need to make sure we're ready. I need you to go to the commissary and retrieve any potions they have—especially healing potions. Can you handle that, wipe?"

Aran blinked rapidly, shaking off sleep. The rest of the company were still in their bunks. "Sir, yes sir!"

He hated the way the words came out, hated that he sounded like the other soldiers. It was so easy to go along with what they wanted, and he knew part of the training was keeping him exhausted enough to do things until they became habit.

"Good. The commissary is on the aft side of the ship. Get moving. No breakfast until you come back with potions." Crewes leaned in closer. "No potions, no breakfast for the entire unit. Move, wipe. Nobody eats until you get back." The sergeant shoved a piece of pink paper into Aran's hand.

Aran tugged on his boots, lacing them as quickly as he could. Crewes loomed, watching as Aran hastily readied himself.

Finally, Aran stood and left the barracks. Crewes hadn't told him exactly where to go, but he knew the commissary was on the opposite side from the firing range. He started in that direction, noting the several platoons of troops drilling between him and the small white building.

He circled wide around the closest group, watching warily as they trotted by. He avoided eye contact, letting the Marines pass before swiftly crossing the area they'd vacated. Aran hurried around a hovertank...right into a squad working on repairing it.

They fanned out to block his path, one of them thumping a wrench into his fist. A couple others held tall brown cans of something he guessed was alcoholic. Aran identified the leader immediately, a tall, blond man with thick shoulders and arms. The others were unconsciously mirroring this man's body language, watching him for cues on how they should react to Aran's arrival.

The blond man folded those arms, staring hard at Aran. "You're out of bounds, techie. You're not supposed to be here. I'm afraid we're going to have to file a report."

"I'm just heading to the commissary," Aran protested, nodding at the building. "It's right over there. Why don't I get out of your hair, and you can go back to...drinking beer around a tank. I mean, I'd hate for you to have to do paperwork on my account."

"Are you making fun of us, techie? Because it sounds like you are." The blond didn't seem amused, and neither did his friends.

"You know what? We got off on the wrong foot. How about you let me...you aren't going to let me by are you?" Aran's few hours sleep had done little to deal with the fatigue, and his stomach rumbled noisily—a reminder that he wasn't the only hungry one. His shoulders slumped. "Fine, if you're going to kick my ass just get it over with."

"Fair enough." The blond guy threw a punch at Aran, but he instinctively deflected the larger man's fist, countering with a punch of his own. The blow caught the blond in the nose, shattering it in a spray of blood.

Aran stared down at his fist in horror, inwardly cursing his lingering instincts. If he'd just taken the beating it might not have been bad. But now that he'd embarrassed their leader? This was going to be ugly.

Sure enough the Marines leapt forward with a collective roar, and Aran went down under a storm of blows. Pain exploded through his vision as a punch caught his temple. A steel-toed boot slammed into his ribs, cracking something.

Every subsequent breath ached more than the last, and still the blows continued to fall. Aran tried to roll away, but another boot kicked him right back into the other attacks. His lip split, spraying blood across the deck.

"Enough," the blond man finally called, cradling his nose. Blood trickled between his fingers. "If you keep that up we really will have to file a report. Techie here is sorry for crossing into the part of the ship reserved for Marines, aren't you, techie?"

"Oh, yeah," Aran groaned, holding his ribs. Blood trickled down his chin, onto the deck. "Terrible. Decision. Won't happen again."

"Let him up," the blond snapped. "We've got a hovertank to fix." Then he leaned down to crouch next to Aran. "And it's 'terrible decision, *sir*.' I'm a captain. Just because you're a mage, doesn't mean you get to ignore that."

The captain reached up with one hand and, with a sharp crack, snapped his own nose back into place. A fresh trickle of blood flowed from one nostril. He held Aran's gaze as he did it, then stood up and walked back to the tank.

Hard core.

Aran didn't question his good luck, stumbling to his feet and away from the Marines. A rib on his right side hurt like it had been cracked, and his chest and gut were likely a mass of bruises. Fortunately the Marines had restrained themselves, and he didn't think he'd suffered any permanent harm.

By the time he reached the commissary, he'd composed himself, though there was no disguising the growing black eye.

A wizened old man with tiny spectacles peered out at him from behind a high counter, frowning. "The infirmary is a level down," he said, turning away dismissively.

Aran fished the pink paper from his pocket, sliding it across the counter. "I'm Private Aran from the tech marine company. Sergeant Crewes asked me to requisition this list."

The old fellow turned a baleful eye on the paper, finally picking it up with a sigh. He rapidly scanned the contents, then stared at Aran suspiciously. "Is this some sort of prank? Six healing potions? A potion of energy resistance? Another for invisibility? We have none of this."

"Oh." Aran blinked and rubbed at his side. "Well, is there anything on the list you *do* have?"

"Hmm." The old man scanned the list again. "I suppose I could part with two potions of lesser image."

Aran wasn't sure what those did, but he gratefully accepted the two pink vials the old man withdrew from under the counter. Each cylindrical vial was perfectly sized to be slotted into a set of spellarmor.

"Thank you..." Aran trailed off, realizing he didn't know the man's name.

The man ignored him.

Realizing he'd been dismissed, Aran limped back toward the tech mage barracks. This time, he took a longer route, circling the edge of the hangar. It added time, but it didn't add bruises and that made it worth it.

By the time he arrived, Sergeant Crewes was standing outside the hangar, armored hands planted on his hips. He glared down at Aran. "Took you long enough. The rest of the squad is hungry. Pity you used up the time they had for breakfast. You've got sixty seconds to get inside and get some slop, then it's back to work. That is, assuming you came back with potions?"

Aran handed across the two pink vials, and was about to plunge past the sergeant when the wall of a man raised an arm to block him. "Did you run into any trouble? You look like you had a fall, maybe."

"No sir, no trouble." Aran shook his head. "The run went smooth as silk, sir. May I be dismissed to get breakfast?"

"Go." Crewes eyed him thoughtfully as Aran entered the mess, and Aran thought he might even have seen a glimmer of respect there.

18

DRIFTER ROCK

Voria buckled on the belt she'd been awarded by the academy, then after a moment's thought hooked her tome over it as well. Tomes were rarely worn outside formal events, but it would be helpful to remind the drifters who and what she was.

She'd discouraged Thalas from calling them pikeys—the pejorative term thrown around back on the capital. It was synonymous with thieves, and unfairly leveled at all drifters. The drifters were nomadic, and it was true that they often solved legal problems by slipping away. But Voria had come to know more than a few, and they had their own rough-spun honor—as much as or more than a blowhard like Thalas. She was counting on that today, but that required she look the part.

Voria strode from her quarters, tracing a path toward the battle bridge. She passed no one, not even the ever-present support staff needed to keep a battleship flying. The battalion had shrunk to less than a full company, really—so few she couldn't even staff guards. Not that guards would matter here, at the heart of the ship.

"Captain Thalas, have Private Aran sent to docking bay three," Voria ordered as she strode onto the bridge.

Crewes blinked down at her in surprise, but said nothing. Instead, he busied himself with his matrix, probably sensing the conflict he was about to witness.

Thalas eyed her askance from across the room, raising a delicate eyebrow. "And may I ask—"

"No, you may not," Voria snapped, tired of his antics. "Follow orders, Captain."

"Of course, Major," Thalas said, the words thick with frost. "Sergeant Crewes, you are relieved. Find Private Aran and have him report to docking bay three."

"Yes, sir," Crewes rumbled, avoiding eye contact with either of them as he slipped from the bridge.

Voria found it curious that a man who inspired such terror in his company was so squeamish about disagreements between superiors.

"Now that we are alone, may I have your permission to speak frankly?" Thalas stepped from the matrix, nimbly avoiding the spinning rings.

"Granted." Voria disliked Thalas, and she didn't have time to deal with him, but if she allowed him no latitude the man would eventually mutiny.

"In a few moments we will exit the Umbral Depths. Instead of arriving at Marid, we'll be meeting with pi—drifters." Thalas closed his eyes for a moment, then took a deep breath. "You are, for reasons you are unwilling to explain, taking with you a fresh recruit of no special note, save that he's new enough to the Marines to still be a flight risk. Major, were you in my shoes, you know what you'd do. We do not like each other, but we both serve the Confederacy. Please, help me understand your actions."

"Very well," Voria said. She deftly stepped inside the

command matrix, tapping sigils as she assumed control of the vessel. "I believe Aran is a war mage. Not just any war mage, either—a seasoned war mage. I'd bet my life on it. He's seen a good deal of ship to ship combat."

"If that's the case, I can understand that he'd make a formidable weapon. But does that make him worthy of your trust? What's the point in bringing him with you?" The sourness had left Thalas's face, but his tone still bore the same arrogance.

"The point," Voria said, slowly bringing systems back online, "is that Aran could be a tremendous asset. He might even make a skilled officer, and we're desperately short of those. We're about to enter the most brutal combat theater in the war to date. We need every asset. It's possible Aran could betray me, and he might even try to run—but I doubt he'll do either. If nothing else, he's a highly tactical thinker. There's no way for him to escape, not with a Confederate battleship parked right outside. And it is absolutely worth the risk. We need to recruit him, Captain."

"Recruit him?" Thalas scoffed. "What are you going on about? He's already a Marine."

"He's been conscripted," Voria shot back. "It isn't the same thing. How can you not see that? The man has no loyalty to us. He doesn't understand the fight or why he might be important to it. I intend to show him those things, because I need his loyalty."

She left out the part about having seen Aran's face in an augury. That would raise a number of uncomfortable questions, distractions she couldn't afford right now.

Voria triggered the final sigil and engaged the ship's spelldrive. Energy, manifested as a tiny, glowing crack, blossomed in the space outside the ship. The crack spread, growing larger even as a cluster of smaller cracks radiated around it. The Fissure cast its hellish glow, bringing light to the Umbral Depths.

Anything capable of sight would see the Fissure from a vast distance, so Voria wasted no time. She guided the *Wyrm Hunter* through the Fissure, and back into reality. The Fissure snapped shut in their wake, easing her tension.

"I still think this is a mistake, but you are in command," Thalas allowed, though grudgingly. "What do you wish me to do while you are off the ship?"

"Have Crewes send a missive to the admiralty," Voria instructed. "See if we can get the most recent combat footage from Marid. That's our next destination." She guided the *Hunter* into the system, toward the station orbiting the fourth world.

From a distance, it resembled the cloud of space debris left in the wake of any space battle, but as they grew closer, that debris resolved into ships. Most were tiny—shuttle class, or even fighter class. Their hulls were scored and discolored, often with several different colors separated by weld marks. None looked spaceworthy, though Voria strongly suspected that was by design.

At the center of the cloud lay a massive asteroid, a sliver of a moon that had likely once orbited this world. The ships congregated around it, drifting in and out as they smuggled whatever illicit cargo they could get their hands on. It really was an unsavory place, the type a Shayan noble like Thalas had been bred to despise.

Voria's own family would be appalled—well, her father's side at least—but in her years of service she'd learned to be pragmatic. Drifters saw things other races did not, and while their brews were often...questionable, they also conveyed powerful magic effects.

She slipped from the rings, then departed the bridge. It

was a long walk to the docking bay, and the closer she came the more people she saw. All stopped to salute her as she passed. Voria returned those salutes crisply, whether given to a private or an officer. She couldn't learn all their names, but she could treat every Marine with honor.

Finally, she reached the docking bay. Aran was already there, chest heaving as he struggled to catch his breath. Crewes had probably told him to run.

Voria smiled.

19

BEER

Aran straightened as Major Voria approached. He snapped instinctively to attention. How much of that was his recent training? Or, had he been military before? So many questions.

The last time he'd seen the major, she'd been in a simple uniform, but now she'd added her parade dress. Her jacket was a Shayan silk, and the belt a dark supple leather. The tome hanging from that belt looked expensive, and likely contained a variety of powerful spells.

The staff cradled in her hand was even more impressive. Magical power rolled off it in waves, whirls and eddies of golden energy. That energy emanated from three teardrop-shaped gems rotating slowly around the tip. The haft was forged from black metal, and a golden cap weighed the bottom. Perfect for smashing an opponent's bones. The weapon allowed self-defense, in addition to whatever magical abilities it conferred.

"At ease, Private," Voria said, eyeing him critically. She moved to stand in front of him, the light catching those striking eyes. She was older than him, though he couldn't say by how much. Nara had said Shayans didn't age normally. He wished he'd had more time to ask her about that. "For the duration of this excursion, you may call me Voria, and you may address me as an equal. When we return, that latitude vanishes. Are we clear?"

"If you want me to treat you like an equal, that means I'm not going to be kissing your boots," Aran replied. He waited a moment to see if she'd react. She said nothing. "Can I ask why we're here, and where here is exactly?"

"I'll explain as we walk. We have a great deal of work to do," the major explained, sketching a sigil in the air before the green membrane that sealed the airlock. It winked out of existence, showing a dim metal hallway leading into some sort of station. "This way. We're aboard Drifter Rock, one of the largest concentrations of drifters in the sector."

"Drifters? Like Kez?" Aran asked, puzzled.

"Yes, just like Corporal Kezia. She does what she can to hide her accent, but she's definitely a Drifter. They're cousins to the Shayans, and worship the same goddess, though most Shayans don't like to admit it. You won't fully understand why until we meet them," Voria said, hurrying up the hallway. Aran followed until the hallway dumped them into a rocky cavern. "We're inside a hollowed-out asteroid, or maybe the remains of a moon. The rock is criss-crossed with tunnels that the Drifters can use to hide, and ultimately escape to their ships. Our arrival sent most of them scurrying, which is why this place looks so empty."

Aran sized up the station they'd entered. This was probably a market, judging by the colorful tents erected in haphazard rows. Most of the tents were empty, but the largest one had a pair of shopkeepers. Voria made for that tent, giving Aran time to study the pair.

The shopkeeper had a well-trimmed beard, and the woman's ample figure spilled out of her bodice. They were even shorter than Kez, coming no higher than Aran's waist.

"Ahh, whatdidya goin do?" the male demanded, the words coming out in such a rush that Aran wasn't sure where one ended and the next began. At least half of it was gibberish, though Aran picked out a few familiar words. "Yadun emptied da marketplace. Allmeh custoomers made for da warrens. Whatcha goona do about that, huh?"

"It's good to see you too, Beadle," Voria replied warmly. She moved to the diminutive figure, offering her hand. The shopkeeper made a great show of kissing the back of her palm.

"Don't ya be getting ideas, or you're goona be smartin' every time ya sit," the woman snapped, moving between Voria and Beadle. "He's spoken fer, ya tart."

"And it's good to see you as well, Magda." Voria gave the woman a smile and bent to kiss her cheek. "This is one of my tech mages. He's only here to observe."

"Ahh, teachin' the young one ta trade," Beadle said, nodding sagely. "Ver wise, ver wise. So, what brings ya ta the rock?" He took on a cunning look, one mirrored by his wife.

"A rather delicate problem." Voria reached into her pouch and withdrew a furry form. The form snored softly in its magical slumber. "A true mage 'morphed this man, and I need to find a way to dispel it. I was hoping you might have a brew that would help."

"Now dat," Beadle said, nodding at the hedgehog, "is one fooked little critter. Best to just put it on the menu, ya know?"

"Maybe, but let's say I absolutely needed to dispel the 'morph. Can you do that?" Voria asked.

Aran finally understood why they'd come, and why

she'd brought him. So far as he knew, only he, Nara, and Crewes knew that Kazon had survived.

"Mmm," the drifter said, leaning closer to inspect the sleeping hedgehog. Its tiny black nose flared with each slow breath. "Couldbe couldbe. Question, though. Watsit worth ta ya? Gonna take big magic ta unfook this fella."

"I have a number of dragon scales," Voria began, "and a handful of soil from the base of Shaya herself."

Aran watched her manner carefully, fairly certain she was holding something back.

"Got lotsa dirt," Beadle said. "Don't need no soil. Dragon scales though? Got any dream scales?"

He peered up at Voria hopefully. Behind her, Aran caught the wife watching—studying Voria. The pair might pretend to be at odds, but Aran knew he was seeing masters work. These drifters treated barter as an art form.

"Life or air, I'm afraid," Voria said, reaching for her pouch. She spilled a few hexagonal scales into her hand. Each scale glowed with its own inner light, and Aran could feel the power in them, waiting to be tapped. "They're high quality, as you can see. Perfect for enchanting. You could make almost anything."

"Except beer. Can't make beer. Keep yer scales. Now that staff, though. That's a pretty piece o' work." Beadle crept closer, looking askance at Voria. The major nodded, and the drifter ran his hand along the haft. "Dis, we'd trade fer. We got some fine beers. Beers that will let you float. Beers that will heal a man. Beer that will make you stronger, or faster."

"That staff is a fully developed eldimagus. She is eleven centuries old." Voria's eyes went cold. "She's worth more than all your beer put together."

"Oh, I don't know 'bout dat. We got lots of beer, not only

what ya see here." Beadle nodded toward a stack of metal kegs in the corner of the room. "There's tree times dis in da back. You kin have it all, for that little stick." Beadle leaned his chair back, delivering a practiced half smile. "It's good beer."

"The finest, I've no doubt," Voria agreed, with an entirely too serious nod. Aran felt lost in the negotiations. "But there's no way I can part with a treasure like this, not even with a guarantee that you could restore my friend."

"Ah, dat's not true. A lady brings a staff like that, she's looking to fook a fellow right up his wallet," Beadle protested. He leered at Voria, drawing a stern frown from his wife. "I tink you're willin ta part with that stick, fer da right price."

"Let's get down to it then," Voria said, dropping her voice to a near whisper. "You want the stick? I want a guarantee you can unfook the hedgehog. Can you do that? No drifting around the point. Give it straight, Beadle."

"Aright, aright. I can't unfook the fella—but I might have something that'd still be worth that stick." Beadle folded his arms, studying Voria. "I got a right special brew from my ma's ma. This beer's so good, men will come back from the dead ta drink it. Been saving it for years, but haven't seen cause to use it."

"You give me that special brew, and every other brew you've got. All of them, no holding back. You do that, and you label it all properly, and the staff is yours." Voria patted the haft of the weapon.

"You can't possibly plan to give him that staff," Aran protested. "A fully developed eldi-whatever you called it...for beer?"

"That's precisely what I intend to do. Do we have a deal,

Beadle?" Voria spat into the palm of her hand, and offered it to Beadle. The drifter spat in his hand, then shook.

"Done deal. I'll tell da boys ta get the brews loaded." He stared longingly at the staff.

Voria handed it to him.

"You're going to give it to him before he pays? What's to prevent him from just running with it?" Aran demanded. She *had* given him permission to speak freely.

"He's a dumb fooker, innit?" Beadle said, pointing at Aran with the staff. It was comically large for his tiny form. "Listen, tall fook. We're drifters. We make a deal, we honor da deal."

"You need to make sure you're very clear on the terms," Voria said, coldly. "Thank you, Beadle. We'll take our leave. She'll serve you well."

Aran followed the major, not speaking until they were out of earshot. He grabbed her shoulder, forcing her to stop. "What the depths was that? You gave up a priceless artifact, and we didn't even get the brew that will turn that hedgehog back into Kazon. What was the point of this? And why bring me?"

She met his gaze evenly. "Release me, Private."

Aran let her go. "Guess the being treated as an equal is over."

"That it is, though I will answer your question. The point of this expedition wasn't to cure Kazon, though that would have been wonderful had it been possible. The battalion needs supplies of every type. The Confederacy cannot supply them, and even if they could, they cannot get them to Marid in time for them to do any good. These brews will save lives. Many lives. Thanks to this deal, you and your squad will go into combat armed with healing potions." She narrowed her eyes, adopting an instructive tone. “A single magical item, even an eldimagus, will only marginally affect the outcome of a battle. But every tech mage and every Marine squad having access to healing magic? Now *that* might turn a battle around.”

20

IT BEGINS

"It's very sweet of you to come see me off, Governor," Nebiat said, leaning in and kissing the man lightly on the cheek.

Avitus shuddered, but didn't pull away. "I have to obey your orders, you know that," he said, glaring. "Given the choice, I'd have already have taken my own life."

"But you don't have that choice, do you?" She smiled wickedly, stepping inside the airlock. "Don't worry though, Governor. I'm not asking you to do anything terrible this time. Simply close the airlock, and jettison me into space."

He eyed her suspiciously for a moment, then slapped the red button next to the airlock door. It slid down, locking with a hiss. A red warning klaxon began flashing above her, and a few moments later the outer door opened, flinging her into the void.

Nebiat embraced the cold, beginning her transformation the moment she left the airlock. Her dress split down the back, and wings jutted from her back even as her limbs thickened and elongated. Her tail burst out behind her as she grew many times in size. A sea of fangs filled her mouth, and her neck elongated.

She was whole once more.

Now a full-sized Void Wyrm, Nebiat glided toward the planet below. She glanced at the station behind her, beaming a draconic smile at the cluster of ships gathered around it. They were tightly packed, gathering supplies and passengers before fleeing the system entirely.

Nebiat reached deep into her well of magic, sketching an amplification spell. Then she breathed, a cloud of pallid white mist engulfing the station and the ships around it. That mist passed right through the metal, sinking into ship and station alike.

Nebiat imagined the curiosity. If any of the people inspected that breath, they'd notice the horrified faces of the damned trapped within—right before the mist engulfed them and their own souls joined the terrible choir.

All except Avitus, of course. Her magic protected him, and him alone. Everyone around him would die, but the Governor would survive. He could still inflict untold damage on the Confederate defense, if utilized properly.

Satisfied that the station was dealt with, Nebiat turned back to her work. She swam through the void, stopping in the planet's Umbral Shadow. She sketched the sigils to open a Fissure, smiling as the space before her fractured. Fat, massive troop carriers plunged through immediately, followed by nearly two dozen Void Wyrms—her father's strongest children.

"You certainly took your time," Kheftut snapped, swooping past her, his tail insultingly close. "We've been waiting in the depths for a full day. Even I do not enjoy that place."

"This must be handled delicately, Kheftut, which is why

father placed *me* in charge, not you. I needed time to pave the way for your arrival." Nebiat reared up over him, fixing him with her gaze. "Now, I am going to head to the planet to verify the Catalyst is where we expect. If it is, I will lay the groundwork for the ritual."

"And what do you want me to do?" Kheftut demanded, petulantly.

"Have your binders harvest the corpses on the station," Nebiat instructed. "When the Ternus fleet arrives, ambush it. Crush them utterly, and do it before the Confederate forces reach Marid. Hold this station at all costs, and do not let the Confederate forces reach the world below. Have I made it simple enough for you to understand, little brother?"

"I hate you so much, you smug wench," Kheftut growled, but there was no real heat to it. "I will do as you ask, for now."

He swooped toward the station, and the rest of the Wyrms followed. By the time the Ternus fleets arrived, the Krox forces would be entrenched. That would make for a very short battle, and would keep the focus in space instead of on the ground.

Nebiat turned from the station, drifting toward the planet below. She enjoyed the warmth of re-entry, her scales heating and turning a pleasant, dull red as she skimmed through the upper atmosphere. Below stretched a sea of clouds, and she plunged quickly through them.

She burst into the sky above an enormous crater with human settlements dotting its inner slopes. The settlements lurked around the edges of a massive swamp, one shrouded in mist every bit as thick as the cloud cover. From deep within that mist, Nebiat sensed a familiar, pulsing power.

Power she would soon claim.

21

THE KROX

"Hey, Nara, come have a look at this," Kez called from across the barracks.

Nara opened her eyes, rising to her feet with a groan. Every part of her ached, and she knew it would all begin again the next morning. She wove between cots until she reached Kez and Bord, who were clustered around a golden disk the size of a dinner plate. It was covered with elaborate sigils, mostly fire-related. She could feel the faint power emanating from the device.

"What's this?" she asked. The magic wasn't destructive in nature, despite being fire-based.

"You're so cute when you're ignorant," Bord said, patting the cot next to him and delivering his infectious smile. "This is a missive. It's one of the most common magic items in the Confederacy."

"A missive?" The word tickled the back of Nara's brain, but she couldn't quite summon the meaning.

"They're like the recordings Ternus uses, basically," Kez explained. "Here, watch." She tapped the largest of the red symbols, and the device began to hum. Tiny flames burst into existence over each sigil, all feeding into a larger flame that danced over the device. The final fire topped a meter in height.

"Soooo...you've discovered fire?" Nara asked, blinking. "That can't be all it does."

"Joost watch," Kez insisted.

Nara clamped her jaw shut, resisting the urge to stalk back to her cot. She needed sleep.

The flames grew taller still, the center going blue as the heat rippled outward. An image appeared—faint at first, but then with more definition.

"What system is that?" Nara asked, studying the blue-white planet. A ring of asteroids encircled it, and a glittering silver station was silhouetted by the sun.

"That's Marid." Kez stabbed a finger at a cloud of vessels rising from the station. "And that's the Ternus defense force."

"There are a lot of them," Nara observed, crouching next to the flames. The heat was intense, but not quite painful.

"They're going to need every one." Bord pointed at the base of the flames, toward the dark side of the planet. Shapes were moving there, perhaps a dozen in total. They varied in size, but even the smallest was larger than the Ternus capital ships. "Those? Those are dragons. Full-grown Void Wyrms, every last one."

The shapes gained definition as they came over the planet's horizon and into the light. Each had a pair of broad, leathery wings. Their dark scales drank in the light, contrasting with the fiery glow coming from their eyes and mouth.

"What are those?" Nara whispered, pointing at the cluster of fat shapes following the dragons.

"Those are Krox planetships. They contain their line

troops, enforcers, and whatever else their binders have enslaved," Kez explained. Her casual demeanor was gone, replaced by a deadly earnestness. "We probably won't see what's inside, not in this missive anyway. First, the state o' things in space has to be decided. Ternus will attempt to defend the station. If they fail, the Krox will board her. From there, they can invade the world below."

The dragons fanned out, slowly moving to encircle the station.

"Why aren't they staying in formation?" Nara asked. "Aren't they opening themselves up to be surrounded?"

"Because Wyrms don't fight fair." Bord's demeanor had also changed, all his playfulness gone.

The first and largest dragon reached a cluster of ships. Those ships launched a salvo of projectiles, hurling hunks of metal the size of a shuttle. Dozens of shots traced paths toward the dragon, crossing hundreds of kilometers in the space of a few seconds.

The dragon vanished. It reappeared behind the Ternus ships, drawing its head back as if sucking in an enormous breath. Then the dragon lunged, exhaling a cloud of ghostly white energy. That energy engulfed the two closest Ternus vessels, passing over each vessel seemingly without inflicting any visible damage.

Their cannons stopped firing, and both ships continued unerringly forward, making no move to alter their course as they neared the dragon. The remaining Ternus ships fired another volley, this time with more success. Hunks of metal peppered the dragon's right flank, and it roared silently as the rounds tore into its flesh. Wherever a round hit, dark scales exploded outward, exposing the orange-white glow inside.

The two Ternus ships that had been hit by the breath

weapon abruptly changed course. They swung back around and opened fire...on the other Ternus ships.

The same thing happened near the other dragons—Ternus vessels suddenly firing on their own.

"What am I seeing?" Nara whispered, hugging herself with both arms.

"The Krox are binders," Kez explained, tapping the sigil at the base to turn it off. She looked up at Nara, her face emotionless. Her hands told another story, whitening as she gripped the cot. "They turn our own against us. That breath? Its a spirit weapon. It tears the soul from a body, leaving us an empty husk. We can't see them, but there's a cloud of Krox spirits following every dragon. They're joost waiting to possess the empty vessels."

"Ternus primarily uses conventional weapons. They have no defense against a weapon like that," Bord said, more subdued than ever. "The Krox took the station, and Ternus only took down one Wyrm."

"That's terrible," Nara said. "Can't someone help them? Shouldn't the Confederacy send reinforcements that can deal with those dragons?"

"They have. That's why we have the missive. They've sent us." Kez picked up the missive and tucked it back in the locker at the foot of her bed. "I don't know why the major hasn't taken us there already, but I'd get whatever sleep you can. Tomorrow, maybe the day after...were going to war with the Krox."

22

JOB HALF DONE

Voria adjusted her coat, smoothing it into place. She waited for the scry-screen to connect, wincing as Jolene's stern face appeared. Like most Inurans she was tall and classically beautiful, but this woman had gone out of her way to blunt that beauty. She had the eyes of a hawk, her beaked nose jutting out over her frown. Her chestnut hair had been shaved to stubble—the five day remains of a proper military buzz cut.

"Finally, you contact me," Jolene snapped. "It can only be bad news, or you'd have slinked back into the light sooner. Tell me. All of it." She folded her arms, eyeing Voria with her ever-present disapproval.

"It's not so bad as you fear." Voria steeled herself. She didn't work for this woman—though theoretically all Inurans did, even half-Inurans. Voria reached into her pouch and withdrew the hedgehog. "Kazon is alive, but, as you can see, not unharmed."

"He's been 'morphed?" Jolene asked, raising an eyebrow. She relaxed into her chair, steepling her fingers against her chin. "You've tried dispelling it and failed, I take it."

Voria was privately thankful that this was taking place over scry-screen instead of in person. She ran her finger along the screen's bronze border, struggling to maintain her composure.

"I've used the only resources at my command without success," Voria admitted. "I know how important Kazon is to you, and to your position. I also know you have both the power and the resources to counter this spell."

"I can see where this is going." Jolene's face soured. "You want me to live up to our bargain, even though you failed to hold up your end of it. The deal was alive and unharmed."

"Yes, well, one for two has got to count for something. I realize this is an unexpected obstacle, but it's one you can solve. I'm afraid I'm going to have to demand full payment." Voria spoke matter-of-factly. It wasn't easy keeping her shoulders square, or meeting Jolene's gaze.

"And if I refuse? What if I only give you half? That would seem fitting, for a job half done." Jolene's gaze became calculating.

"I'm afraid I must insist on the full payment—and, further, I must insist you bring it to Marid immediately."

"More? You're asking for *more*?" Jolene sputtered. Her face flushed, and her nostrils flared. "I could have you stripped of rank with a single missive. I could—"

"Mother."

That single word stopped Jolene, long enough for Voria to speak. "I'm heading to Marid. I will arrive in roughly seventeen hours. When I do, I plan to engage the enemy forces. If you want Kazon back, then you will bring every last provision I have requested."

"Very well," her mother snapped. "You've bound me like a Krox. I have no choice and you know it."

"Goodbye, Mother. I'll see you tomorrow."

Voria terminated the connection and glanced at her bed, giving a longing sigh. Not yet. She reached into her satchel and retrieved the missive that had 'ported in that morning. She'd dreaded hearing it, but couldn't put it off any longer. One more unpleasant task, and she could sleep.

She set the missive on her desk, touching the prime *fire* sigil. It roared to life, displaying the image of a heavy set man behind a shayawood desk. The dark wood was magnificent.

"Major Voria," Colonel Brett began, "I regret that it's come to this, but as you've ignored our last two missives I have no choice." His jaw tightened. "The Confederate Marines hereby strip you of rank and position. You are to immediately turn over control of the *Wyrm Hunter* to Captain Thalas. Further, you are to be confined to the brig until such time as—"

Voria shut the missive off. There was only one thing that could save her career: overwhelming victory at Marid. That victory was unlikely in the extreme, but if she died at least she'd escape punishment.

She removed her coat, dropping it on the floor at the foot of the bed. Then she crawled in, closing her eyes and losing herself to sleep.

When she awoke, it would be time for war.

23

KHEFTUT

The Fissure cracked open before them, exposing the Marid system. Voria guided the *Hunter* through, conscious of the collective relief across the bridge. No one said it, but they were all grateful to be out from under the oppressive weight, even if it meant going immediately into battle.

Voria studied the data on the scry-screen. “Sergeant Crewes, give me your assessment,” she ordered.

“Uh, it looks like the Ternus forces have retreated to the asteroid ring around the planet,” Crewes supplied. The scry-screen zoomed in, showing Ternus cruisers flitting nimbly through the rocks. The dragons’ size became a hindrance, and Voria smiled when a massive chunk of rock careened off a Wyrm’s skull. “They’re spitting right in the Krox’s face. They can fall back forever, using the asteroids as cover.”

“So our allies are secure for now,” Voria mused, guiding the *Hunter* closer to the blue-white world. “Aran, stand second to me. Nara, stand second to Captain Thalas. Prepare for combat.”

"To fight *what*?" Thalas asked, eyeing her with his usual disdain.

"That," Voria nodded up at the scry-screen. The largest Wyrm had broken off its assault, and was winging swiftly in their direction. "On second thought...Nara, relieve Thalas."

"Are you mad?" Thalas demanded, glaring at her through the rings. "I am a seasoned officer and you want to replace me with a freshly wiped tech mage?"

"Captain Thalas, we are in a combat situation. If you disobey another order, I will execute you. Stand clear of the offensive matrix. Now." Voria turned to Nara. "Once he's clear, I want you to step inside. I will talk you through this."

Nara nodded hesitantly, but ducked inside the rings just as Thalas exited the opposite side. Voria noted Thalas's particularly violent scowl, but focused on Nara instead.

"Before you were wiped, you used an invisibility spell to make your entire vessel disappear. I need you to use that spell right now, to make *us* disappear. It's the only way we'll get past that Wyrm and into the asteroids."

"I don't remember how." Nara said, her eyes going wide as she stared up at the rings rotating around her.

"The spell is still there," Voria explained calmly. She was all too aware of the approaching Wyrm, which grew larger with each passing moment. It might be the largest she'd ever seen—larger even than Nebiat. Eight hundred meters from tail to snout, at least. "When you mastered it, you inscribed that spell onto your very essence. Were you a diviner, you could see that spell tattooed on your—for lack of a better word—soul. All you need to do is access that power. Begin with the part of you affiliated with *dream*. The energy will feel pink or light purple."

"I can't," Nara whispered.

Voria took a slow, deep breath. How should she handle

this? Too much pressure, and Nara cracked. Not enough, and the dragon would be upon them.

Aran cleared his throat. "Nara, I saw you cast the spell, like it was child's play. You can do this. I know you can. You're a true mage, just like the Major. You know what Xal feels like. There's something else inside you—like that, but attuned to another aspect. Find it. Use it. We need you."

Voria was mildly surprised by his support, if his tale about Nara being a pirate was true. This woman had used him, but if that bothered him he didn't show it. That boded well, suggesting he was willing to put the unit's needs over his own desire for revenge. That would be important, if she were to promote him.

Nara closed her eyes, and her hands moved in a flurry, touching sigils on every ring. Purple-pink dream energy rolled out of her in waves, soaked up by the rotating rings.

"Now add air, it will feel ethereal, and well...airy," Voria instructed.

Nara's eyes closed and a bright, blue energy flowed from her, into the matrix. The ship vibrated around them as the two energies mingled, then the spell completed in a silent explosion.

"Did it work?" Nara asked, her eyes fluttering open.

"We're about to find out," Voria replied, focusing on the scry-screen as she guided the *Wyrm Hunter* through a tight turn.

The dragon came up short, colossal eyes narrowing as it scanned the space where they'd been. Voria licked her lips, lowering her voice to a near whisper. "I recognize that Wyrm. That's Kheftut, one of the oldest Wyrms in the sector."

Voria moved the *Hunter* in a wide arc, away from the dragon and toward the asteroids below. She took an indirect route, knowing Kheftut couldn't easily anticipate their course. The Wyrm knew they needed to reach the asteroids, but not what route they'd take to get there.

Kheftut began sketching symbols in a tight glowing pattern in the air in front of it. The energy gathered quickly, more quickly than any mortal mage could duplicate, then discharged. It birthed a thousand motes of light, and those motes broke into several schools, each swimming toward the area where the *Hunter* had disappeared.

"That last group of motes is headed our way," Thalas cautioned, his voice half an octave higher than usual. "Evasive maneuvers!"

"What do you think I've been doing?" Voria snapped, coaxing the *Hunter* into a steeper dive. She poured energy into the spelldrive, increasing their speed—but at a cost. That energy couldn't be used to defend themselves.

The last school of motes burst into several smaller clouds, and one of those clouds found their aft hull. It clung to them, outlining them in much the same way Crewes's clinging flames had outlined the slaver vessel. Kheftut gave a silent roar of triumph, and dove in their direction.

"Aran, step inside the matrix," Voria ordered, accelerating toward the asteroids below.

"Uh, okay." Aran ducked through the rings, standing awkwardly next to her. "What do you need me to do, sir?"

"I'm going to focus on counterspelling whatever Kheftut throws at us. I need you to guide the ship. Take her into those asteroids, and use them as cover like the Ternus are doing." Voria touched several sigils in anticipation of the Wyrm's next spell.

Aran shot a nervous glance at the scry-screen. For a moment, she thought she might need to prod him, but then his features hardened.

"Done," Aran said.

She felt him connect to the *Hunter*, assuming control as if he'd flown her for decades. It confirmed at least part of her suspicions. He *was* a war mage.

The Wyrm breathed a cone of white-grey death; the energy raced toward their stern. Voria tapped *spirit*, and its opposite, *dream*. She fired the counterspell, and the pink ball arced into the breath. It detonated, harmlessly dispersing the white-grey energy.

The *Hunter* dipped into the asteroid field, temporarily obscuring Kheftut.

"Now what?" Aran asked, winging past several more asteroids.

"Keep us on the edge of the field, so we can see Kheftut," Voria ordered, watching the scry-screen as Aran executed her order. The *Hunter* circled to the edge of the field, moving out far enough to afford an unobstructed view.

Kheftut hovered over the edge of the field, scanning; the instant he saw them, the Wyrm charged. Rage twisted his draconic features, making the already terrifying impossibly more so.

"Fall back into the field," Voria ordered. "Keep far enough ahead of that thing to avoid its breath."

They zipped between asteroids, rolling around large ones while smaller ones careened noisily off the hull. Behind them, Kheftut crashed into the field, knocking away a rock that dwarfed their ship.

"Major, we must retreat to the Ternus lines, immediately. We are not equipped to fight that thing." Thalas had regained his dignity at least; his voice had returned to a more normal level.

"Captain Thalas, please relieve Nara," Voria ordered.

"You did well, Nara. Please stand second, in case you need to relieve Thalas."

"And what, precisely, do you want me to do about that?" Thalas said, stabbing a finger at the Wyrm. It clawed an asteroid out of its path, breathing another cone of white death their way.

The *Hunter* smoothly rolled around another asteroid, interposing it between them and the breath.

"Wonderful piloting, Aran," Voria said. She turned to Thalas. "This is a Confederate warship, Captain. We're going to use the weapon she was created to employ."

"You want to fire a bolt of disintegration? We're not staffed for that. We'd need at least three more fire mages, and one more void mage," Thalas protested. "It will fail, draining us dry in the process. Even if it succeeds, at best we have one shot. One the dragon could easily dodge."

"But not counterspell," Voria shot back. "Kheftut is old, and powerful. He is not used to being opposed, and he'll underestimate us. We're going to capitalize on that."

"And just who do you expect to pull off this little stunt?" Thalas demanded.

"Aran, turn over control of the ship to me," Voria ordered.

Aran obliged, and Voria eased back into piloting. She guided the *Hunter* around another asteroid, conscious of the Wyrm's looming form. It would be on them in moments.

"Aran, use your void energy to initiate the spell. It's a fifth-level spell, the most powerful this vessel is capable of firing. Once you've initiated, each mage will add either *fire* or *void* to the spell."

"All right," Aran said, a note of hesitation creeping into his voice. He stared up at the rings, then back at her. "Are you sure about this? I have no idea what I'm doing."

"Trust me. Start the spell, Aran."

Aran nodded, touching the sigil for *void*. Power rolled out of him, into the rings. Voria touched the sigil for *fire*, adding her own power to the spell. All around them, the others did the same. Crewes with *fire*, Thalas and Nara with *void*. That power collected deep within the ship, thrumming like a cosmic heartbeat.

Behind them, the Wyrm knocked away the final asteroid. It reared back, sucking in the breath that would end them.

"Fire," Voria commanded.

Aran loosed the spell, and a torrent of crackling red-black energy poured from the spellcannon. The Wyrm raised a titanic claw, sketching the sigils to a counterspell. Had it dodged, it might have survived. Instead, the bolt of disintegration caught the Wyrm full in the waist.

The spell rippled outward, enveloping the entire Wyrm. Kheftut burst into billions of particles, dissolving into a cloud that quickly swept away into the asteroid field.

24

A PLAN

A ragged cheer overtook the bridge, and Voria didn't bother to hide her smile. "Aran, guide us to the main Ternus force. Crewes, what are the Krox doing?"

"Their Wyrms are falling back toward the station." The scry-screen shimmered, then showed two large Wyrms guarding the rear as the rest retreated back to the station.

Then the view was obscured by asteroids, as Aran guided them toward the pitifully small cluster of Ternus ships. Now and again an asteroid pinged off the outside of the hull, but their armor was thick enough to deal with anything but one of the largest.

Voria deftly stepped from the rings, moving to stand before the scry-screen. It would make her appear larger on the other side. Petty, but effective.

The scry-screen resolved into three partitions, each containing a very angry official. The man in the middle spoke first, his gaunt cheeks and tousled hair a testament to how hard the Ternus had been fighting.

"It's about bloody time," he roared, spittle flying from his mouth. "Where were you, Major? Where were you while our ships burned? We begged your government, and they claimed they sent you days ago."

"You have my deepest apologies, Admiral Kerr. I mean that, sincerely. I faced a very difficult decision, and I made the best choice available. I could either show up without the weapons necessary to win this war, and lose it alongside you, or delay a few days to gain those weapons." Voria plunged ahead before he could speak. "I realize the time was costly. I know you have many dead—and again, you have my sympathies. But I'm here now, and ready to help. I've already killed Kheftut and bought you time to regroup."

"True." The woman on the left panel of the scry-screen was a younger officer with a trio of grey bars giving her rank as Captain in the Ternus military. "I'm willing to hear her out, at least. What are these weapons you were securing?"

"They should be arriving shortly. I've made an arrangement with the Consortium." Voria let the words settle, waiting for their reaction.

"You've dealt with the Inurans, outside the bounds of the Confederate military?" the last man said. He wore a starburst pendant over rich Shayan silk, denoting his rank.

"Governor Avitus, respectfully, your world is being overrun by the Krox. This is the very first and largest Ternus colony, is it not? Do you really feel now is the time to quibble about the source of your reinforcements? You called for Confederate aid, and I am here," Voria said. She folded her arms, adopting as neutral a stance as she could manage. "I will be receiving four hundred Inuran smart rifles, six hovertanks, and enough supplies to mount a ground defense of this world."

"Ground defense?" Avitus barked a sharp laugh. "They haven't even attacked us on the ground."

"Shut up, Governor," the admiral snapped. "You're starting to grate on me." He nodded respectfully to Voria. "I understand why you needed to delay your arrival, and I apologize for my...outburst. It's regrettable—but you're here now, and we need all the help you can offer. You have a plan for preventing the conquest of our colony?"

"First, I need to understand why the Krox are here," Voria said, folding her arms behind her back and pacing before the scry-screen. "Kheftut is the brother of Nebiat. That means she's here, and she wouldn't come unless she wanted something badly enough to risk herself. Have the Krox landed yet, and if so where?"

"They set down at the edge of Malgora Crater," Admiral Kerr said, "the most densely populated part of the planet. We have a thriving mining operation along the slopes of an extinct impact crater. The crater is filled with a tropical swamp. I'd guess whatever Nebiat is after probably lies toward the heart of that swamp. I've ordered our forces to set up a defensive perimeter around the city. There are too many locals to evacuate. How long before the Krox attack?"

"Not long." Voria clenched a fist, stifling her feeling of powerlessness. "Before we can retake the world, we need to retake your station. Otherwise, Nebiat's Wyrms will pounce on anyone trying to reach the planet. That has to be our top priority. Once we've secured the station, we can start thinking about supporting the surface."

"And how do you plan to retake the station?" the governor snapped. His watery green eyes narrowed. "If we leave the asteroids, we have to face the Wyrms unprotected. You must have seen the missive we sent. You know what will happen to the remains of our fleet."

"I realize that." Voria ceased her pacing. "That's why my people are going to take care of it. We'll seize that station.

You refit, and get ready to aid your people on the surface. We need to get down there. Be ready."

All three officials looked surprised by that, and it was the woman who finally spoke. "You're a gods-damned hero in my book, Voria, as big as your legend. I still remember seeing you fight at Vakera. If you can pull this off—if you can get that station back—then we'll be ready to crush Nebiat on the surface. Dreadlords bleed, too, and we're bringing that bitch down."

"Wonderful. After we meet with the Consortium, we'll begin our assault. Major Voria, out." Voria nodded respectfully, then Crewes terminated their connection. Voria looked at her assembled officers. "We have one last stop to make, but I promise you'll enjoy this one. We're going to be picking up a whole load of new toys."

Crewes dabbed at his eye and his voice rose a full octave. "We're getting healing potions, and new guns?" He cleared his throat. "I think I'm going to need a minute."

"Sir, are you crying?" Aran asked.

"No," Crewes growled. More tears fell. "Now you wipes get down to the hangar."

"Aran," Voria said, pulling attention from an embarrassed Crewes. "I'll have a dress uniform sent to your barracks. Get dressed as quickly as possible and meet me at the airlock."

25

KAZON

Aran adjusted the parade uniform the major had provided. The collar was too high, the jacket too confining. The sky-blue fabric restricted movement enough to be a real hazard in combat.

"You look passable enough. Stop fidgeting," Voria ordered.

She strode briskly up the corridor, and Aran hurried to keep up. He hadn't been to this section of the *Wyrm Hunter*. They passed a single technician bent over an exposed conduit, yanking wires from the wall. Voria said nothing, so Aran ignored the man.

"Sir, where are we going?" Aran asked, infusing the request with respect. She'd earned that much from him after leading them against Kheftut.

"We're meeting with the richest matron in the Inuran Consortium. She's here to retrieve her son, the man you rescued." The major patted her satchel, where Aran assumed she was carrying the sleeping hedgehog. "You started this, I think it fitting you see it to its end. Kazon only survived because of you."

"I owe him my life as much as he owes me his," Aran said, remembering the brief fight with Yorrak. "Kazon was my only ally, and the only reason I lived. It could have just as easily been me that got 'morphed."

The corridor narrowed, finally ending at a large steel airlock door with a small porthole cut right above the center. Aran could see several figures standing inside the airlock. Voria waved a hand, and the steel door rose silently into the ceiling.

The major executed a perfect bow. "Hello, Matron Jolene. Thank you for coming to meet me."

Jolene looked a great deal like the major, with the same high cheekbones and chestnut hair, though hers had been cut to a severe—and very unflattering—stubble.

"This is one of my tech mages, Private Aran."

"I don't care about your subordinates," the matron snapped, her mouth tightening. "Let's get this over with. Where is your brother?"

"Brother?" Aran asked, before he could stop himself.

Fortunately, both women ignored him. Voria reached into her pouch and handed over the sleeping hedgehog. It curled in on itself, fluffing up its fur as it settled into Jolene's hand.

"You're right about the 'morph," Jolene murmured, studying the hedgehog. "This is one of the most powerful I've seen. This will take a moment." Jolene raised a single delicate finger, and sketched a fiery symbol in the air. She added a *dream*, then a *water*. The sigils piled up, swirling about in a way that made them difficult to track. Finally, the sigils drew in on each other, growing into a nimbus of light above the hedgehog.

When that light faded Jolene quickly set the hedgehog down on the floor and took a large step backward. The hedgehog's body rippled as the spell Yorrak had cast was slowly reversed. Perhaps half a dozen heartbeats later, the bearded—and very naked—man lay where the hedgehog had been.

He blinked sleepily awake, sitting up. Seeing his surroundings, he flipped to his feet with a roar, spinning to put his back to Aran. "Stand with me again, brother. Where are we? What happened to the bald mage?"

"It's all right," Aran said. "We killed Yorrak. You're safe now."

Kazon, still ready for a fight, shot Aran a look. "Who are these women?"

"I am your mother," snapped Jolene. "And mind-wipe or no, I will not allow such behavior. I've come a long way to find you, and that's taken me away from legitimate business for entirely too long. We're going home, and we're going to salvage as much of your memory as we can."

"Why should I trust you?" Kazon demanded. His legs tensed, and Aran recognized a man who was about to run.

"Because you have little choice," Jolene said. Her eyes narrowed. "My patience is wearing thin, Kazon."

"Kazon. That's my real name?" He looked to Aran for verification.

"So far as I know," Aran said. "That woman is your mother, and I guess Major Voria here is your sister."

"That's right," Voria confirmed. "Kazon, I know you're confused, and the gods know I wouldn't want to go with Mother either. I'm sorry for this, but I had to do it."

"What do you mean?" Kazon asked, suspiciously.

"She sold you, to me," Jolene interjected, fixing Voria with an amused smile.

"You sold me?" Kazon asked. "And you're my sister?"

"Half-sister, and I didn't sell you." Voria sighed. "Mother

put out a contract paying anyone who could recover you. I merely took the contract. I'm sorry, Kazon. My battalion needs the weapons, and this was the only way to get the Consortium to provide them. Without these, there's no way we'll be able to liberate Marid. This means saving millions of lives. I hope you understand."

Kazon eyed her searchingly for long moments. "If you're being honest, and I believe you are, then your intentions are noble. I'm willing to go with this woman—my mother, I guess. Provided you give me some clothes, and a moment to thank the man who rescued me."

"Good," the major said. "Now, Mother, about those weapons."

Both women were clearly strong-willed, but the major's usual confidence seemed lacking.

"You'll get them." Jolene waved a hand, and several pallets lifted into view. The came through the corridor leading back onto the Inuran vessel, floating inside the airlock, and then into the the corridor behind Aran. "Right now I have two pallets of smart rifles, a case of missiles, and enough ammunition to equip your thugs. Consider this a down payment until I can bring you the rest."

"Mother, I need those weapons now. In case you haven't noticed, the Krox are holding that station." Voria pointed at the porthole, which showed the station bathed in the glow of the planet. An asteroid drifted past, briefly obscuring the view.

"I cannot simply wish them here. I am not a god," Jolene snapped, her eyes blazing. "I promised them, and I will deliver them. The vessel carrying them won't arrive until tomorrow evening. That's the best I can offer." She raised a hand, and it disappeared into a void pocket, emerging with a long jacket. She handed it to Kazon. "Cover up; you're embarrassing yourself. Then say your goodbyes, and do it quickly. We have business to be about."

Kazon shot Jolene a suspicious glare, then finally turned to Aran. "I don't know you, not really. But I know you saved me, and you tried to save the other slaves. If you hadn't acted, I'd be dead. I owe you my life, and I promise I will find a way to pay you back, my friend."

Kazon offered a hand, and Aran took it. "There's no need for thanks. You'd did the same for me. I couldn't have taken Yorrak alone."

"Probably." Kazon laughed. "But it doesn't change what happened. I don't know what the future holds for me, but if you survive and we meet again, we'll share a drink."

"If we survive." Aran released Kazon's hand and turned back to the major. The last of the pallets had already drifted onto the *Hunter*. "Take care of yourself, Kazon."

"Take care of yourself, brother." Kazon nodded respectfully, then turned and headed through the airlock into the Inuran ship.

26

ROLL THE DICE

Aran ducked into the war room, unsure what to expect. It had been constructed with a large crew in mind, with enough room for two or perhaps three dozen officers to gather at the round table dominating the room.

The size of the table made the smattering of people standing around the major appear that much more sparse, highlighting how outnumbered they were. The company was there, and Captain Thalas. And a grizzled man with a salt and pepper beard.

Aran studied the last of those. The man was perhaps fifty, his broad shoulders gone a little soft but impressive nonetheless. He wore forest-green fatigues, with a bulky pistol belted to his side. His arms were folded, and he stared at the major in a way that suggested he wanted her to know his patience was at an end.

The uniform was different from the Confederates, confirming what Aran had pieced together. Ternus had their own separate government, but from what Aran had seen they were also part of the Confederacy. He was pretty sure the blond officer who'd kicked his ass had been from Ternus, but beyond that wasn't sure what separated them from the Shayans.

It would probably be a while before he started to grasp the complexities of Confederate politics. Of course, that wouldn't be an issue if anyone had bothered to spend a little time explaining how they worked.

"Welcome, Private. Now that everyone's here, we can discuss our strategy for boarding the station. This room is warded, so we can speak freely," the major explained in her clear, powerful voice.

"A moment, please," the grizzled man said, the words clipped in what Aran was coming to understand must be the Ternus accent. He reached into a pocket and withdrew a white pen, depressing a button on the end. "There. I've added a white noise generator to augment your wards. I know you trust your magic, but I'm more comfortable using something I know works."

"Are you implying that our wards are insufficient?" Thalas asked. The words were delivered politely, but acid boiled up under every one.

"We welcome the additional security, Admiral Kerr," the Major interjected smoothly. She gave Thalas a look that promised swift retribution, but if it swayed him at all, Aran certainly couldn't tell. "Now then, the plan."

"Apologies, Major. I have one more issue to resolve before we begin." Kerr ran a hand through his hair, looking distinctly uncomfortable. "The planetary governor has requested you be arrested and censured, claiming they've received word from Confederate High Command. Now, obviously that isn't going to happen. The Governor can't give me orders, but he can tell my superiors. You've already bought us time, and my colleagues and I realize you are our only chance to take back that station. I'm doing the same for you, but I won't be able to keep them off you forever."

Thalas grew very interested at those words, and Aran didn't at all like the predatory way he studied the major when she wasn't looking. Nor did he fully understand what he was hearing. Why wasn't Kerr trying to remove the Major from power? Maybe he considered it an internal Confederate matter. Or maybe he was just practical.

"So what is it you're asking, then?" Voria folded her arms, all good humor vacating her expression.

"The governor wanted to be present for this meeting. I can patch him in using my portable communications array, if you are amicable."

"I am not," Voria snapped. Her eyes narrowed, and Aran flinched in spite of himself. Damn, she could be scary. "The entire point of planning this meeting in person is so it could not be anticipated or intercepted by our enemies. The governor is a civilian leader, is he not?"

"Yes, but ultimately Marid's militia answers to him," Kerr explained. "My superiors will expect me to include him in the meeting. I don't like it, and I don't like asking you to do it, but I have little choice."

"That's fair. You asked. I refused. We are fighting the Krox, Admiral. Do you understand what that means?" Voria asked coldly.

"Not entirely, no. This is the first time Ternus has faced them directly," Kerr allowed. "We have a few veterans who tried to help Starn when the Krox overran it, but other than some battle footage I haven't really seen what they can do."

"I understand that your people embrace technology, and many mistrust magic." Voria unfolded her arms, resting her palms on the table. "That doesn't mean you should be ignorant of what it can do. The Krox are binders, Admiral.

That binding can take many forms. They can bind spirits into the bodies of the dead, sending those corpses to kill their former companions. But they can also shackle the souls of the living. A binder can wrest control of your body away from you, forcing you to do terrible things to those you love. Or they can make you fall in love with them so completely that you will forsake your heart vow just to please them."

"So you think the governor could be compromised?" Aran found himself saying. He blinked when everyone in the room looked at him. "I mean...that's who I'd turn if I wanted the perfect spy."

"Precisely," Voria agreed. She nodded encouragingly at Aran. "I don't suspect the governor of anything other than incompetence at the moment, but we will not allow anyone to hear information that could damage us unless we are absolutely positive they have not been bound. I had Sergeant Crewes inspect all of you when you entered the room, and he cleared everyone."

The admiral nodded approvingly. "I can't say I disagree with your strategy, Major. By showing us the plan in this room you guarantee that no one gets wind of it before it's implemented. So what is that plan precisely?"

"The plan is fairly simple." The major's gaze roamed the room, resting briefly on Aran. "We are going to send our tech mages to the station, in secret. Captain Thalas will lead Sergeant Crewes, Aran, and Nara. They'll bring a teleport beacon. Once they arrive, they'll damage the station's anti-teleport wards, then set up the beacon. We'll open a portal and flood that station with our Marines, and set up our armor around the portal as a defensible permitter."

"Won't the Krox just turn their dragons on the station?" Aran asked. Again, everyone looked at him. "I'm sorry if I'm speaking out of turn. No one explained the protocol for these meetings."

"I'm glad you're showing initiative, Aran. We need more of that." Voria nodded approvingly. "To answer your question: yes, the Krox would normally turn their dragons back on the station. However, if we provide a distraction, we might keep the dragons at bay long enough for the Ternus forces to launch a counterattack."

"Okay, I see where this is going," the admiral said, stroking his beard as he considered. "We can have our fleet waiting at the edge of the asteroid field. I still don't think we can reach the station in time, though."

"This plan is madness," Thalas said. He shook his head sadly. "In the time it takes the fleet to stop cowering behind these rocks and engage the enemy, they'll have already wiped out anyone on the station."

"Unless the dragons are no longer at the station," Voria said. She gave a grim smile, resting her palms on the table. "While the tech mage company is moving into position, the *Wyrm Hunter* and two Ternus ships will make a break for the surface. We'll plot a trajectory to the place where the Krox landed. This will, I suspect, force the dragons to leave the station and engage us."

"If they all come they'll overwhelm us," Thalas protested. "Again, madness."

"You use that word entirely too often, Captain." Voria folded her arms again, eyes glittering coldly as she studied the Shayan. "The *Hunter* will be prepared to fall back. We have better speed than those Wyrms, so all we need to do is lead them away from the station. With Kheftut dead, none of the dragons can best us in a one on one fight, and they know it. That will make them hesitate, giving us the time we need."

"And if your plan fails?" Thalas demanded.

"Then we will die in battle, like warriors," Crewes barked, scowling darkly. It seemed to take him a moment to realize who he was talking to. "Uh, sir."

"Admiral, do you have anything to add to the plan?" Voria asked, ignoring the exchange.

"No, I think this is the best plan we've got. There are several major points of failure, but we're going to have to roll the dice and hope. You've got one hell of a reputation, Major—a reputation I saw upheld when you executed Kheftut today." The Admiral gave Voria a respectful nod. "I'll return to my ship, and get our fleet into position."

"Excellent. I will ready my assault." Voria turned back to the squad. "Thalas, take Crewes, Nara, and Aran and get set up. Bord, Kezia, report to the battle bridge."

27

CLOSING FAST

"Listen up, wipes," Crewes bellowed, stabbing a finger in Aran and Nara's direction. "We are about to engage in your first real combat. If you screw this up, not only will *you* die, but everyone on that planet below will die. Do. Not. Screw. Up."

"Yes, sir!" Aran and Nara chorused together.

"Now get into your armor, and let's move out," Crewes rumbled, moving toward the membrane near the rear of the airlock across from the barracks. Thalas had already moved to the membrane, his arrogant face obscured by his mirrored helmet.

"You notice Thalas doesn't ever speak to us directly?" Nara said in a low tone, moving to the back of her armor.

"Yeah." Aran moved to the back of his own armor, pausing to inspect the potion loaders. All three were now full, two with a shimmering white liquid, and the last with a bright, fluorescent green. "All his orders are relayed through Crewes, I've noticed. The only people he'll speak to are direct subordinates, or superiors. He didn't even speak directly to Admiral Kerr, because he isn't Confederate."

"Doesn't exactly fill me with confidence." Nara sketched the *void* sigil in front of her armor, and the armor went translucent. She paused to look at him, giving a tentative smile. "Listen, we're about to do something that could get us both killed, so if I'm going to say this, now is the time. I don't really know what the history between us is. I gather I screwed you over pretty badly. I just wanted to say...I'm sorry that happened. But I'm not that woman anymore. I've got your back out there, Aran. I hope you have mine."

That took Aran off guard. He cocked his head, considering. "I can't lie, Nara. Trust comes hard. You weren't a good person before. Maybe I wasn't either; who knows? All we've got is the people we are now. You watch my back out there, and I promise I'll do the same."

"That's enough for me." Nara stepped into her armor, and the armor solidified.

Aran sketched his own sigil, drawing the barest amount of energy to do it. He stepped into the armor, sighing as it solidified around him. Being in the armor brought him to life in a way nothing else had, and while the prospect of boarding the station terrified him, there was a note of excitement too.

The armor's HUD flared to life, showing the paper doll representation and the potion meters. Those meters were all green, but Aran still had no idea what they did.

"Sergeant Crewes, I notice we're loaded up with potions," Aran said, using the armor's built in comm unit instead of the external speakers.

"It's good to know you wipes aren't completely blind. Aran, you're loaded up with two healing potions, and a potion of magic resistance. That moment when you're wetting yourself, ducking acid bolts? Yeah, that's when you use that potion."

"Good to know." Aran walked over to stand next to Crewes and Thalas, noting that the captain's armor didn't pivot even a millimeter to acknowledge his presence.

"Sir, what about mine?" Nara asked. She was still more hesitant than she'd been before the mind-wipe, but Aran could hear the confidence returning. He wondered how much of the old Nara remained.

"You've got a potion of healing, and two potions of invisibility. You're going to use those to cloak our unit, all four of us. Any use of magic will disrupt the invisibility, so once we're under way no one casts anything. Stick close. If you leave the radius of the spell, you'll become visible." Crewes set his helmet over his head, then tightened it. "Get your suits sealed. We're moving out in fifteen."

Aran took a deep breath, watching as Nara moved over to join them. Sending a pair of untrained tech mages to assault a Krox-held station? Maybe Thalas was right. Maybe it was madness. But Aran noticed that once the major had decided, Thalas had accepted the order. He was here, leading a charge he thought suicidal, even though he knew the Confederacy had technically relieved the major of her command.

"Sergeant Crewes, deploy your men," Thalas commanded. He leapt through the membrane, into the cold void beyond.

"Move, mages. Move!" Crewes roared.

Aran leapt through the membrane, and Nara followed. There was no change in temperature, but Aran felt somehow colder outside the ship. Just the knowledge that there was only a thin metal suit between him and the unforgiving vacuum outside terrified him.

Thalas had begun a slow burn toward the edge of the asteroid field, drifting toward the outer edge. Crewes had followed, increasing thrust to draw even with the captain. Nara fell in beside Aran, about forty meters back.

They followed Thalas to the back side of a city-sized asteroid, slowly spinning toward the edge of the field. Thalas glided to a graceful crouch at the top of a ridge. Beyond them lay only a few smaller asteroids, and then the empty space leading to the station. A cloud of hazy, winged shapes danced around that station—nine in total.

"Two Wyrms are unaccounted for," Thalas said over the comm.

"Should I send a messenger to the major, sir?" Crewes asked.

"Negative. It's not worth the risk or the energy. The plan does not change. Have Private Nara engage the first invisibility potion."

"You heard the man, wipe. Use the first potion." Crewes moved a bit closer to Nara, so Aran did the same.

"How long will the spell last?" Nara asked.

"And how far from her can we get before it will drop?" Aran added.

"One at a time, wipes. It will last about ten minutes, enough time for us to reach the station," Crewes rumbled. "Stay within twenty meters of Private Nara. Your armor will show the locations of the company on a mini-map, as soon as you enable that feature."

Aran looked at his HUD, but saw no obvious way to do that. After a moment a mini-map sprang up in the lower right corner, showing blue dots representing the three other company members. Apparently, it responded to thought. Handy.

"Okay, here goes," Nara said.

A wave of tingling energy pulsed off her, rippling outward in all directions. It passed with no visible effect, but Aran could sense the residual magic energy around them.

"How are we still able to see each other?" he asked, reluctantly risking another question. Crewes did not seem to like questions.

"Man, every time I think you can't ask a dumber question. It's an invisibility sphere, wipe. Anything outside the sphere will see empty space. Anything inside can see as normal."

"Let's deploy, Sergeant," Thalas barked. "We have a mission to be about."

"Move!" Crewes stabbed a finger at Nara, and she leapt off the asteroid, into the gulf between them and the station.

Aran touched the energy in his chest, feeding enough to guide the armor after her. They quickly accelerated, and the asteroid field receded between his feet. He glanced upward —well, relatively upward. The station was approaching swiftly, but they were several minutes out.

"Here she comes," Crewes barked into the comm. "The *Hunter*. Ain't she glorious? They're making their approach."

Aran watched the wedge-shaped ship break from the rock field and angle toward the planet below. A pair of battered Ternus cruisers fell in behind her, ripe targets any enemy would find tempting. All the pieces were in motion.

He looked up at the station again. Closing fast.

28

SURPRISE

Voria exhaled a long, slow breath. She schooled her features, knowing both Bord and Kezia were watching her from their respective matrices. Neither was adept at starship combat. Neither had fought a full-sized Void Wyrm. Both would be tested today. She could give them a rousing speech, but sensed that would be a mistake. It would call attention to their impossible task.

Instead, she would treat it like any other day. Then, perhaps, they would also treat it as such.

"Specialist Bord, pour your strength into the spelldrive. We need every bit of speed the *Hunter* can manage." Voria eyed the scry-screen through the rotating rings that enclosed her in the battle bridge's command matrix. "Corporal Kezia, normally I'd handle defense myself. Today, I entrust that to you."

"Yes, sir." Kezia gave a tight, confident nod.

Excellent. Thalas rode her relentlessly, with his prejudice clear at all times, yet Kezia seemed immune to his constant badgering. She just worked harder to be the best in her unit.

Voria touched a fire sigil, then a second on another ring.

The scry-screen rippled, showing the space behind the ship. Two battered Ternus cruisers limped in their wake, one still battling a very real structural fire. The admiral had handpicked them; each was staffed with a skeleton crew of wounded heroes who knew they wouldn't be returning from this.

"They've noticed us," Kezia said, biting her lip. "That happened faster than I'd expected."

Several dragons had lifted off from the station's outer hull like a flock of birds startled into flight. More joined them, until the entire flight had gathered. They were already growing larger on the scry-screen.

"More speed, Bord," Voria ordered, not looking at the specialist. He had a deplorable array of personal weaknesses, but he was a talented life mage. The very rarest type of mage.

Fortunately, his chief weakness was a fondness for women. He'd do anything to impress Kezia, including admitting to that fact.

A bead of sweat trickled down Bord's forehead, then a slow, golden luminance built around him. It flowed into the matrix as liquid pulses of light. The *Hunter* accelerated, creating a gap between it and the cruisers.

The dragons streaked toward the cruisers, unable to resist fleeing prey. Especially wounded prey.

"Won't they suspect some sort of trap?" Kezia asked, reaching up to grab the stabilizing ring in her matrix.

"A few of them might, but they won't be able to stop the swarm from attacking." Voria studied the approaching Wyrms as they neared the slower of the two vessels. "Losing Kheftut has enraged them, and they'll take any opportunity to vent that rage."

As if to punctuate her words, one of the largest wyrms

breathed a cone of white at the cruiser. The damaged vessel was far too slow to dodge, and the breath enveloped the entire ship, extinguishing all life within.

The cruiser detonated, a ballooning wave of fire and debris expanding in all directions. The closest dragon's eyes widened comically, then the wave overtook it, blasting the creature backward. Its wings were shredded, and a large chunk of burning hull punched through the Wyrm's chest, right above the heart.

Two other wyrms were caught in the blast, though both survived. They circled behind their dying brethren, wounded and seething.

"Kezia, prepare a counterspell," Voria barked. She brought the *Hunter* about, toward the wounded Wyrms. Voria touched the sigil for *earth*, then added *void* from another ring. Finally, she tapped *earth* again.

Deep brown power rolled from her chest, surging into the rings around her. The *Hunter's* spellcannon hummed, then fired. A blob of dark, pulsing energy shot toward the two wounded dragons. They evaded, swooping clear of the energy's path.

Voria smiled. The gob of energy expanded, and streaks of purple lightning crackled within. The wyrms slowed, then halted. Then they were pulled toward the ball of energy, sucked inside by the spell's immense gravity. Voria brought her hand down in a sharp chopping motion, and the ball of energy zoomed toward the planet. By the time the Wyrms broke free, the planet's gravity well would already have caught them. In their wounded state, they'd be too weak to make it back to orbit for several hours.

"They're firing spells, sir," Kezia called, her voice cracking.

"Intercept, Corporal," Voria ordered. She shifted the

scry-screen to show the incoming spells—a trio of deadly blue clouds—and maneuvered the *Hunter* into a tight dive, toward the planet. She used its gravity to slingshot them forward, increasing their momentum.

The spells were still closing, adjusting their course to match the *Hunter*. "There's no outrunning them. Kezia!"

The tiny corporal gave a fierce roar, her hands flying across the rings. Sigils lit up, and a streak of silver energy boiled out of the spellcannon. It caught the closest enemy spell, dissipating it harmlessly.

The second and third slammed into the *Hunter*, knocking Voria from her feet. She fell into the rings, and her head rebounded off the silver one.

Voria pulled herself back to her feet, shaking her head to clear the stars. "Bord, damage report."

"Both shots hit the spelldrive. We're down to less than a third of normal strength." Bord sounded panicked, and a glance confirmed it. His eyes were wide, knuckles white. He was ready to break.

"Steady yourself, Specialist." Voria allowed some compassion into the words. That got his attention. He looked up at her. "Use what remaining power we have," she said. "Limp back toward those asteroids."

"I'm sorry, sir," Kezia said, quietly.

"Excellent work on that last volley, Corporal. Prepare another counterspell." Voria concentrated on the rings again, synched with the matrix, and guided the *Hunter* back toward the asteroid field, as if abandoning her attempt to reach the planet.

The remaining Wyrms followed, far closer than she'd like. The plan was unravelling. The Wyrms would reach the *Hunter* well before she made it to the asteroids.

"Let's hope our friends are ready," she muttered grimly.

29

BATTERED

Voria tapped *spirit*, then *life*. She fired the counterspell, and a moment later the spellcannon echoed it with Kezia's. They streaked into the cluster of incoming spells, ending them in a silent explosion.

"Yes!" Kezia cheered, pumping a fist in the air. "That bought us some time."

"Let's hope it's enough," Voria said, watching the scry-screen. Six dragons pursued them, straining against the planet's gravity to reach them before they could find shelter in the ring of asteroids.

They'd ignored the second cruiser, and in fact had flown wide around it, slowing their progress. Wisely, as another explosion lay waiting.

"The dragons are unleashing another volley," Kezia murmured, her smile fading to a flat, worried line.

"Counterspells," Voria barked. Her fingers flew across the sigils with practiced ease. "We're nearly there."

Kezia nodded tightly, paling as she tapped the sigils in her own matrix. Another volley of blue spells shot in their direction, and two more counterspells rose to meet them. This time it wasn't enough. Two of the spells were stopped, but four more continued on, unhindered.

They slammed into the *Hunter*, and the bridge titled wildly. This time Voria was fast enough to grab the stabilization ring and prevent herself from falling. Neither Bord nor Kezia were as lucky. Both were tossed into the rings and battered about as they fought to regain their footing.

Something groaned deep within the *Hunter*, a sound like the deep clawing of metal tearing from metal.

"Bord, are you conscious?" Voria demanded, slipping from the rings and moving to Kezia's side. The tiny warrior's eyes were closed, and a lump swelled on her forehead.

"Coming," Bord called weakly. He crawled the distance to them, stopping next to Kezia. "She's not too bad off. I can fix this."

"Do it." Voria rose smoothly to her feet, and ducked back into the matrix.

The scry-screen told a grim tale. The dragons had closed, and were moving into position to deliver a killing blow. The *Hunter*'s shields might stop the first breath weapon or two, but the third or fourth would kill them all.

Fortunately, the *Hunter* still had plenty of momentum, and their course carried them toward a continent-sized chunk of dark rock—the asteroid where the Ternus forces lay waiting.

Voria touched a *life* sigil, then a *water* sigil. She reached into her satchel, withdrew a glowing blue bottle, and upended it, savoring the mouthful of grape-flavored potion. Then she touched a *void* sigil.

Even with the potion's energy augmenting her own, casting the spell was a near thing. It hollowed her out, drinking the last of the power residing in her chest. In its wake came a towering wave of exhaustion, knocking Voria to one knee. She grabbed the stabilizing ring, staring up at the scry-screen.

A swirling bubble of black-white energy sprang up around the ship, obscuring the dragons. Screaming faces swam through the white, the lingering echoes of spirits summoned by the spell. She found such magic disquieting, though in this instance the spirit ward was their only chance of survival.

A keening wail echoed through the ship, so loud it drowned out all other sound. Voria's hands shot to her ears, and she gritted her teeth as she waited for the horrible cacophony to fade.

"What just happened?" Bord asked, rising from Kezia's unconscious form. The lump on her forehead was gone, and her breathing was deep and even.

"I summoned a spirit ward around the ship. The wailing was the sound of the Wyrms using their breath weapons. Without the ward, we'd have had to deal with the spirits themselves." Voria rose shakily to her feet, slipping from the matrix. She wasn't strong enough to pilot in any case.

"You saved all our lives, ma'am." Bord gave her a respectful nod, then seemed to realize who he was addressing. He snapped to attention, sketching a salute.

"At ease, Specialist." She looked at at the scry-screen, laughing.

The spirit ward had faded, showing the space around them once more. White streaks, the signatures of the Ternus gauss cannon, swarmed around each of the dragons. Hunks of dense metal slammed into the Wyrms, peppering them with myriad small wounds. Individually, the wounds weren't fatal, but if one accumulated enough of them, even a dragon would die.

The dragons were falling back, overwhelmed by the unexpected attack.

Voria took a deep breath, then stepped back into the matrix. There was one more matter she'd very nearly forgotten about in her haste to deal with the Wyrms: the *Hunter* was barreling toward an asteroid, and if she didn't slow their progress the Wyrms wouldn't have to kill them.

"Specialist, I need you back on that spelldrive." Voria rested both hands on the stabilizing ring, smiling grimly as the dragons fell back before the Ternus fleet.

The smallest Wyrm had lost a wing, and fluttered helplessly as six cruisers peppered it safely from range. The Wyrm desperately tried to reach them with its breath weapon, but the cruisers danced nimbly away.

"Yes, ma'am." Bord ducked back into his matrix, and the spelldrive rumbled reluctantly to life. "She feels damaged, ma'am. I'm not sure how much she can give."

"I'll take whatever's available." Voria shifted the scry-screen to show the asteroid. It had grown alarmingly large, and she guessed their distance at no more than forty or fifty kilometers.

Voria tightened her hands on the ring, and bonded to the ship. A wave of vertigo threatened to send her to the deck, but she righted herself. Piloting took very little energy, and she only needed to give one more order.

She focused, willing the *Hunter* to veer away from the asteroid. It slowly drifted wide as she fought to pull away. The asteroid blotted out the entire view now and continued to grow. The *Hunter* strained, the deep groan from the hull becoming a painful screech as the keel cracked.

The surface loomed; a wall of mountains blocked their path. She forced the *Hunter* to rise, fighting desperately to clear the mountains. She juked around a peak into a narrow valley between two stone giants. The *Hunter*'s prow rose and began to gain altitude again. They zipped past the peaks, leaving the asteroid's light gravitational field.

"That is as close as I ever want to come to death," Bord said, panting. He rested against the stabilizing ring. "I think this ring is the only thing keeping me from falling. I'm just going to stand here for a while."

"I think you've earned the break, Specialist." Voria waved a hand, and the scry-screen shifted to show the Ternus fleet. They'd driven the dragons into high orbit, away from the station. "As long as Thalas and his squad can take the station, we can call today a victory."

30

ENFORCERS

"This feels too easy," Aran muttered. The station loomed ahead of them, close enough that he could now pick out individual docking berths. Almost all were empty.

"You consider this easy?" Nara asked over the comm.

"Don't worry, wipes," Crewes boomed. "The hard part's about to start. Make for the secondary access port right below station control."

"Won't the Krox center their defenses around station control?" Aran asked, willing his suit to magnify around that area.

"Sergeant, inform your squad that questions are not tolerated during combat," Thalas snapped.

Silence followed.

Crewes took point, the thruster on the back of his armor firing as he zoomed toward a narrow, unremarkable door. He flipped his suit around, and his massive metal boots slammed into the deck then locked with a *thunk*.

Thalas slowed gracefully, hovering next to the door.

Aran duplicated the maneuver, with Nara following a few meters behind.

Aran waited silently, stifling a million questions. This was the last place he'd have picked to assault. They would meet heavy resistance and force the enemy to commit everything they had to the defense. Better to establish a beachhead at an unoccupied part of the station, where the Marines could create a perimeter.

Thalas raised his gauntlet before the door, and the door opened silently. The captain darted inside, and Crewes motioned for Aran to follow. Aran ducked through, snapping his spellrifle to his shoulder as he took in his surroundings.

They'd entered a small airlock, with a large window set in a thick steel door. Beyond that window stood a pair of terrifying guards, though neither had noticed their entrance. Each draconic creature easily topped two meters, and bore a pair of wings and a tail very similar to the Wyrms outside. They were facing away from the airlock and didn't seem to be paying much attention to it.

Unlike the Wyrms, these creatures wore body armor and carried some sort of heavy spellrifle. Otherwise, they were basically small dragons, so far as Aran could tell.

"What am I looking at?" Aran asked quietly into the comm.

"Those are Krox enforcers," Crewes muttered. "They're strong, resistant to magic, and have armor thick enough to stop conventional arms. They can fly, and even their tail is a weapon. Also, most are powerful mages."

"Get the company in order, Sergeant," Thalas said, crouching next to the airlock panel. He raised his gauntlet. "We'll use explosive decompression to throw them off guard, then I need you to deliver me two dead enforcers."

Aran found it more than a little terrifying that explosive decompression was merely a distraction to these things.

"Brace yourself," Thalas ordered. He grabbed a rung on one side of the airlock, so Aran moved to the opposite side. The others took rungs as well, vacating the doorway. Thalas raised his gauntlet, and the door whooshed open.

Atmosphere flooded past them in a fierce wind, tugging at Aran's armor as it burst out into space. Both Krox were unprepared, and one was sucked through the hole, into space. The other wrapped its spiked tail around a bulkhead.

Thalas raised his gauntlet, closing the airlock and trapping one of the enforcers in a full vacuum.

"Kill that thing," Crewes barked. He leaned through the door, aiming his cannon at the remaining enforcer. A high-pitched whine came from his armor, and the rifle glowed bright orange like a volcano then kicked backward, lobbing a lump of superheated magma.

The Krox raised a wing to block, bracing itself for the attack. It screeched when the magma splashed across its wing, but raised a spellrifle and let off a flurry of pale white spirit bolts in the sergeant's direction. Crewes ducked out of sight, narrowly avoiding the Krox's return fire.

Aran took the opportunity to line up a shot, centering the targeting reticle over the Krox's face. He flipped the rifle's selector to level two, grunting as the weapon extracted a significant chunk of power from his reserves. It kicked into his shoulder, discharging a thick black bolt.

The bolt took the Krox in the right side of its face, and its eye and cheek boiled away to dust. The creature screeched, raising a hand to the wound. It glared hatefully at Aran and raised its own rifle.

Nara dropped to one knee beside him, gripping her pistol with both hands. She shot off a quick trio of level one spells, forcing the Krox to abandon his shot. Aran rolled behind a rusting metal console that had been half-stripped for parts.

"Sarge, how do we drop this thing?" Aran panted into the comm.

"More effort," Crewes roared, stepping from cover. He thumbed the selector on his cannon to three. The weapon gave a deep, deafening roar that thrummed through Aran even inside his armor. The cannon belched a wave of liquid fire that rained down over the Krox's entire body. Wherever it landed, the Krox's scales sizzled and hissed.

It tossed away the now useless rifle. "You arrogant mortals think you are winning." The sizzling creature boomed out a laugh, then sprinted toward Aran.

Aran stepped backward...into the Krox who had been jettisoned into space. Somehow, it had gotten through a closed airlock door. The Krox seized him, then hurled him toward the wall. Aran experienced a brief moment of weightlessness as the world spun outside his helmet. He crashed to the floor on the far side of the room, skidding into the wall in a tumbling spray of sparks.

Something snapped in his left leg, and he cried out in agony. Aran forced away the pain, gritting his teeth as he rolled behind another terminal.

Nara leapt from cover, firing the same grey spell she'd used to immobilize Aran back on her ship. The energy rippled over the Krox's back, but was pushed backward in a spray of mana fragments. The spell dissipated, and the Krox turned to face Nara.

Aran glanced at Crewes, but the sergeant had moved to grapple with the other Krox. There was no one but Aran to help Nara. He leaned against the terminal, hastily lining up a hip shot with his rifle, thumbed the selector back to one, then squeezed off a quick void bolt. It caught the Krox in the back, driving it back a half-step.

Nara rolled away, popping back to her feet and peppering the enforcer with void bolts of her own. The creature looked back and forth between Nara and Aran with a snarl, then sprinted back the way it had come. It leapt into the air, using its wings to glide to the far side of the room.

Aran squeezed off a shot that ricocheted off the doorway, just as the enforcer fled deeper into the station.

"Are you all right?" Nara asked, squatting next to him.

"My leg is broken," Aran said, through gritted teeth. He writhed back and forth as shards of pain lanced through his entire leg, puffing out a series of quick breaths.

"So use a healing potion." Nara pointed at the canisters on his armor.

"Oh, yeah." Aran willed the armor to activate the first canister, sighing in relief as the golden fluid disappeared from the tube. It flooded the armor, which directed the flow to his wounded leg.

Intense heat surrounded the wounded area, and the pain faded to numbness. Then the warmth faded, taking the pain with it. He suddenly understood just why the major had been willing to trade away her staff.

Aran flipped to his feet, sprinting forward as if he'd never been wounded. He moved past Crewes, who was still wrestling with the wounded Krox, and circled wide to flank it. He thumbed the selector to two, then unloaded a near-point-blank void bolt into the back of the Krox's skull. The Krox tumbled to the ground, the back of its head simply gone.

"Sergeant, secure this room," Thalas commanded. Aran had almost forgotten the man was there. "Ensure that nothing comes through that door. I'm going to erect the teleport beacon." He reached into his suit's void pocket and pulled out three curved metal rods, each a glittering silver that reflected the lights above.

"You heard the man. Move, wipes. Take up positions on either side of that door. Nothing gets through."

Crewes trotted forward, stopping behind a bulkhead that offered hard cover against anyone coming through the door.

Aran sprinted to the right side of the door, dropping into a crouch a few meters away. Nara mirrored the motion on the other side of the door. She had her pistol at the ready.

In the distance, Aran heard moans. Lots of moans. He looked curiously at Nara, who merely shrugged. The moans were getting closer and louder, so Aran crept to the doorway and peeked around the corner.

"Oh crap." Aran ducked back into cover. "There are about seventy dead Ternus Marines incoming. Looks like they're mostly using conventional rifles."

"Damned corpses. Even more useless than zeroes, but dangerous if they get through that chokepoint. Light 'em up, but make your spells count. These guys are gonna soften us up, then the Krox will be back with his buddies." Crewes extended a meter-long blade from one wrist and ignited a spellshield on the other. His eyes went savage, and he smiled. "Sometimes it's nice to mix it up a little bit. Here they come."

31

MAKE EVERY SPELL COUNT

The first corpse emerged through the doorway, stepping into the room with a ferocity that made Aran want to take a step backward. A pallid glow came from its eyes, proof of whatever fiendish intelligence had animated the body.

The corpse's gaze locked on Crewes, and it brought up its rifle smoothly, as it would have in life.

Aran was faster. He lunged, bringing the stock of his rifle down on the corpse's face.

The blow smashed the corpse to the ground, shattering the left side of its face. The corpse started to rise again, so Aran finished it with a void bolt.

"Inform your men to conserve their spells," Thalas called, without looking up from the rods he was assembling.

"Are you mentally deficient, wipe?" Crewes bellowed, turning to Aran. "We do not use spells against corpses, unless there is no other choice. Their whole purpose is to bleed our magic away."

"Sorry, instinct," Aran said, bending to pick up the

soldier's rifle. Two more corpses came through the doorway, and Aran raised the unfamiliar weapon. The firing mechanism was easy to understand—a simple trigger, very similar to what he'd been given back at the Catalyst. The safety was already disengaged.

The weapon fired a hail of slugs at the first target, making it dance like a puppet as the shots carried it back into the hallway.

Crewes barked out a laugh. "That's more like it."

More corpses were coming through. Aran fired again, but the weapon clicked. Empty. He tossed it to the ground as several corpses advanced in his direction.

Crewes waded into the fray, cutting down former Ternus soldiers. The bodies wore standard environmental armor, most without a helmet. The sergeant's chrome spike punched through easily, pinning his targets long enough for him to dismember them with his gauntlets.

"You either gotta shred these things." Crewes demonstrated by pulling the arms off another corpse. His elbow shot back, crushing another corpse's skull. "Or you pulp their brains."

Aran darted forward, seizing a corpse by the side of the head and slamming it into the deck. He looked away from the gore, convinced the corpse wouldn't be rising.

More dead soldiers came through, forcing him back from the doorway. Their bodies piled in, one after another. He glanced at the Captain, but thus far none of the corpses had broken through.

Aran darted forward again and yanked one from the mass, then willed open his void pocket, seizing his spellblade and delivering a wicked slash to the corpse. The headless body toppled to the ground, drawing a grim smile.

"I think the blade is actually enjoying this," Aran said, slicing the legs from under another corpse. The spellblade, its enchanted metal more than a match for whatever composite Ternus used, hummed through the armor. Exhilaration flowed from the blade, up Aran's arm. Whatever it was felt even better than adrenaline. "You're right, Sarge. Mixing it up does feel good."

"Don't get cocky," Nara said, a tinge of panic to her voice. She'd fallen back, and was using controlled bursts from a Ternus rifle to discourage the corpses swarming in her direction. "There are a lot of these things, and I don't have a melee weapon."

"Improvise, wipe," Crewes barked.

The gun clicked empty, and Nara started using it as a club. Her suit's enhanced strength made every blow lethal, skulls popping like melons.

"Yes, sir," she said.

Aran decapitated another corpse, then brought up his spellshield to block a hail of bullets fired by a pair of corpses who'd just entered the room. They staggered their fire, forcing him to retreat to cover or risk real damage to his armor.

"Those two are using something a lot higher caliber," Aran called, ducking behind a terminal. "We need to take them down fast."

Aran glanced from cover, noting the trio of corpses that rushed past the ones with the heavy assault rifles. These ones weren't carrying rifles, but they did have a grenade clutched tightly in each fist. The corpses fanned out, and started lobbing those grenades in their direction.

"Scatter!" Crewes boomed.

Aran dove from cover, using his suit to accelerate into the air. He hovered near the ceiling, watching in horror as two of the corpses lobbed grenades at Crewes. They detonated in quick succession, hurling the sergeant backward into the wall.

Thalas glanced up from his ritual, but continued assembling silver rods. This appeared to be the last of three, and Aran hoped that meant they'd have reinforcements soon.

Both corpses with assault rifles were focused on Crewes, firing a stream of deafening rounds that left deep craters in the rear of his suit.

"Nara, see if you can helps the sergeant," Aran called. "I'll hold them off."

He knew these things were designed to use up his magic, but if the four of them died because they didn't use spells it wouldn't matter. He snapped his rifle to his shoulder, thumbed the selector to level one, and picked off the first grenade-throwing corpse before it could throw.

The grenade clattered to the ground at the corpse's feet. The explosion sent corpses flying, including the pair with the assault rifles. Aran swooped low, slashing the head off another corpse with his spellblade. The mass turned in his direction, forgetting about Crewes.

Nara landed next to the sergeant and stood over his body with her makeshift club. She knocked corpses away, keeping Crewes safe while he clawed his way into the corner.

"I've got my back to the wall now. Don't worry about me. Healing potion's already working." Crewes forced himself to his feet.

Aran wasn't worried about Crewes; he was worried about the Krox enforcer who burst through the door. It aimed a spellcannon in Aran's direction, squeezing off a crackling black-brown hunk of boiling stone. The rock expanded in the air, and was larger than Aran's suit by the time it impacted.

The rock's incredible mass slammed Aran into the far wall, and a crack ran down his faceplate. The paper doll in his HUD burst into a riot of reds and yellows, showing all the places that were damaged.

"No," Nara roared, swooping up above the enforcer. "Not on my watch, you scaly bastard." She gripped her pistol in both hands, squeezing off a level two void bolt. It tagged the Krox in the face, melting scale and bone.

Somehow, the blow didn't kill the enforcer. It sketched a black symbol in the air and flung it at Nara.

Aran forced himself back to his feet, pouring power into his armor. He soared into the air and interposed himself between Nara and the spell. Raising his shield, he caught the black sigil, which exploded into a wave of darkness, billowing out around them like mist. A wave of exhaustion crashed over him.

"Get out of that cloud!" Crewes bellowed, striding back into combat. "It will sap your magical energy!"

Aran zoomed backward, suddenly able to see as his suit burst from the cloud. There was no sign of the enforcer, and only a few corpses were still on their feet. He flew lower, completing the grisly work he'd begun with his spellblade.

"Well done, Sergeant," Thalas called, pointing proudly at the assembled portal. "We've succeeded. Now we have fodder of our own."

Aran looked up from the carnage to see Thalas standing next to a trio of curved metal spires, their tips forming an archway. Within those silver spires, a bright blue glow had begun to coalesce. There were shapes within, vague and indistinct.

Then those shapes—the battalion's Marines—burst out

one by one. Each was armed with a Ternus assault rifle, and a set of armor identical to those on the corpses. That made Aran shiver. They could very easily become enemies, if they weren't protected.

The Marines fanned out in the room, each squad taking up cover and setting up firing lanes on the doorway.

32

FODDER

Aran removed his helmet, shaking sweat from his forehead. His breathing had returned to normal, and the adrenaline was already fading. The fight had taken more out of him than he'd like—particularly since that had been the enemy's entire goal.

"Who's in charge of this...rabble?" Thalas asked, surveying the platoon of Marines with a critical eye.

"I am, sir. Captain Davidson. We've met. Several times." Davidson stared Captain Thalas down, his body language tight and aggressive. "This 'rabble' is the 707th Company. We're ready for your orders. Sir."

Aran blinked, recognizing Davidson as the man who'd kicked his ass on the way to the commissary. His nose had a single small bandage across the right side, the only evidence of the fight.

"You know him?" Nara asked. She'd removed her helmet, and sweat had plastered her dark hair around her face, framing it into a perfect oval.

"Yeah. He kicked the everliving shit out of me when the sergeant sent me to get potions the other day."

"Ah, I figured you'd made some friends when I saw the bruises. Bord said they were a lot worse before he took care of them." Nara gave him a sidelong glance. "You're...kind of a smartass. And you have this smug *I'm superior to you* thing going on. So, uh, I can't say I'm surprised they kicked your ass."

Aran barked out a quick laugh, shaking his head. "You know, I like new Nara a whole lot better than old Nara. You're a lot more honest."

"You want us to do what, sir?" Davidson's voice thundered, interrupting their conversation.

Aran turned to see Davidson getting in Thalas's face. Thalas seemed completely unruffled, though he did eye Davidson with a mixture of distaste and annoyance.

"I believe my orders were quite clear, Captain. I want you to start ordering platoons through that doorway. Each time a platoon goes through, we'll bring in another from the *Hunter*. Repeat this until all fodder are through that doorway. Am I clear?"

"What did you call us?" Davidson blinked. He cocked his rifle and turned to his men. They wore ugly looks, and Aran could smell the violence frothing just under the surface.

"I called you *fodder*." Thalas took a step toward Davidson, eyes narrowing. "If you do not execute my order, immediately, I will execute *you*. Then, I will have your second carry out that order. I will continue to execute fodder until you follow orders. So tell me, Captain, will you follow orders? Or must I give command to another?"

Suddenly Aran understood exactly why Davidson and his men had assaulted him. Could he really blame them? He wasn't even aware that his feet were moving until he was nose-to-nose with Thalas.

The captain eyed him balefully. "What is it, Private?"

Aran kept as tight a rein on his anger as he could. “Sir, sending our Marines through that door will result in near total casualties. We’re assaulting a heavily fortified position, and every time one of our troops goes down the other side gains a soldier.”

“Leave the strategy to me, Private,” Thalas said. The words dripped venom.

“Sir,” Crewes rumbled, limping over to join them, “I know you don’t like having subordinates question you, but sometimes it’s smart to listen to the people under your command. Men die in war, but it shouldn’t be like this. Sir.”

“I will make this single allowance for your impertinence, Sergeant.” Thalas’s expression grew even blacker. “We send the fodder in, knowing the enemy binder will use them against us. We do it for the same reason they send fodder: to bleed their resources. Converting corpses into minions takes both time and a large amount of magic. We send in our fodder, so by the time we reach the binder they are weak enough to be killed. I realize the callousness, and I salute those men who sacrifice their lives.”

“But not enough to actually learn the names of our officers.” Davidson spat on Thalas’s boot. “The way I see it, if we’re going to die anyway, what’s the difference if it’s fighting you or fighting them? I can’t really see a way that makes them any worse than you.”

Thalas’s armored hand shot out, seizing Davidson by the throat. He hoisted the captain slowly into the air and raised his sidearm in his other hand. He turned to face the Marines, holding their officer before them. “Let this be an example to the rest of—”

Aran barreled into Thalas from the side, knocking the captain to the deck. Davidson tumbled away, scrambling back from the augmented combat.

"This is mutiny," Thalas hissed, knocking Aran away and rising into a crouch. He pulled his spellblade from a void pocket. "And there is only one way to deal with mutiny."

"Wait," Crewes bellowed, stepping between them. "Captain, don't do this."

"So you're standing with him then?" The captain's eyes narrowed.

"Yeah, guess I am." Crewes scowled at Thalas.

"Listen," Aran said, though he doubted there was any getting Thalas to see reason. "There's another way. Nara still has a potion of invisibility. We can launch a quick, surgical strike to deal with this binder. We sneak past their defenses and put them down fast and hard. It uses less resources, and you can save the *fodder* for the assault on the planet below."

Thalas glared hatefully at Aran. "You assaulted an officer in a time of war. After I have executed you for treason, I will take your plan under advisement."

Aran never saw Nara move into position, but he did see her strike. It was exactly the same move she'd used on Yorrak's guards, right down to the pink spell fired from her spellpistol.

The energy washed over Thalas, and he blinked in surprised, turning to face Nara. "What did you c-casht?" he slurred. Then his eyes closed, and he collapsed to the deck. A moment later, he gave a tremendous snore.

Aran gave an appreciative laugh. "Nicely done."

Even Crewes smiled. "He's going to kill us for this. I mean that literally. But until then we get to fight smart. Aran, your plan is solid. Take Nara and sneak up to the command level. It will be at the top of the mezzanine, a big glass sphere. Find the binder, and kill them. Our only hope of saving our asses is killing that binder. Maybe the major will be able to talk Thalas down, if we pull it off."

"Sir?" Davidson asked tentatively.

Aran realized the man was addressing him. "I'm pretty sure you outrank me, Davidson. In fact I distinctly remember you pointing it out after you planted a boot in my face," he said, laughing.

"What I said back in the hangar was bullshit. No Marine outranks any tech mage. Ever." Davidson shook his head bitterly. "Listen, I just wanted to say thank you. For saving our lives. It's bad enough that most of us were conscripted. If we're going to die, we at least want our deaths to matter."

Aran clapped Davidson on the shoulder. "For what it's worth, I'm sorry. You've been given a raw deal. All the Marines have."

"You're the first tech mage I've seen ever acknowledge that fact." Davidson offered his hand, and Aran took it.

"I don't want to interrupt your date, but we have a binder I need dead. Go make it dead. *Now*," Crewes roared, so loudly it echoed.

33

THREE. TWO. ONE

Nara snapped her helmet back into place, relieved that it insulated her not only from the violence, but from the hostility boiling up all around her.

The corpses she could tolerate, and the Krox—but the absolute lack of empathy Thalas had just demonstrated shook her to the core. It underscored how little she mattered, and that she *only* mattered that little bit because she happened to have the right magic.

Who were they even fighting for?

"Are you ready?" Aran asked. He'd already donned his own helmet, and stood near the doorway.

"No, but every moment we stand here I'm less ready, so we may as well go." Nara moved to stand near Aran, then willed her suit to use the second potion loader. Warm, purple-pink energy filled her. It passed through her like a conduit, flowing back into the suit as a spell. That spell rippled outward around them, and the energy flowed out to establish the sphere of invisibility.

"Okay, I'll take point," Aran said. He didn't wait for an

answer; he merely glided forward a meter or so above the deck.

Nara rose into the air as well, following Aran as cautiously as she could. She was already learning her strengths, and head-on combat wasn't one of them. Fortunately, Aran excelled at it. He tended to rush in. That allowed her to hang back, she could generally throw a critical spell at the right moment.

She wished she knew which spells, of course. But she'd settle for panic-casting at opportune moments. It had worked so far.

The room past the door was littered with corpses, about half of which were actually dead. The other half lay on the deck with slitted eyes, waiting for someone to pass by so they could leap up and attack. The fact that they didn't react to Aran and Nara reassured her, and she let out a breath she hadn't realized she'd been holding once they'd passed.

They drifted up the corridor, exiting into a mezzanine—or she assumed the big, open marketplace was a mezzanine. She'd never heard the word before today. Dozens of stalls dotted both sides of a raised floor that curved out of sight in the distance. A set of stairs led to a level above it, and a second set to a level below.

"Up there," Aran whispered over the comm.

Nara looked up to see a five-story building dominating the center of the mezzanine, placed like an axle at the center of a wheel. Large bay windows ringed the very top, allowing whoever sat there to view the entire mezzanine with relative ease. Whoever had built this place loved control.

"Shall we?" Nara whispered, pointing up.

Aran nodded, rising slowly into the air. The light filtering down from the ceiling revealed how much damage Aran's armor had suffered. A crack ran the entire length of the faceplate, and more of the surface was scorched than wasn't. He seemed to be moving fine, but Nara worried how much longer his armor would protect him.

They drifted quickly past each of the five levels, peering through the windows as they rose, Most were opulent apartments she guessed belonged to dignitaries or wealthy corporate magnates. From here, they could oversee their acquisitions, and watch the little people conduct day-to-day business.

"Moment of truth," Aran whispered, accelerating slightly. He rose over the building's ledge, and Nara quickly followed.

They hovered outside a wide bay window, looking into a lavish office. Shelves that appeared to be real mahogany flanked a simple glass desk. A redheaded woman with dark skin sat with her feet up on the desk, eyes wide and unseeing. A tiny trickle of drool leaked from one corner of her mouth, and her chest rose and fell slowly. A faint residue of power surrounded the body. The aftereffects of some sort of spell, Nara thought.

"I wonder what she's doing." Nara moved to the window, peering through the glass.

Aran landed next to her. "Maybe controlling the corpses somehow?"

"The spell does have a spirit residue. Either way we'll never have a better chance." Nara withdrew her pistol. "How about I put a hole in the glass, then you unload everything you have on her?"

"Sounds workable. Go in three?"

She nodded. "Three. Two. One."

Nara shot the glass with a void bolt, disintegrating a two-meter circle. Aran rolled through, flipping to his feet and unloading a level two bolt on the catatonic binder. The bolt hit the woman directly in the heart. It unraveled her blouse, scorching the skin underneath to a charred black.

Aran was already firing again, aiming for the same spot. The woman's eyes, twin pools of orange flame, snapped open. She sketched a sigil in the air, a counterspell that zipped into Aran's void bolt just before it hit, then she rolled backward out of the chair, using it as light cover.

"How did you reach me without being detected?" she hissed, glaring at them over the chair.

"She's stalling," Aran roared, sprinting wide around the left side of the desk.

The binder tracked his path, ignoring Nara.

Nara smiled and moved silently to the right, lining up a shot with her pistol. Concentrating, she channeled something that drew from the dream magic inside of her and fired a bolt of intense violet from her spellpistol.

It hit the binder in the back of the head and disappeared instantly. The binder screamed. Her hands shot to her head, and light poured from her mouth and eyes.

For a moment Nara felt elation, then it fell to ashes. The flood of light slowed to a trickle, then flickered out. The binder turned her hate-filled gaze in Nara's direction.

She'd resisted the spell.

"An untrained binder in a tech mage's armor. Interesting. I may let you live, just so I can rip your story from your mind."

34

BREATHE

The binder twisted to face Nara, leaving her back exposed to Aran. He glided forward, his armor only a few centimeters off the ground. Reaching deep, he pulled from his diminished pool of magic. Black and purple lightning crackled down the blade.

Aran rammed the sword between the binder's shoulder blades, leaning in with both hands and all the force his suit could muster. The blade sank in, but reluctantly. Only the tip disappeared into the wound. The void lightning crackled into the wound, and a thin streamer of smoke curled from the blackened flesh. Confusion emanated from the spellblade.

The binder's hand shot out behind her back, seizing Aran's blade. He fought desperately to yank his weapon loose, but realized the binder was far stronger than she appeared. She flung him backward, and he released his spellblade, tumbling into a disused terminal in a heap. The crack across his faceplate spread another centimeter.

"Ow." Aran rolled back to his feet, knowing he didn't have time to lay around.

The move saved his life. The binder had pulled Aran's sword from her back and was now using it to attack. She slashed at him in a wide arc, but Aran hopped backward, just out of reach.

"That thing is supposed to be bound to me," Aran muttered, circling wide to buy himself a few seconds to think. "What does that mean exactly? Okay, spellblade. Do something bad to her, before she kicks my ass."

"Again." Nara called, unhelpfully. She fired another void bolt, but the binder ignored the impact. It burned away clothing, but left whole unbroken skin underneath. "Uh, Aran I'm not really sure how to stop her."

"Yeah, I'm out of ideas tooooo." The last word drew out as Aran fell backward. He avoided the slash, but was now prone with the binder standing over him.

She raised the spellblade, grinning at him predatorily. "It was a valiant effort, tiny human. You wounded me, and that's something no one has done for over a century."

The hilt of the sword flared a blinding purple, and the scent of sizzling flesh billowed outward. The binder dropped the weapon with a pained shout, clutching her wounded hand to her chest. Aran's hand shot up, and he caught the hilt of the weapon. He brought it around in a low slash, but the binder hopped over it.

She danced backward, her features boiling over into rage.

"This is no longer amusing." She sucked in a deep breath, and roared.

The roar deepened, and her body rippled. She grew, her limbs becoming thicker and heavier. Her skin darkened further, then broke into a sea of midnight ridges. Those ridges grew into dark, bony scales.

A pair of impressive wings sprang from her back, and

her neck elongated. Within moments, the binder was gone, replaced by a full Void Wyrm. She raised her wings, shattering the windows on all sides of the room.

Aran dove over the desk, dodging a tail strike that smashed the bookshelf behind him. He rolled forward, then leapt through the empty space where the window had been, twisted in midair, and flipped so he could track the dragon's movements.

"It's smaller than the ones the *Wyrm Hunter* fought," Nara offered, zipping into the air about thirty meters above him.

"Yeah, somehow I don't find that comforting. I guess that explains why she's so tough. Any ideas?" Aran dove, barely dodging another tail swipe.

"I have one," the Wyrm rumbled. She opened her mouth, breathing a cloud of fetid white mist. Aran tried to tumble backward, but knew he was too late.

Nara dove in and seized Aran around the waist. There was a moment of vertigo, then they were thirty meters higher than they had been. The cloud passed harmlessly under them.

"Displacement spell," Nara said, releasing him. She hovered above the dragon, weaving erratically. "I think I knew it from before."

"I saw Kazon do that to Yorrak. Fancy." Aran sprinted low along the ground. He kept a parallel course to the dragon, looking for a way to make an attack. If they couldn't hurt this thing as a human, what the depths were they going to do to it when it had centuries-thick armor?

Aran glanced up. The station's observation dome vaulted above them, giving a spectacular view of the planet below. In the distance he could see tiny streaks of white pounding into massive dragons, under fire from the Ternus fleet.

"I've got an idea." Aran shot straight up, narrowly dodging another cloud of pallid white fog. "When we first met, you used a spell that enlarged several people. Is there any chance you can use that on me right now?"

"Uh, maybe. Hold on."

Aran spiraled around a swipe from the dragon's foreclaw, but was too slow to dodge the tail. It curled around his leg, slamming him into the metal floor with bone-breaking force.

His paper doll went mostly red, but it was himself he was worried about. He could only take shallow breaths. Something was broken in his chest. He couldn't move.

Black spots swam through his vision, but dimly he remembered to trigger the next healing potion. Relief flooded his chest, and he started climbing to his feet.

The dragon landed several meters away, sending up a wave of wind from its titanic wings that knocked Aran backward. He rolled across the floor and struggled to his feet, diving over another cone of dragon breath.

"Any time, Nara," he yelled, ducking under a claw swipe.

"If this kills you, it isn't my fault," she yelled.

From the corner of his eye, Aran saw a flash of blue. The magic washed over him, sinking into his armor. The armor responded by drinking it up. It grew larger, and Aran grew with it.

He flipped back to his feet. Four meters tall, then five. He wasn't as large as the dragon, but he was close enough. Aran triggered the last potion—the magic resistance one. Then he poured every remaining bit of power into *thrust*.

His suit shot upward, catching the dragon in the chest. Together they flew up, picking up speed as they neared the dome.

Aran smiled through his cracked faceplate, laughing at the binder. “Have fun surviving the Ternus navy.”

“Have fun trying to breathe,” the binder roared back.

Then they slammed into the glass, and outward into space. A spray of atmosphere and glass increased their momentum, and they spun away from the station.

Aran’s hand shot to his face to cover the crack spreading across his helmet. Tiny puffs of white oxygen leaked out between his fingers.

“It’s all right,” the dragon crooned, wrapping her thick limbs around him. “You’ll be dead long before you have a chance to suffocate.”

“No, he won’t,” came Nara’s laughing voice. She appeared next to Aran, seizing him with both hands. There was a moment of vertigo, then they were above and behind the dragon as the displacement spell completed. “Go, go! That was the last of my spells.”

She shot toward the station at full speed, and Aran fell in behind her. He laid his arms flat against his body, willing the armor to greater speed. Air continued to pour from the crack in the faceplate, but all he could do was try to reach safety before it ran out.

Aran glanced down, and relaxed slightly when he saw the dragon moving away from the station. Her form was silhouetted against the planet, moving toward the cloud covered continent below. He turned back to the station, zipping through the hole they’d created in the observation dome.

That hole was already closing as the station’s repair drones rebuilt the damaged section. Aran landed in a crouch, putting his hand over his faceplate again.

Nara landed a moment later. “That hole should be

sealed in about sixty seconds. Sit tight, and try not to breathe. Much."

Aran waited patiently, taking slow, even breaths. He tried not to focus on the air hissing out of his faceplate, and tried even harder not to watch the drones work above. They'd maneuvered a flexible green patch into place, and were bolting it over the hole.

Spots danced across his vision, and his breathing became quick and shallow. "Nara."

"Don't talk," she snapped. "You'll be fine. Just a few more seconds."

The drones completed their work, and the air processors kicked on again. Air began to refill the mezzanine, though not quickly enough for Aran's tastes. He popped off his helmet, gulping at the too-thin air.

Finally, he was able to breath normally. He leaned against the wall behind him, slumping to the ground. "I can't believe we pulled that off. We just beat a Void Wyrm. Well kind of."

"We also blew the entire mezzanine into space," Nara pointed out.

Aran looked around, surveying the destruction. "Huh. I hope we don't have to pay for that."

35

CONSEQUENCES

"... And I hope you are prepared to pay for that station," Governor Avitus roared from his half of the scry-screen. "Your people destroyed a multi-billion-credit observation dome, and vented the entire mezzanine into space—including my office, which contained an irreplaceable library."

"You're welcome, Governor," Voria said coldly. She narrowed her eyes, glaring up at the governor's image. "Yesterday at this time you'd lost the entire station. Your world is already under assault, your citizens in danger. Yet you're chastising me for collateral damage? Need I remind you that my people drove a fully grown Void Wyrm off your station?" She wove around the command matrix, closer to the scry-screen. If the governor had been here in person, she'd have used one of several choice spells to show him exactly how she felt about the matter.

"Please, Governor," Admiral Kerr quickly interjected, from the other half of the scry-screen. "Major Voria arrived in system and immediately killed Kheftut. Then she risked the *Wyrm Hunter*, pulling off a maneuver that slew three

Wyrms and forced the rest to the surface. Thanks to the major, we now have orbital superiority against the Krox. No one has orbital superiority against the Krox. Not ever."

"Point taken, Admiral," the governor replied, as coldly as Voria. "You have our thanks, Major. While I may question your methods, I cannot argue with your results. Now, if I could suggest a strategy going forward, I think you should bring your troops down to reinforce the capital. It's the densest population center, and the one the Krox are most likely to assault."

"Until we know what the Krox are after, I'm hesitant to commit to a strategy," Voria ventured, speaking more to the admiral than the governor. "This invasion isn't like the others. In those cases, the Krox's goal was carnage. They slaughtered everyone, even those who fled."

"And you don't think they're doing the same here?" The admiral's image flickered, then stabilized. He opened the top button of his uniform and rubbed at the back of his neck. "I'll admit I've never directly fought the Krox before, so I'll defer to your opinion, Major."

"Each time the Krox have hit a world, they've been systematic. They begin by establishing orbital superiority, crushing all resistance in space. This ensures no one can flee." In her mind's eye, Voria replayed the battle of Starn, saw the Shayan ships raining down into the atmosphere like burning embers. "Then they'll ground their enforcers near the densest population center. They'll raze the city with dragons, then flood it with whatever minions they've bound. Corpses are common, but so are local megafauna. Only then will the Krox engage directly, usually to surgically destroy a target. The longer the battle goes on, the more troops they can create from the bodies of dead opponents. Time is always on their side."

"The Krox grounded eleven hours ago." The admiral folded his arms, leaning back in his chair. She could see how tired he was, even through the screen. "I begin to see your point. They could have mobilized far more quickly. Why haven't they?"

"I don't know," Voria admitted. She walked back around the matrix, still within view of the scry-screen. "I agree with the governor that the capital is a likely target, though I don't understand why they haven't already hit it."

"All the more reason to get your troops down here immediately, Major."

"You're already down there?" Voria asked, blinking.

"I can't desert my people," Avitus snapped. "They need to see me, see that I am not afraid. Now if you will excuse me, I have preparations to make."

The governor faded from the scry-screen and was replaced by the admiral as his image took over the whole screen. "I'm sorry, Major. I don't understand how you've accomplished what you have with the resources you've been given."

"We fight with what we have, Admiral. You're a direct man, which is one of your better qualities. What is it you want to say, exactly?" Voria respected this man, the finest of the Ternus commanders in her view, but time was pressing in on her. It always did.

"Your government sent me another missive. They've insisted again that you be removed from command, and I work with Captain Thalas." The admiral sighed. "I'm not really sure how to handle this, Major. Putting him in charge is madness, to borrow one of his words. You are our only hope of resisting the Krox, even if it isn't much of a hope."

"I see your dilemma. If you work with me, you strain the relations between Shaya and Ternus. Given how recently

Ternus joined the Confederacy, that's likely to make your government nervous." Voria shook her head sadly. Fighting the Krox while standing in political quicksand was a recipe for defeat.

"You have my full support, but there will be a reckoning when this is all done. I can't stop that." The admiral leaned in closer to the screen, giant now. "Major, give it to me straight. What can you bring to the field? What kind of numbers are we working with? And do you have ammunition and supplies? We don't have enough to share."

"I realize the Confederate Marines have a reputation for being beggars, but I've secured my own supplies and material. I'll be fielding a company of Inuran tanks, supported by three hundred of your own Marines. Backed by a company of tech mages, of course."

"So nearly a full battalion, then." The admiral wore his relief openly. "That's good news. Very well, Major. I'll let you get some rest before you get down to the surface. I apologize for the governor's behavior. He isn't normally this...odious. I think the stress is bringing out the worst in him. He's been erratic since the Krox arrived."

"I see." Voria cocked her head thoughtfully. That could mean nothing—or it could be a sign of a binder. She didn't want to voice her suspicions. Not yet, not until she had evidence. Or proof she was wrong. "Thank you, Admiral, I'll see you shortly. Major Voria out."

The scry-screen went dark. Voria stretched. She wished she had time to sleep, but her mother had already arrived; she didn't even have time to clean up, a fact she was positive her mother would make mention of.

Voria sighed and trudged from the battle bridge, forcing herself to head to the officer's mess.

36

ONE MORE CONDITION

Voria scanned the officer's mess, cataloging her mother's entourage. Jolene had brought only a few people, all pale-skinned Inurans—and all nobility, judging by their elaborate robes and stiff hair. Each wore the colors of their house, with a neutral black trim to signify their loyalty to the Consortium above all.

"Hello, Matron Jolene." Voria nodded respectfully, moving to sit in the chair opposite her mother. She ignored the looks of disdain from the attendants, having long since stopped caring how they felt about half-breeds. "Hello, Kazon."

Her brother sat next to their mother, looking awkwardly around him as if for a way to flee. He merely nodded at Voria in response. Kazon also wore a set of robes, the azure and black perfectly matching their mother's.

Jolene answered just as Kazon opened his mouth to speak. "Let's dispense with the pleasantries, Voria. We'll conclude our transaction, and I will be on my way. I know you have a war to die in, after all."

"Very well." Voria closed her eyes for a moment. Dealing

with her father bore its own share of headaches, but she still preferred it to dealing with her mother. She opened her eyes. "I'm assuming you've brought everything I've asked for?"

"Of course." Jolene slid a scry-pad across the table. "See for yourself. Everything you've requested, and a bit more."

"More?" Voria snorted. "You've never given anyone anything you didn't have to. Even your own children."

"Yes, well, I wasn't given a choice." Jolene glared at Kazon. "Your brother insisted. He said he'd enlist in the Marines and refuse to return home, if I didn't provide...additional resources. I've included some of our newest weaponry, in addition to the ammunition."

"Don't forget my other condition," Kazon said, speaking for the first time. Voria had a hard time finding her brother under the unruly beard, but his eyes were the same—blue and steady.

"Other condition?" Voria asked.

"Kazon would like to reward the man who saved him," Jolene explained. "He wants this...Arack?—Aran?—whatever his name is...to be honorably discharged, with full pay." She shrugged apologetically. "It's only one soldier. Even losing a tech mage won't noticeably affect your chances of victory. Give Kazon his little concession, and we can go our separate ways."

"Why do you want him discharged?" Voria demanded, meeting Kazon's gaze.

"Everyone I've met so far has sought to use me," Kazon shot back, eyes blazing. "First that treacherous snake Nara, then you, and now a woman claiming to be my mother." He leaned over the table, his tone sinking to a low growl. "Aran saved my life at the Skull of Xal. If he hadn't, that place would be my tomb. Instead, he picked me up and carried me to safety. He didn't do it because he knew I'd reward him; he was being a good person. And how was he rewarded? After being kidnapped and forced to a Catalyst, he was enslaved and forced to fight in your war. It isn't fair, and I have a chance to fix it. So I am. Let Aran go, or I'm withdrawing my support for this deal. As I understand it, Jolene can't do this without me. No Aran, no weapons."

Voria gave a deep sigh, slowly massaging her temples. She looked up at Kazon. "I can see the mind-wipe hasn't changed you, brother. You've always championed those who can't defend themselves. Please reconsider. Aran isn't just any tech mage. I don't know who he was before, but he's vital to my confrontation with the Krox. He's the only reason we took back that station. Aran can save countless lives on the surface, maybe help me put down Nebiat once and for all."

"He didn't ask to be part of your war," Kazon countered. "I know what it's like to be enslaved and mind-wiped. I know your war is important, and that's why we're giving you the extra weapons. Let my friend go."

"Fine," Voria snapped. "I'll have him sent for immediately."

37

THE PENALTY IS DEATH

Aran flopped down on his bunk, groaning in relief as his back settled against the cool metal wall. It was the first time he'd stopped moving in what felt like weeks.

"Thank gods for healing potions," he muttered. "Every part of me aches, but at least all my pieces are in the right place."

Nara sat down on the bunk next to him. "Oh, I don't know about that. I can think of a few parts that probably aren't sore." Nara's eyes twinkled mischievously.

Aran was brainstorming a witty comeback when Kez came flouncing over, her short hair as wild as ever. "Bord, get over here. Two big, bad heroes joost walked into our barracks. You're going to want to tell your grandkids about this."

Nara burst out laughing, and Aran found himself grinning.

Bord trotted over, his usual animosity a bit softer. He extended a hand to Aran and offered a half-smile. "I hear you fought hard. A lot of people owe you their lives. They're probably grateful enough to overlook how ugly you are."

"That's why I kept the helmet on." Aran grinned as he accepted his handshake. "We can't all be blessed with your amazing charms."

"I know. Natural beauty is a curse, but its my burden to bear." Bord released Aran's hand and gave him a mocking smile. "I didn't realize you actually had a sense of humor. In fact, I had a bet going that you were one of them Ternus robots that can pass for people."

Kez reached up and punched Bord in the side. She was barely able to manage it, despite how short Bord was. "How you remain so confident, I will never know."

"Joking aside we do have news," Aran said, lowering his voice. He looked at the doorway, but there was no sign of any officers. "I, uh, sort of disobeyed a direct order. So did Nara. And Crewes."

"You guys defied Thalas?" Bord said, blinking. His smile vanished.

Nara shifted uncomfortably. "Aran tackled him and I may have used a sleep spell on him."

Kez gave a low whistle. "There's no way Thalas will stand for that. That fooker's probably already gone to the major. As if she didn't have enough to deal with."

Everyone fell quiet as familiar booming footsteps approached. Crewes poked his head through the doorway of the barracks. His armor was still dented and scored, but he'd taken the time to wipe the soot from his face.

"Sarge, is that blood all over your chest?" Kez asked.

"What?" the sergeant looked down. "Yeah, it's blood. It ain't mine. Aran, Nara. Front and center."

Aran rose with a reluctant groan. "Sarge, is there any

chance we can get a nap before whatever torture you've got planned?"

"Nope. Davidson just sent word that Thalas headed for the officer's mess, where the major is meeting with the Consortium." Crewes's dark skin was paler than usual, but he hid his exhaustion well. "We need to get up there and defend ourselves. You don't know Thalas like I do. He'll call for our execution, and he'll bring in his father if the major refuses."

"Is there a form I have to fill out to get a day off?" Aran muttered, following Crewes out of the barracks.

"Yeah it's called form *shut the depths up and follow orders.* You can file it in the latrine, under *I don't give a shit.*" Crewes glared at Aran. "Now move, mage."

Aran snapped to, quickening his step. He followed Crewes, and Nara fell into step beside him.

"Aran," Nara whispered quietly, putting a hand on his arm. "We haven't really talked about...before. I mean, I know I brought it up before the station, but we didn't really get a chance to chat."

"Do you really want to do this now?" Aran whispered.

"We may not get another chance. They could execute us. So, yeah, now's the time. I want you to know I'm sorry for whatever I did to you. I've pieced together, from the nightmares, that I was a slaver. I don't really understand the details." Nara's head was held high, but she refused to look at Aran. Her eyes shone, but she keep her voice even. "I don't know who I was before, but I think I was a bad person. A really bad person. I don't want to be. Since I woke up, I've tried to help everyone. And I'll keep doing that."

Aran glanced sideways at her. He was silent for a long moment. "Nara, you risked everything back on that station. You saved my ass, and everyone else's. And you're still here fighting. I don't think you're the same person you were, and I'm sorry I've treated you like you are. I don't care who she was. I care who we are. You've got my back. I've got yours."

Nara shot him a quick grin, then looked straight ahead.

Crewes took them through the crew mess, where two dozen long tables were packed with Marines. Much to Aran's shock, the closest table started clapping. That clapping rippled through the room, and someone yelled from the back. "Tech mages!"

"Tech mages!" the room chorused, and the cheering intensified.

Aran was dumbfounded. "What did we do?"

Crewes—for the first time in his life, so far as Aran could tell—was smiling. "You two wipes kept them from having to suicide against the Krox lines."

The temporary high faded the moment they reached the end of the crew mess and stepped into the officer's mess. Two adjoining tables were occupied, and the tension was only covered by thin veneer of forced politeness.

Kazon and Jolene sat on one side of the tables, Voria on the other. Thalas stood next to her, his expression murderous. Several Inurans stood behind Jolene, all of them doing a magnificent job of avoiding eye contact.

"Ah, Sergeant. Thank you for coming. You saved me the trouble of having to send for you." The major gestured at the three of them. "Thalas claims that all three of you disobeyed a direct order during a time of war. He's citing Confederate military law, which is quite clear on that point."

"The penalty is death," Thalas said. The words were drawn out. Smug. "To be meted out immediately, by the commanding officer. Shall I tend to them, Major, or you?"

"Captain Thalas, are you aware you are in the presence of an Inuran matron? And you want to conduct military justice right this instant?" The major maintained the quiet dignity Aran was coming to expect from her, but a dangerous earnestness underlay it now.

"I'm afraid I must insist, Major." The words were even more smug. A smile played at the corners of Thalas's pretty mouth.

"Thalas, please. I understand why you are upset, and promise you we can deal with it. They will be punished." The major's expression softened to...was that pity? "If you make an issue of this, you will be killing fully half of our tech mages on the eve of a major battle with the Krox—a battle we are already unlikely to win. Are you really willing to deny the battalion their strength? Knowing it will be the deaths of many, or possibly all, your brothers?"

Thalas met Aran's gaze, and the fury Aran saw there almost made him take a step back. The depth of hatred was immense. The captain wasn't looking at either Crewes or Nara. He was focused solely on Aran.

"What if I take responsibility?" Aran asked. "I'll accept the punishment. It's fitting, since I was the first one to question the captain's orders. Execute me, but let Nara and Crewes return to the squad."

"I'd find that an acceptable compromise," Thalas said, quiet as the void.

"If you touch him, I will split your skull like a melon," Kazon roared, leaping to his feet. He stabbed a finger at Thalas. "Control your dog, sister. I told you: no Aran, no weapons. If you execute him, then you fight the Krox without our help."

Aran's mouth worked as the magnitude of the dilemma sank in. He watched the Major, trying to guess how she might react.

38

A HIGH COST

Voria took a long, slow breath. She surveyed the room, but reserved most of her focus for Thalas. These next moments would be critical, and while she feared what she was about to do, she also understood it was the only choice that would allow the world below to survive.

"Captain Sandoval Thalas, are you insisting I put these tech mages to death, knowing full well it will compromise our ability to wage war?" she asked. "Think carefully about your answer."

"I'm not insisting all three die, just Aran." Thalas's gaze was still locked on Aran.

The totality of his rage sickened Voria. It blinded him to the enormous damage he was inflicting on the military he claimed to love.

"You've heard the Inurans. If we kill Aran, they will deny us the weapons and material we need to wage war. I ask you one final time: are you insisting I put a mage to death, knowing that doing so will compromise our ability to wage war?" Voria's hand slid slowly to her sidearm.

Thalas finally broke his gaze away from Aran, turning to Voria. He licked his lips. "Yes, Major. I am insisting."

"Captain Thalas, as the commanding officer of the *Wyrm Hunter*, I find you guilty of treason during a time of war. Sentence to be carried out immediately."

She drew her spellpistol and executed Thalas.

The void bolt hit him cleanly in the heart, making death instantaneous. His body slumped to the ground, blood pooling around his corpse. Aran, Crewes, and Nara all wore shocked expressions. The Inuran attendants were even more horrified, and two ran screaming from the room.

"I'm proud of you, Voria." Jolene rose to her feet, giving an inappropriately cheerful smile. "It's unlike you to be so...pragmatic."

Voria ignored her mother, turning to Aran. "There's still something we need to deal with. Aran, you heard Kazon. He's insisting we discharge you. You'll be free to go wherever you wish."

Kazon clamped his hand into a fist over his heart. "I'll see you're well taken care of, brother. I will never be able to repay my debt to you."

"Before you choose, Aran, hear me out." Voria's tone was pleading, and she hated it. But Aran was too canny for any sort of subterfuge or manipulation. That left begging. "I've just executed Captain Thalas, weakening your company. Tomorrow we're all—Nara, Crewes, Bord, Kezia—going into battle to keep the Krox from wiping out this world. Davidson and his Marines will be there too, spending all the lives you saved on that station to push back the Krox. We'll probably fail. But you know what? Our chances are a whole lot higher if you're with us."

She trailed off, knowing any more wouldn't help her case. Aran was analytical, like she was. He'd weigh the decision, then make it. She'd have to live with that choice, whatever it might be.

"Sir, if I can chime in?" Crewes asked. Voria nodded, more than a little surprised by his initiative. Crewes licked his lips, directing an appraising eye at Aran. "This wipe did something today, that almost made me respect him. When Thalas tried to order our Marines into a suicidal situation, Aran stepped up and stopped it. He did it while I stood by. The kid saw what needed to be done, and did something about it. Then, he and Nara drove that Void Wyrm from the station."

"Where are you going with this, Sergeant?" Voria asked, aware that her mother was impatiently tapping her foot.

"Aran's an excellent choice to command the company. He's rough around the edges, but he's actually willing to give orders that don't get people killed. That's a huge plus. Give me some time to break him in, and he'll be the finest officer in the battalion—excepting you, of course, Major."

Voria raised an eyebrow, and Crewes gave her a helpless smile. "You want me to promote him...from private to lieutenant? Just like that?" Privately, she remembered the augury. Aran was going to be instrumental in the final battle with Nebiat, somehow. Perhaps him being in command was a part of that.

"He ain't the best commander to ever live," Crewes said. "But how many options do we have? I'm good in my role, but I'm not fit to run this company. Put him in charge, and I'll get him up to speed."

"All right. If you'll stay, Aran, I'll promote you to lieutenant," Voria offered. She didn't believe the rank would tempt him, but the idea that his friends were going into combat without a leader might.

Emotions warred across Aran's features. He looked from Voria, then back to her brother. "You say you owe me?"

"Always." Kazon nodded.

"You and I were both screwed by the same people," Aran said. "Both mind-wiped and manipulated. But this is bigger than either of us. There are millions of people down there, and I've seen what the Krox will do to them. Those people can't protect themselves. But *I* can protect them. Or try, at least."

"I understand. As long as this is your choice, not theirs." Kazon rose, and walked around the table to embrace Aran in a fierce hug. After a moment Aran returned it.

Voria was genuinely touched. Her brother wasn't one to show such emotion in public—or hadn't been before the wipe.

Kazon finally released Aran. "Mother, I'm afraid I have to make yet another stipulation."

"Really? Another one? I'm shocked." Jolene rolled her eyes. "For the love of money, what is it now?"

"I want our best suit of spellarmor. I want our most expensive potions. Anything we can give Aran to help him fight the Krox." Kazon rounded on his mother. "Just that, and I swear you have my agreement to these terms. I'll return with you, and do whatever you ask."

Jolene paled. "Do you have any idea how expensive our finest suit of armor is?" She sighed. "You won't care. Very well, I will prepare a suit of Mark XI armor personally, and I give my word it will contain the finest we have to offer."

"Then everyone is in agreement?" Voria said. She hadn't realized she'd been holding her breath.

Everyone looked around, nodding.

They'd done it. The battalion finally had the weapons it needed to fight.

Voria stared down at Captain Thalas's still-cooling corpse. The cost had been high—a good deal of it deferred until after the battle. Even if they won, she'd pay dearly for her actions today.

39

TELL ME

Trotting up the servant's stairwell, Nebiat released her invisibility spell. She moved briskly along the hallway, slipping quietly inside the office at the end.

The governor was already there, hands clasped behind his back, staring out the bay window at the swamp below.

"Tell me," she snapped. She'd felt her brother's death, but not the making of it. She'd been too focused on the preparations for the ritual, and now Kheftut was dead.

"The station is lost," Avitus explained, with a touch of smugness. "Voria's tech mages lured your brethren into a trap, and they were ambushed by the Ternus fleet. During the confusion, she slipped a company of tech mages onto the station. They battled your binder and drove her off the station. The Confederates now own the skies."

"That pleases you, doesn't it?" Nebiat asked, crossing to join the governor at the window. She rested a hand lightly on his forearm. "I *know* it's difficult betraying everything you believe in. I just don't care."

She stepped to the window, gazing down at the town. An

idea occurred to her, a further obstacle she could toss in Voria's path to slow her. That was all she needed really: a simple delay. The ritual was very nearly ready.

"I want you to have a celebration, Governor." She turned to face him, reveling in the sudden horror that bloomed in his eyes. "Tell your people the Confederates are coming to save them. They've won in space, and now they're going to crush the Krox on the ground. Build up the Marines. Tell your people how invincible they are, and that they'll easily push the Krox back. Really emphasize that point. Can you do that for me, Governor?"

He gritted his teeth, but he nodded in spite of himself.

She put her hand back on his arm. "I also need you to get Voria down to the surface immediately. Have her mobilize and land next to the starport. I want a pathway lined with civilians, leading all the way to that park right there. You're going to give a speech, Avitus. A wonderful, rousing speech about how amazing and powerful the Confederates are. You'll enjoy that, I'm sure. I'm told you're a wonderful speechwriter."

"You're going to ambush them."

"Of course I am." Nebiat patted his cheek. "And I'm going to slaughter a great number of your citizens. If all goes well, we'll wipe out the Marines, too. That would be wonderful news for you, Governor, because it will mean I don't need you anymore."

"So you'll kill me then?" Avitus asked.

The words were clipped, but she still read the hope there.

"Oh no, that would be such a waste. But I will allow you to travel with me. Over time, you'll learn to love service to others. I can promise you that." She shot him a wink, and he leered back at her, in spite of himself. "You see? You're already losing control of your body. In time, the same will be true of your mind."

She turned from him, sketching another invisibility spell as she moved to the door. She needed to return to the ritual. Now that she'd arranged her little present for the Confederates, it was time to begin.

40

MARK XI

"It's here," Nara said, leaning excitedly into the barracks. "Come on, they're unloading it."

Aran rolled to his feet, more eager than he'd expected. He hurried from the barracks into the hangar. A crowd of Marines had already gathered, though they kept a healthy distance from the Inuran techs delivering the weapons the Consortium had promised.

A line of sleek black hovertanks floated down a ramp, off their shuttle, filling almost a quarter of the hangar. There were no rivets, or any obvious clue as to how those hovertanks had been created—the hallmark of Inuran technology, apparently.

"Incredible, aren't they?" Nara asked, laughing. "I'm glad they're on our side. Your armor is this way."

Nara led him to a tech unloading a tall black crate from a pallet. He nodded at them, then waved at the pallet. It floated after him as he trotted back over to the Inuran transport.

"Let's take a look," Aran breathed, moving around the

crate. There was a large red button on the front. "Seems pretty self-explanatory."

He pushed the button, and the crate hummed and whirred, pulling back and away to expose a suit of midnight-hued spellarmor, the same color as the tanks. It wasn't dissimilar to the suits they'd already piloted, but this one was a little bulkier in the chest.

"Oh. My. *Gads*!" Kez yelled, sprinting up to the armor. She caressed a leg lovingly. "Do you have any idea what this is? This isn't joost a suit of spellarmor. This is the Proteus Mark XI. The military don't even have these. I don't know who you know among the Inurans, but someone has a *lot* of pull. You are such a bastard. I can't believe they gave you this."

"It looks...intimidating. Why is it so special?" Aran slowly circled the suit. The limbs were a little thicker, too, presumably because the armor was heavier.

Kez ran a hand lovingly across the chest. "For starters, it allows you to cast third-level spells, even if the tech mage isn't normally capable of doing so. They drain you quick, but they can also turn the tide in a lot of fights."

"It has five potion loaders, like Sarge's," Aran said, squatting down behind the back. "They're all full."

Kez hurried around to take a look, eyes widening. "Oh, I don't believe this. You are such a lucky fooker. Who did you sleep with?"

"What's this?" Nara asked, tapping the one on the far right. It contained a soft white fluid with motes of gold floating within it. The motes swam toward Nara's finger, gathering in a curious circle.

"Oh not much." Kez shook her head, giving a lopsided grin. "It's only a potion of Shaya's Grace."

"A what?" Aran asked. Two of the others appeared to be healing potions, but he didn't recognize the glimmering blue ones.

"Shaya was a goddess," Kez explained. "Her death created the world my people are from. Before her death, it was a lifeless moon, but her magic transformed it into a paradise. Potions o' Shaya's Grace are drawn from her blood. You are, quite literally, drinking the blood of a goddess."

"And what does that do, exactly?" Aran asked, rising from the armor. "When should I use it?"

"You should use it," Crewes bellowed from behind, "when it will save our collective asses. That potion will make you faster. Stronger. Quite literally smarter. You will be, for a very short time, a god. Sir."

"Sir?" Kez blinked.

"Blame him," Aran said, pointing at the sergeant. "He and the Major cooked this up, not me. I literally cannot remember last Thursday, but they think I should be in charge."

Bord threw up his hands. "You cannot be serious. You are serious. Damn it. You already have too many advantages. How's a short guy supposed to compete?" He stalked away, heading over to his own spellarmor.

Crewes followed, leaning down into Bord's face. "You already have too many advantages, *sir*. You are addressing a superior officer, Specialist. How do you address a superior officer?"

"By—"

"*By addressing them as* sir." Crewes roared. "Now get your ass geared up. We're heading down to the planet." He nodded at the airlock membrane, which showed the world rising toward them.

A mass of swirling clouds covered the entire southern continent. Lightning flashed occasionally. The *Hunter* made straight for the storm, beginning to shake as they brushed the upper atmosphere.

"All right, people," Aran called, turning to face the company. He hoped for a sudden surge of confidence, some sign that his old self had been a leader. There was nothing. If he was going to do this, it was on his own merits. Aran took a deep breath and mustered his confidence, trying to adopt an air of command. "Get geared up and ready to deploy."

"We're already gearing up." Kez stuck her tongue out at him. "Uh, sir," she added, as Crewes loomed over her.

"Well, uh, gear up harder." Aran couldn't help but laugh.

"You're not helping, sir." Crewes said, hovering like a disapproving hen over a wayward chick.

Aran sketched the sigil for *void* over the chest of his new armor. It turned translucent, and he slid inside. The armor solidified much more quickly than his previous suit, and was more comfortable. Instead of sweaty leather, he was encased in something that molded itself to his body. It felt rubbery, and warm.

The heads-up display was similar, but with five canisters instead of the three he was used to. There was also a golden icon on the far side for something called *spell amplification*.

Aran took an experimental step, which turned into a gliding hop. The armor was more responsive, but required a much greater degree of control. He zoomed awkwardly to a halt, trying to get his balance.

"This is our fearless leader?" Bord said over the comm. "Nara, tell me you're not going to fall for this idiot."

"Cut the chatter," Crewes snapped. "We're a military outfit, not a bunch of gods-damned kids."

"Yes, sir," Bord said, only a little sullenly. Then, under his breath: "I'm healing that bastard last."

Aran turned the armor to face the planet. They had descended into the wall of white clouds; whorls of grey and black whizzed by. Finally, they broke the cloud cover. Below lay an enormous mountain range, part of a crater that stretched for hundreds of kilometers.

Terraced buildings covered the mountains on the southeastern slopes, enough buildings that it had to be the capital. A few skyscrapers poked up like weeds, but almost all the structures were built into the mountainside. A series of gondolas connected them, cars slowly rotating on a track to carry passengers from level to level.

Beyond the buildings lay a swamp, with clusters of tall trees dotting the water. Low mist hung between them, growing thicker then vanishing into a wall of white.

"Why do I get the feeling the Krox are going to make us go in there," Aran said, sighing.

"Guess you should have taken Kazon's offer." Nara laughed.

"I will *literally kill* you people," Crewes rumbled. "*Sir*. It's not that hard. He's an officer. You're in the military. Seriously, how hard is it?"

The *Hunter* continued to shed altitude, slowing as she approached a starport where several Ternus cruisers were already berthed and moved smoothly into a berth on the far side of the station. The ship shuddered for a moment as she came to rest against the station's gravity harness.

"All personnel, this is Major Voria." The major's voice rang through every corridor of the ship. "Prepare for deployment. Apparently, the governor wants us to conduct a little demonstration, to raise morale. I'll be down in Bay Three in ten minutes."

“All right people,” Aran boomed, this time not needing to feign the confidence. “You heard the Major. Let’s do her proud.”

41

TOTALLY NOT A TRAP

Voria marched at the head of a column of infantry that snaked all the way back to the *Hunter*. Davidson marched two steps behind her, and behind him came the gleaming hovertanks Kazon's rescue had purchased from the Inuran Consortium.

Aran and Nara zoomed by overhead, using their gravity magic to great effect. Both had improved noticeably as pilots, and each flew with a conscious awareness of where the other was. That teamwork would save lives. It was too soon to tell how Aran would adapt to his new role, but she remained cautiously optimistic.

Sergeant Crewes trotted underneath them, Kezia and Bord flanking him on either side. They kept back a bit, using Aran and Nara to scout as they would in a combat situation.

A hovertank glided quietly up next to her, the pulsors making a low *whum, whum.*

"Is that a Mark XI?" Davidson asked, gawking up at Aran from the tank's turret.

"Indeed it is. A present from a powerful backer," Voria said, knowing Davidson could connect the dots.

Ahead lay a broad thoroughfare that sloped gently down, finally disappearing into the swamp where it met the crater floor. It provided them a spectacular view of the swamp, but it also provided the swamp a spectacular view of *them*. Enemy snipers could wreak havoc on them out here.

Voria quickened her step, forcing the rest of the battalion do the same. She didn't like being so exposed.

Their destination lay at the end of the thoroughfare, which emptied into a coliseum full of civilians. Voria frowned. This was a total security nightmare, and one she had no control over.

The odds of an attack at this exact moment were slim—unless the enemy had spies here. But then, that was a near certainty, which meant even now the enemy was learning the Confederate troop movements.

A cluster of officials stood near a stairwell leading into the coliseum. Voria immediately recognized the salt and pepper haired man in the center. She schooled her features, trying to suppress her distaste for Avitus.

"Ahh, Major," boomed the governor, dignified in the simple business suit worn by most Ternus officials. His hair was slicked back, untouched by the stiff breeze. "Please, if you'll follow me. I was hoping you might address my people."

"Governor, I must protest. You should dismiss these people at once. This is an unnecessary risk." Voria tried to be respectful, but hoped he picked up the steel in her voice.

"You're already here. What's the harm in a short ceremony?" He smiled warmly at her. "Please. I know we didn't begin well, but I'm hoping to repair my mistakes. You've come to protect us. The people revere the Confederate Marines, and many have heard of your exploits at Vakera and Starn. Just give them something to cling to."

"Very well," Voria said, stalking past him and down a narrow stairwell that emptied onto a wide stage. All eyes were on her as walked slowly to the center. The moment she reached it, a simple cantrip activated, amplifying her voice.

"Citizens of Marid, my name is Major Voria, and I've brought a battalion of Confederate Marines to help aid you against the Krox." Voria was forced to pause as an explosion of applause washed over her. She waited several moments, raising a hand to calm them. "Please...please..."

Eventually they quieted, and Voria continued.

"We will do everything we can to protect you, but understand that the Krox greatly outnumber us. You are all in terrible danger, and the safest thing you can do is return to your homes. Avoid going out. If you have scouts, or anybody with a good set of eyes, have them watch the swamp. The Krox will come for you sooner or later, and sooner is my guess. I don't know how much time we have until—"

"Contact!" Aran's voice boomed over the coliseum, and he glided over the stage in his Mark XI. "Major, there's a wall of mist advancing out of the swamp. It's already creeping into the lower part of the city."

"Damn it," Voria roared, the cantrip amplifying her voice. "This is exactly what I was afraid of. Governor, evacuate these people, immediately!" The magic made her words thunderous. "Davidson, get your Marines out on that left flank. Have the armor set up here, around the civilians. Lieutenant Aran, take your unit and circle wide on our right flank. The first thing they'll try is probably a pincer attack, and we need to break at least one of those pincers. If we allow them to encircle us, we're done. Governor Avitus, who is in charge of your militia?"

"That would be me, actually," Avitus said, clutching at

the tails of his shirt. "I'm sorry, but I have to admit we are entirely unprepared for this invasion. Why, I—"

Voria stopped listening. Her fears hadn't been confirmed, but the evidence had certainly mounted. An attack at the exact moment of their arrival, and an ineffectual militia leader placed in the path of the Confederate forces? It could be a terrible coincidence, but she doubted it.

Unfortunately, she wasn't in a position to determine the answer. Detecting a binding on the governor would require the use of a spell, and she needed her strength for combat right now. Besides, even if she exposed him she had no way to convince his supporters that he'd been corrupted.

Voria turned and sprinted back up the stairs, making for the top wall of the coliseum. The civilians had, predictably, panicked. They were stampeding for the exits, trampling their own in an attempt to flee.

The battalion moved fluidly into position, each unit executing its orders with precision and focus. They moved swiftly, watching the advancing tide of fog. It had already covered the base of the slope and now blanketed those buildings in a cloud of impenetrable white.

"Ready yourselves," Voria called. The comm clipped to her collar picked up her voice and transmitted it to the unit. "Hold your fire until I give the word."

A Void Wyrm swooped up from the mist, the wind from its passage so strong that many civilians were thrown from their feet. The Wyrm paused at the apex of its flight, breathing a cone of death upon the audience.

Pale grey fog whirled around them, the keening of souls whispering faintly wherever the breath touched. Hundreds of people—everyone in that wedge of the coliseum—died instantly. Just gone. The survivors went into a frenzy, trampling each other to claw their way out of the coliseum.

"Fire!" Voria bellowed, stabbing a finger up at the Wyrm.

The tanks opened up, their gauss cannons emitting a high-pitched whine each time they fired. The cannons shot two-hundred-and-fifty-kilo rounds, the heavy ammunition her mother had provided.

The rounds streaked into the Wyrm, punching through its wings and chest. It staggered backward in a desperate attempt to flee. Another shot streaked into its head, ricocheting off the skull.

The Wyrm gave a panicked screech and disappeared back into the mist.

A moment later four more Wyrms burst out, each breathing on the largest segment of fleeing locals they could reach. The carnage sickened Voria, and the sense of powerlessness made her long to crush something with her bare hands.

"Push. Them. *Back*!" she roared.

The tanks surged forward, peppering the Wyrms. On the left flank she heard the automatic weapons fire as Davidson's Marines opened up. There was still no sound from Aran's company, but that could be a good thing.

If her tech mages could surprise the Krox on that flank, they might stop the enemy advance long enough to counterattack.

42

SACRIFICE

Aran glided over a row of squat buildings, only a few meters above the wooden shingles. Any higher, and he couldn't make out Crewes leading Bord and Kez up the narrow street. The mist hard already grown too thick to see more than a dozen meters.

Nara hovered on the opposite side of the street, scanning the mist with the her spellpistol.

"I don't like this, sir," Crewes rumbled. "This has got ambush written all over it. These bastards were waiting for us."

"I don't like it either, but we're going to have to spring their trap," Aran said, zooming ahead of the column. The mist only thickened. It made excellent camouflage, and he privately applauded the enemy commander.

In the distance he could hear a smattering of automatic weapons fire and the occasional gauss cannon. Under those were the more persistent screams of fleeing refugees. "Nara, move ahead seventy meters and increase your elevation by five."

It was officially the first order he'd given in a combat situation, and he tried not to be self-conscious about it. He'd had plenty of skills prior to the wipe, but being an officer had clearly not been one of them. So why had Voria agreed to put him in charge?

Crewes had endorsed him, and that probably counted for a lot. Why had the sergeant done that?

"Yes, sir," Nara said, zipping past him. Her form was swallowed by the thick white clouds, which showed not even a hint of her location. It was a few seconds before she spoke again. "I've got something. Movement. Lots of movement."

"Krox troops?" Aran demanded.

"No. Not exactly, anyway. It's...it looks like vermin. Rats. Bugs. Other things native to this world, I imagine. They're carpeting the street, heading in your direction."

"I've seen this before, sir," Kez said, more somber than usual. "A binder can animate joost about anything. Sometimes what they'll do is kill everything, then send it all in to harass a town. They used this tactic on a colony where I lived. The Krox attacked right after the vermin."

The screams were getting closer—much closer. Aran glided backward, scanning, as dozens of figures plunged through mist.

"Looks like we've got civilians, sir," Crewe said. "Are we protecting them or focusing on the Krox?" His tone didn't suggest that he favored either course.

"Sergeant, I want you to get a fire field down across the street. Hopefully that will divert the vermin." Aran willed his external speakers on. "Citizens of Marid, you're rushing into a Krox offensive. You need to take shelter immediately. There's a large stone structure across this park. Make for that, and my company will keep them off you long enough to get inside."

Most of the fleeing civilians started veering roughly in the direction Aran had indicated, but more than a few wandered about lost, screaming in panic.

"Guide them in, people. Nara, keep an eye on that fog. If anything more than vermin shows up, let me know. Like the sarge said, this looks like a great place for an ambush." Aran dropped lower in the mist, above one of the clusters of panicked refugees. They looked up at him, so he slowly guided them toward a three-story building that he guessed must be a temple of some kind.

People were streaming in now; those too far away to see the building followed the people ahead of them. The line seemed endless, like it might stretch all the way back to the major's position.

"The vermin are almost on you," Nara warned. "They're coming up the street now."

"On it," Crewes barked. His cannon kicked, lobbing a single flaming ball into the mist. A blinding wave of light refracted around the explosion point, then died down to merely bright as the fire continued to burn within the mist. "Man, I love this job."

Aran jerked instinctively to the right, narrowly dodging a gob of sickly green acid as it zipped by him. Two more gobs shot out of the mist, but he rolled low and avoided both. "Contact. Nara, see if you can get eyes on our attackers. They're firing acid, so earth magic. I'd guess Krox enforcers."

"You're probably right, sir. How do you want to handle this?" Crewes moved defensively in front of the stream of refugees still sprinting into the temple.

"They can see through the mist, and we can't," Aran said,

glancing at the temple. He zipped upward, then to the right. Every few seconds he moved erratically, knowing the enemy was out there trying to line up a shot. "That favors close range fights, but we can't take it to them if we don't know where they are. Anyone got a suggestion?"

"Sir," Bord piped up on the comm, "two of the potions on your Mark XI are counterspells. That can be used retroactively to cancel a spell after it's been cast, if it has persistent effects."

"I can dispel the mist? Great suggestion, Specialist." Aran glanced down at the potions displayed on his HUD. "That's the blue potions?"

"Yes, sir," Bord confirmed.

Aran willed one of the potions to activate. His entire suit vibrated as the liquid flowed into it. A blinding sapphire glow radiated from the armor, painting the mist a hazy blue. The power was immense, beyond anything Aran was capable of casting.

"That's a third-level potion," Kez breathed in awe.

The light exploded outward in every direction. Wherever it touched, the mist simply dissolved. For over a hundred meters around them it was simply gone. Beyond lay a perfectly spherical wall of fog, swirling about the edges of the counterspell.

The expression on the trio of Krox enforcers now standing in the open was a comical blend of shock and disbelief.

Aran used that instant to devastating effect. He shot forward, lining his rifle up with the lead Krox's face. He flipped the selector to two, then remembered the fight on the station and flicked it to three. He braced himself, unsure how such a powerful spell would affect him.

The rifle tore nearly a quarter of his magic away,

launching a fat void bolt into his opponent's face. Where the level two had damaged the Krox, the level three simply disintegrated everything above the shoulders. The headless enforcer slumped noisily to the ground.

A wave of vertigo washed over him, but only for a moment. He recovered quickly, panting as he surveyed the results of the spell.

Crewes stepped up underneath him, lobbing another ball of flaming liquid. It detonated in the air over both remaining enforcers, coating them in superheated flame. Both screeched, leaping in separate directions as they desperately sought cover.

"Aran! On our right. There's more coming from the fog." Nara panted into the comm. "I count four so far."

"Kez, get in there and see if you can keep them busy. Crewes, move to support her. Nara, I want you to harry the two wounded Krox." Aran rattled off the orders mostly on instinct. "Bord, stick close to the temple. Do you have any defensive spells?"

"I can ward this place, yeah," Bord said. "It should protect the people inside from spells or dragon breath, but it's difficult and takes a bit of time. I'll get to work." He trotted off into the mist, disappearing as Aran turned back to the combat.

Kez sprinted to the Krox's position, deflecting a gob of acid with her spellshield. She brought her hammer down on the closest enforcer, who raised a wing to block; her blow crushed the wing and knocked the enforcer prone. She followed up with a kick to the gut, and the enforcer instinctively moved its hands to cover its belly.

"Not smart, scaly," Kez taunted, bringing her hammer down on its skull with a sickening crunch.

A gob of acid caught her in the back, and she stumbled forward.

"Oh, no you didn't," Crewes roared. He fired a hunk of magma, catching the enforcer who'd shot Kez. "How's it feel? You don't much like being shot in the back, do you? Don't worry. I'm gonna shoot you in the face, too." The sergeant fired off a second shot, ending the Krox.

A titanic screech came from the fog above them, outside the counterspell, and a full-sized Void Wyrm descended into view. It swooped in a tight arc, its course taking it over the temple. The Wyrm breathed a cloud of pallid fog; the cone moved to envelop the temple.

A sea of glowing white sigils sprang up, forming a perfect dome around the temple just before the breath hit. The Wyrm's breath washed harmlessly over the ward, shunted away from the refugees.

"Nice work, Bord." Aran zipped upward, circling wide as he studied the dragon. How would it react? And what was the best way to take it down? Could they even?

The dragon roared its fury, then dove. It crashed into the ground right outside the temple, cracks radiating out around its feet like miniature fissures opening.

"I do not enjoy being thwarted, little human."

The beast's tail shot forward in a blur, impossibly fast. The spiked tip punched through Bord's armor, erupting out the back and continuing for a full meter. The end was slick with Bord's blood, and his hands wrapped around the spike buried in his chest.

"Is that a healing potion? Let's get rid of that." The dragon's clawed hand shot out and crushed the potion loaders, splattering the potions uselessly on the outside of Bord's armor. Its tail came up, then smashed Bord into the ground, face first.

The faceplate shattered on impact, showing Bord's ruined face. He coughed violently, spurting a mouthful of blood.

Then the dragon slammed him into the ground again, snapping his neck.

43

PAYBACK

"Noo!" Aran roared, already diving toward the Wyrm. He aimed his rifle at its face, firing a second level three void bolt. It ripped at his reserves, and a new sigil appeared on his HUD: a half-full ball of blue.

The Wyrm dodged, but the bolt still caught it in the right wing. A wide swath of leathery scales simply ceased to exist, and the suddenly flightless Wyrm crashed to the ground outside the temple, crushing several refugees. It flipped over faster than any cat, its long tail circling above it, seeking prey.

"You are the one who drove my little sister from the station in orbit," the Wyrm roared, glaring up at Aran as Aran circled around it. "You will not find me so easily bested."

The Wyrm's claw came up, and it began sketching sigils—but not like Aran would have, or even Voria. The sigils flowed from the tip of the dragon's claw in a wave, forming a spell more complex than Aran had ever witnessed. Infinitely more complex than even a level three spell.

Aran had no idea what the spell would do, but if it was stronger than a level three he was positive he didn't want to find out.

"Let's hope this works," Aran muttered, willing the suit to use the last blue potion. As before, his suit began to radiate sapphire light. He dove toward the dragon, twisting to narrowly avoid the tail as the tip plunged past him.

Aran focused the counterspell into one gauntlet; the glow pooled there, blazing. He rolled over the Wyrm's slash at him, discharging the counterspell at point-blank range. It slammed into the delicate sea of sigils, shattering them into mana shards.

Kez sprinted up the stone street behind the dragon, leaping into the air and coming down high on its back. She raised her hammer, screaming wordlessly as she brought it crashing down on the dragon's shoulder, right where the wing met the body. Bone shattered, and the second wing slumped.

"I will devour your souls and pour my young into your vessels," the Wyrm screeched, rearing up on its hind legs. It sucked in a deep breath, preparing to breathe.

"Nah." Aran's rifle snapped to his shoulder, and a level three void bolt zipped into the Wyrm's mouth. Gums and teeth disintegrated, and the Wyrm shrieked. The dragon thrashed about wildly, crushing more refugees as it writhed toward the mist.

"What's your hurry?" Aran taunted. He poured on the speed, and the Mark XI responded in a way the Mark V never could. It crossed the distance in seconds, putting Aran directly over the Wyrm. He reached into his void pocket, removing his spellblade. The weapon greeted him eagerly, ready for use.

Aran forced the armor into a steep dive, bracing the

sword against the leg of the suit. He drove the blade through the Wyrm's skull, pinning it to the stone, then reached deep into his reserves and poured a torrent of void lightning directly into the dragon's brain. The dragon writhed beneath him, a massive claw slamming into the stone behind Aran.

The stench of cooked meat filled the air around him, and the dragon stopped thrashing.

"Sergeant," Aran called tiredly. "Do you have word from the Marines? Is their line holding?"

"They're taking a beating," Crewes replied. "There's another binder on that flank, and she's throwin' some sort of giant snakes at them. But their line is holding, for now."

"Okay, that gives us a little time. Mount up, people," Aran called with as much confidence as he could muster. "We're moving out."

"Aran, Bord is *dead*," Nara cried. "Aren't you going to do anything?"

"We can't joost leave his body here." Kez wept softly, emotion thickening her voice.

"You think I don't know that?" Aran said, fighting to get the words out around a growing lump in his throat. "There's no time for guilt, or shock, or even anger. The war isn't going to wait for us to recover. We honor Bord by protecting this city. Let's move, people."

Crewes was the first to recover. "You heard the man. Get back in formation, and get ready to head back into that fog." He started confidently up the street toward the mist.

"What about us?" a matronly woman called. She leaned heavily on a cane. "Are you just going to leave us?"

Aran turned to face the woman. "The best way we can help you is by eliminating binders." He drifted closer, hovering in the air near her. "We don't have the manpower to guard you here, but now that the binder is dead you're probably safe. Stay inside the temple until we come back."

He didn't wait for an answer, but flew up over the squad, catching up as they plunged back into the mist. He immediately missed the extended visibility, especially knowing their enemies could probably see through this muck.

"You got a plan, sir?" Crewes asked, the way he emphasized *sir* suggesting that he didn't think so.

"Yep, nice and simple. We can hear the Krox assaulting the major's position. We're going to come in behind them. We're looking for true mages. Consider us a kill squad until further notice."

"You want to hit their backline." Kez laughed sharply into the comm. There was a deadly edge to that laughter. "I think I'm going to enjoy this particular bit of payback."

They pushed through the fog, moving up narrow alleyways to hide their silhouettes from the enemy. It didn't take long to reach the edge of the battlefield. The mist broke around the major, evidence of a counterspell identical to the one Aran had used.

Six tanks were arrayed across the courtyard in a reverse horseshoe, each with a firing arc designed to protect the center. The major stood atop the shattered remains of a building, surveying the battlefield with the focused gaze of a raptor.

A wave of corpses burst from the mist, charging the tanks. Squads of Marines rolled from under the tanks, bringing their brand new Inuran rifles to bear. They lit into the charging corpses, cutting them down as quickly as they emerged. The bodies piled up, quickly reaching a height that made it difficult for the ones behind them to move forward.

"Perfect," Aran said, smiling. He floated back into the

mist. "Let's head a hundred and fifty meters south, then move west. That should put us somewhere around where the binder is."

The squad moved with unified intensity. No one spoke. No one said the name. But they were all thinking it. Bord would be avenged. Killing the Wyrm wasn't enough. This binder was going to pay the price, too—and so were the rest of the Krox on this world.

"Freeze," Nara snapped.

Aran froze. So did the rest of the company.

"There," Nara whispered, "in the building across the street. On the fourth floor, at the balcony."

Aran scanned the area she'd indicated, finding the outline of the building in the mist. He drifted a few meters closer, picking out a shape on the balcony.

"Nara, take the shot," he whispered back, slowly raising his rifle to his shoulder.

"Copy that," Nara's armor zipped over the balcony, and she fired a level two void bolt.

The binder, this one in human form, raised her staff over her head. The void bolt rebounded off an invisible shield, and a ripple of iridescent sigils flowed out from the point of impact. Fortunately, the shield was directional, angled upward to block Nara's shot.

Aran fired another level three bolt directly at the binder's exposed side. It caught her in the midriff, vaporizing flesh and bone alike. Her hands flew to the ghastly wound, just in time for a wave of magical napalm to blanket the balcony. Her agonized scream drowned out the distant screams of the refugees.

"This is for Bord, you bitch," Kez roared, leaping onto the balcony from the street below. She brought her hammer down, ending the binder's cries.

They all stood around her body, panting. It didn't help at all with the pain.

"Let's link up with the major's position," Aran ordered, struggling to keep the weariness from his voice. Dimly, part of him wished he'd taken Kazon's offer. He shoved that part down. Being here was important, and things would be even worse if he'd backed out like a coward. He forced himself to look at the aftermath.

Bodies carpeted the streets around them, some killed during the initial attack, others bound and sent to fight before being put down again. The screams in the distance made it clear that more bodies were joining them, every moment. Just like Bord had.

Aran balled his fingers into a fist. The Krox had to be stopped, the personal cost be damned.

44

A HUNCH

Voria smile grimly when the transport-sized serpent simply collapsed, like a puppet whose strings had suddenly been cut. All over the battlefield, corpses fell bonelessly.

"Captain Davidson, what's your status?" she asked, scanning the wall of mist outside her counterspell. There was nothing visible, of course, but she could feel them out there: powerful binders, most of whom were also Wyrms and therefore ancient and nearly impossible to kill.

"We've taken devastating casualties," Davidson yelled back, his voice almost drowned out by the gauss cannon on his tank. "I've rallied the remaining Marines around the armor, and we're falling slowly back to your position. If you've got a way to relieve us, we'll take it."

"I think that can be arranged. This is Voria to armored company. Move to Captain Davidson's position, and offer relief."

All six tanks rose into the air, then zoomed toward Davidson.

"Lieutenant Aran," Voria asked, "what's your status?"

"We're returning now, sir," Aran replied, his unmistakable Mark XI armor bursting from the mist into the area cleared by her counterspell. "We've downed two of the enemy binders, one of whom was an adult Void Wyrm. There were...casualties."

The rest of the company limped into the mist, shoulders slumped.

"Bord?" Voria asked, naming the only person she didn't see. She frowned, remembering his place in the augury.

"He took a tail spike through the chest," Aran explained rigidly. He was bottling it up. That kind of compartmentalization was important during combat, but she'd need to speak to him after the battle. To make sure he didn't lock up, as so many new officers did when losing someone in their command for the first time.

"We'll honor his sacrifice later, Lieutenant. For now, we need to finish securing this city. Captain Davidson's position is tenuous, though I've sent the rest of the armor to relieve him." Voria turned to face that direction, absently tapping her chin. "I don't understand this tactic. Nebiat has more binders, and she could have assembled a much larger army of corpses. I expected her to either ignore us or hit us with overwhelming force."

"Sir, it can't be a coincidence that she hit during our landing," Aran said. "Maybe she wasn't ready, and sent only what she could field quickly."

"Or maybe this was designed to keep us bottled up here, on the defensive. Maybe it's a feint, concealing whatever she's after out there." Voria frowned as the mist suddenly began to recede. "Captain, status report."

"The reinforcements have arrived and pushed back the corpses," Davidson said, his voice thick with the inevitable exhaustion that followed adrenaline. “It looks like they’re in full retreat now, and the mist is going with them.”

“They’re falling back?” Aran asked. He zoomed up above the city, facing the swamp.

“Sir, I don’t get it,” Crewes said, shaking his armored head.

“I think I do, and I don’t much like it,” Voria said, staring down at the swamp. The mist had already flowed back to the base of the slop, and was beginning to lose its supernatural thickness. “Captain Davidson, fall back to the landing site. Establish a defensible perimeter, and set up triage stations. Anyone with medical skills is relieved and expected to volunteer.”

“Yes, sir. I’ll make it happen.” Davidson’s voice was confident, which pleased her. He hadn’t been shaken by the carnage. Of course, he was a veteran.

Aran might be another matter, and Voria wished she could see his face. Had Bord’s death shaken his confidence? This was, after all, his first battle as an officer. Of course, the man had also killed two enemy binders in quick succession, more than anyone else in the battle.

Hopefully he saw that too, and didn’t focus solely on Bord.

“Aran, take your squad and direct as many survivors to shelter as possible. Look for any lingering threats. Report to me once you’ve secured the area.” That would give her time to investigate, then she could speak to him about Bord’s death.

“What are you going to be doing, sir?” Aran asked.

“I’m going to investigate a hunch, Lieutenant. I suspect I know what Nebiat is after on this world, and I need to confirm it. Now get to work.”

“Yes, sir,” Aran replied. He and his unit moved off in the

direction they'd come, into the smoking remains of the city proper.

Voria turned and peered up the street toward the governor's palace. Right below that palace stood the university, and at the university she'd find the local archives. She picked her path up the ruined street, forcing herself to look at the faces of the fallen. Their bodies would be burned soon, and she honored them a final time. They were gone, but some tiny part of them was remembered in her. It wasn't much, but it was something.

She climbed slowly, finally reaching a wide marble building. A picture of an open book stood over the doors, confirming that this was the archive. Voria pushed open the door, and stepped into a near-silent room.

Stacks of books sat on dark wooden tables, and row upon row of shelves disappeared into the distance. This place was bigger than it appeared; it was probably built deep into the mountain. Very pragmatic.

"Can I help you?" A broad-shouldered man stepped in front of her. His salt-and-pepper hair had been cut short, and matched the stubble on his face. He wore an outfit almost identical to her own, right down to the mage's satchel.

"I take it you are the local archivist?" she ventured. Voria could use her rank, but the best way to attain what she wanted was cooperation. If this man felt threatened or marginalized, he could simply neglect to share his decades of knowledge about this world.

"You take it correctly. And I take it you are Major Voria of the Confederate Marines. What do you seek in my archive, Major?"

She noted he hadn't offered a name.

"I need to know about this world's oldest myths. Specifically, how this crater was formed and what lies at the center of the swamp." Voria folded her arms, deciding to trust him with the entire truth. "Krox dreadlords do not leave jobs half-finished. They do not launch raids. They annihilate worlds. The attack today was a distraction, and I believe it was to cover up whatever the Krox are seeking. I'm hoping you can help me determine what that is."

"I have an obligation to help," the man said, sitting down at a nearby table. He motioned for her to join him. "Please, sit. Why don't we begin with introductions? I am called Horuk."

"Pleased to meet you, Archivist," Voria said, perhaps a touch impatiently.

"Let's get to the meat of it, then. This world is old. Very old. It's been settled by half a dozen different species over a period of twenty millennia. Before any of that, it was the site of a battle between two ancient gods. They fought in the space above the world, and the loser was hurled to this world, creating the crater you now see. That god, we believe, is still here. Its heart lies near the center of the swamp."

"Nebiat is too crafty to be here for a simple Catalyst, even one as powerful as this," Voria mused, steepling her fingers under her chin. "She can gain a little strength from it, but won't be able to do much else. So why sacrifice so much to claim it?"

"There, I have no answer." Horuk shrugged apologetically. "I can do more research, and might be able to find something. But off the top of my head? I have no idea what the dreadlord is seeking at the Catalyst."

"If we want this world to survive, then we need to find the answer. For the time being consider me your research assistant," Voria offered. "Help me find what she's after, and I promise we will stop her from getting it."

"I think we're in agreement then, Major." Horuk smiled grimly. "Let's get to work then."

45

THE POWER OF BEER

Aran tucked his helmet under his arm, resisting the urge to put it back on. Nara had suggested it might help if the refugees could see his face, so he kept it off. He'd considered taking the armor off entirely, but the idea that the Krox could come back at any time made him think better of it. They needed to be ready for a follow-up assault, even if it seemed unlikely.

They'd managed to direct a few hundred refugees to the makeshift shelters, but it felt like so little amidst the carnage.

"Aran, did you want to talk?" Nara glided to a stop next to him. "I mean, about Bord. We collected his body..."

He considered the question. Did he want to talk?

"Thank you for that." Aran looked away from her. "I'm going to go check in with the major. Would you mind keeping an eye on things here?"

"Sure, but I think Davidson's people have everything in hand. The barricades are up, and watches have been assigned." She raised an eyebrow. "Sooner or later, we're going to need to talk. This isn't your fault."

"I know, trust me. I'm not doing the 'oh god I'm a terrible leader' thing." He forced himself to look at her. "It's just a lot to process, you know? I need a little time. I'll be fine. Thanks for looking out for me. It helps knowing you have my back."

"All right, I'll let you off the hook." She laughed. It crinkled her nose, drawing the freckles together. "Now go do your officer stuff. But when you get back, come see me, okay?"

Aran smiled. "I'll do that. We'll raise a glass to Bord."

"He'd have liked that." Nara tucked her helmet firmly under her arm, then zoomed off in the opposite direction. They both pretended that Bord's death wasn't tearing them up, a kind of mutual defense against grief.

He turned toward the archive at the top of the hill, zooming slowly in that direction. He kept his elevation at a precise thirty meters, within easy view of everyone below. The effect was somewhat spoiled by the pillars of smoke rising from the buildings around him.

Had he made the right decision in having Bord protect the temple? Could he have reacted more quickly when the dragon landed? Heat bubbled up in his gut. He shouldn't have even been in charge in the first place. He had no experience at this, and that lack of experience might get the whole company killed.

But what was the better option? The Major couldn't assume control, and Crewes had made it clear he didn't feel up to the job. So what option did that leave? Stepping up. Putting aside his own bullshit emotions, and focusing on the job. Before someone else died.

Aran drifted down to the wide double doors leading into the archive. He touched down right outside and gently pushed open the door on the right. The interior was dimly lit, but after his eyes adjusted he made out the rows of bookshelves. They smelled heavenly, tickling a memory he couldn't quite grasp.

The cavernous room was deserted except for Major Voria and a mage he took for the archivist. He walked boldly in their direction, nodding at the major when she looked up at his approach.

"Sir. You asked me to report to you when the area was secure. Shall I come back later?"

"Now is fine, just give me a moment." She touched the archivist on the shoulder. "See if you can find more about the Guardian, and about whatever these strange skies are. What we have so far is maddeningly unspecific. I'll be right back."

Aran moved out of earshot and waited for the major to join him. She approached briskly and stopped a meter away, folding her arms. She watched him evenly, waiting for him to speak.

Aran led with the report, to stall the question as long as possible. "The barricades are set up, and watches are assigned."

"Excellent. Now let's get to the real reason I asked you here." Voria's face showed a rare note of sympathy. "Losing someone under your command is tough. I know you're strong Aran, but strong can also mean brittle. I need to know you're okay, and still able to command."

"Bord died because he followed an order I gave." Aran licked his lips, struggling to verbalize the tapestry of emotions. "I know rationally that the order was correct. I'd give it again, if I had to. I did what I needed to do, and we accomplished the mission."

"But?" Voria asked.

"Bord is dead."

"You're wondering how you deal with the fact that Bord is dead, because you expended him like a resource." The major seized Aran's shoulder, locking eyes with him. "*You* are a resource, Aran. *I* will expend you like a resource. So is Nara, and Kez, and Crewes, and every last one of the Marines under Davidson. We are all of us resources, all part of a larger whole. You sleep at night, Aran, because you know when the time comes you're going to go out with the same dignity and courage Bord exhibited. And because of his sacrifice, billions of Confederate citizens sleep safely, not having to worry about the Krox darkening their skies."

Aran nodded, considering her words. "That doesn't sound like an easy thing to reconcile, but I can do it, sir. I can't lie. His death tears me up. But I won't let it cause me to hesitate. The Krox have to be stopped. If Bord's death taught me anything, it's that. Those bastards have made this personal. I figure instead of guilty, or sad, I'll just get pissed off."

"Anger will insulate you, for now at least. Unfortunately, I'm about to take that anger away." Voria released him. Her entire demeanor shifted, the dour expression replaced by a broad smile. "I waited to do this, because I wanted you to experience loss as an officer. I realize how cruel that sounds, but I needed to know you wouldn't break. Besides, I'm not certain what I'm about to attempt will work. Come with me. I don't want to get your hopes up, but we may be able to fix this situation."

"Fix the situation?" Aran prodded, but the Major ignored him as she exited the library. He badly wanted to ask where they were going, but stayed silent as they headed to the temporary morgue that had been erected next to the battlefield.

Walking those rows of bodies chilled Aran in a way the void never could. Someone had taken the time to close their eyes, at least. It dimmed the horrified expressions many wore.

"I found him." Aran called numbly, from the third row. He waited for the Major to make her way over, forcing himself to look at the olive-skinned medic.

Bord's face was pale, his eyes closed and peaceful. The hole in his armor gaped, the edges stained black with blood and dust. Aran wiped the corner of his eye, refusing to look away. This was on him.

"Do you remember our visit to the drifters?" Voria asked. She reached into her satchel, removing the small black keg of beer they'd acquired.

"Vaguely. The drifter claimed that was his best beer, right? I didn't really understand most of what he said."

"He said, very specifically, that the beer would wake the dead." Voria slapped a tap into the top of the keg. "Now I don't know if he was as good as his word—but most drifters are, despite what people think. It's one thing to make a healing potion, quite another to make beer that can call a person's spirit back to their body. That's a fifth-level spell, and usually requires a full ritual casting at a Catalyst to accomplish. We're talking half a dozen powerful mages, all working in tandem, at a place of immense power. Even then, such rituals often fail. This brew may do nothing, but I can't think of a better time to use it. I figure nothing is lost in the attempt. And, if it works, it will definitely prove that trading my staff was worth it."

Aran ruthlessly culled the hope. He wasn't ready to deal with the disappointment, not so soon. The idea that magic powerful enough to call someone's soul back to their body even existed...it refused to take root.

"Hold his head," the major ordered.

Aran did as instructed, tilting Bord's head back and holding his mouth open as the major poured in a steady stream of thick, black beer. She trickled it into Bord's mouth for an eternity, so long that Aran's arms began to cramp. Still he held Bord perfectly still, saying nothing.

A tremendous burp rolled from Bord's throat. His body spasmed, then he coughed violently. His eyes fluttered open, and he stared up at Aran. "Oh gods. You're the last face I want to wake up to." Bord's hands shot down to his chest and his voice rose three octaves. "I'm dead."

"You *were* dead," Voria said, with more than a touch of pride. "Did you think I'd find dying an acceptable excuse, Specialist? You still have work to do among the living. You may stay here and rest until morning, then we'll get you back in the fight."

"Getting killed got me a day off?" Bord mused, leaning back and interlocking his fingers behind his head. Then he grinned. "Worth it. Totally worth it." He leapt from the slab as though unable to sit still. "I feel incredible."

"It's the aftereffects of the brew. You're drunk, Specialist." Voria turned to Aran, grinning in a way that—on anyone else—Aran would have called girlish. "Get your company prepared, and tell Davidson to stand ready in the square. Spread the word to all the shelters that we'll be gathering in an hour."

"Uh huh. Sir." Aran gawked at Bord, still reeling. "You just brought him back from the dead. Like...he was dead, and now he's not."

"Well, technically, the drifters did it. It wasn't my spell." Voria shrugged. "Now get moving. When I promoted you to lieutenant, I expected initiative. We have a long, dangerous road ahead of us. You've got your healer back. Now start delivering me dead Krox."

Aran sat there, bewildered. He'd run the gamut of emotions, from helplessness, to overpowering grief, and finally anger. Now, he wasn't sure what to feel.

"Dead Krox," he finally said, "is something I can do."

46

CONFRONTATION

Satisfied that Aran would do his job, Voria allowed herself a rare moment of reflection. She set down the tome she'd been reading, stretching as she rose. She'd placed a great deal of faith in the augury the Tender had given her. Including using a priceless potion to bring Bord back from the dead. The augury showed him at the final battle. Had that not been the case, she'd never have used the potion.

Voria stifled a yawn. She still had an important task to deal with, one that would require she keep her wits about her. She didn't know how long Nebiat had been in that swamp, or how close the binder was to her goal. Even now, the dreadlord could be completing whatever ritual she was out here to perform. Perhaps she was out here in search of an artifact from the godswar.

Whatever Nebiat's motivation, Voria needed to pursue her immediately. That meant dealing with the governor in the most expedient way possible, while still retaining a mostly functional government in this city. Stopping Nebiat, but having the world fall to anarchy, would be a bitter victory—one she'd prefer to avoid.

She slung her satchel over her shoulder and departed the archives. Horuk had agreed to her request and would report to the square as soon as he'd locked the archives. That meant the last piece was in place. Voria marched briskly back down the steep thoroughfare, only relaxing once she'd re-entered the perimeter Captain Davidson had established.

"Captain, a word please?" Voria called, her loud, clear voice echoing over the still-smoking market square.

Davidson disengaged from a trio of subordinates, striding over to her with brisk purpose. "Yes, sir?"

His deep green fatigues, like those of the men around him, were stained with blood and sweat. His men looked at him with a mixture of respect and adoration.

Up close, his weariness was easier to spot. She found it in the dark circles under his eyes and the tremble in his hands. He needed sleep, and probably a hot meal.

"Are you confident you have a perimeter in place around this square?" Voria asked. She reached for the familiar comfort of her staff, then lowered her arm when she remembered for the millionth time that she'd traded it. At least she'd gotten something fair in trade.

"As confident as I can be," Davidson replied, scrubbing his fingers through his sweaty blond hair. "If the Krox launch another attack, we'll be aware of it, but I can't promise we can repulse it. The new rifles and armor helped us push them back, but we're short on manpower. The locals aren't going to be any help. Their morale has never been lower."

"That was my next question." Voria gave a quick nod. "I

want you to pass the word. Have all the shelters gather, and bring their people here. Inform me when they've arrived."

"Sir?" Davidson asked, confusion leaking into his expression.

"Just do it, Captain. You'll understand why once you see what I have planned, I promise you. In the meantime, I have to meet with the governor."

"Of course, sir." Davidson colored and snapped a hasty salute, which Voria returned. "I'll have all refugees here in the next fifteen minutes."

Voria gave a pleased nod, then continued through the square. She stepped over the corpse of a Krox enforcer, part of its chest simply missing where a void bolt had finished it. Bodies littered the square, though thankfully they were all enemy bodies now. Davidson had been extremely efficient in getting their own casualties off the field.

To Voria's mild surprise, Governor Avitus had already arrived at the stage. If he really were bound, she'd have expected him to flee now that his work was done. The fact that he hadn't troubled her. It suggested he had more mischief planned, or that she was simply wrong about him.

She walked boldly up to the stage, mounting the trio of steps on the right side. The stage had escaped the combat largely unscathed, an island of calm amidst utter chaos.

"Ahh, Governor," she called, infusing the words with warmth she didn't feel. "I'm pleased to see you survived the battle."

"Yes, no thanks to you," the governor snapped, rounding on her. "A full third of my people lie dead, and our city is in ruins. All within minutes of your arrival. Is this the best your vaunted Confederate Marines can do?" He raised an arm, gesturing expansively at the destruction around him.

Voria walked to the center of the stage. Refugees were

already trickling in, gathering at the edges of the square. Davidson worked fast. "An excellent question, Governor—one I imagine your people would be very interested in having answered."

She sketched a sigil, activating the stage's latent magic. Her voice was instantly amplified, booming across the square, and hopefully beyond. "Citizens of Marid, hear me. We have been assaulted by the Krox, attacked by some of their most ancient Wyrms. Many have fallen. We've lost friends, and family. Some have lost homes. Many of you are asking why. I've brought the governor here to discuss the cause of this attack."

She turned to the governor, slowly folding her arms. He rose imperiously, his finery impeccable in the aftermath of the battle.

"Yes," he said, "some very troubling questions have arisen. The Krox made no move to assault us, conducting whatever business they have here in peace. Then the Confederates arrived, and we were instantly attacked. The Marines failed to protect us, failed in their duty."

Dark murmurs came from the Marines, but Davidson silenced them with a look. He stood proud, and his men mirrored the gesture. Voria's opinion of the man rose another notch.

"Have you anything further to add, Governor?" she asked mildly, the magic amplifying her voice many times over.

"I do." The governor walked to the edge of the stage, clasping his hands before his chest. "Much as it pains me, I have made the difficult decision to contact the Shayan government directly. I have reported the major's gross negligence, and been informed that she has already been stripped of command. These Marines aren't here legally, and the major has an outstanding warrant for her arrest. Command was to be given to a Captain Thalas, a man the major murdered in cold blood. I do not know if she is in league with the Krox, or simply serving her own interests at the expense of our people. But I will have no part of it. I demand you withdraw your forces from our world. Leave us in peace, and the Krox will too."

Voria waited, letting the speech wash over the crowd. Many were murmuring confused questions.

"You've heard the governor's words," Voria called, also stepping to the edge of the stage. "Now hear mine. A mere few hours ago, many of you were fleeing for your lives. You ran because the Krox launched an unprovoked assault. They killed your people, and burned your buildings. The governor paints this attack as somehow linked to the arrival of my battalion, and I believe he is right. I believe the Krox chose that exact moment to attack, because they'd been informed of our arrival. Further, I believe the governor gathered you all here, knowing you'd be in tremendous danger. The more of you who died, the better."

Murmurs passed through the crowd, more heated now.

"And what could I possibly hope to gain from the slaughter of my own people?" Avitus scoffed. The way he looked at her suggested he thought he was winning this little debate.

"You hoped to serve the ends of your true master, the dreadlord Nebiat," Voria calmly explained. She let that sink in for a moment, then continued. "Your will has been shackled, and everything you've done preceding the Krox invasion has been at the behest of a full Krox dreadlord."

Voria knew a moment of fear. She was *almost* positive she was right, but the possibility still remained that the governor was merely incompetent, not bound. If that was the case, everything she was hoping to achieve here would fail.

"That's your defense? You're labeling me some sort of binder puppet?" the governor asked, chuckling. "Where's your proof? This is nonsense. An attempt to deflect blame, criminal."

"Ahh, here we go," Voria said, pointing at Horuk as the archivist stepped onto the stage. "Citizens of Marid, most of you recognize Archivist Horuk. He's served in that role for most of your lives. Horuk, you are a true mage, are you not?"

"I am." Horuk's deep voice boomed out over the square.

"And you are capable of reading spell sigils to detect the nature of a spell, are you not?" Voria asked calmly, watching the governor closely. He'd begun to shift, his gaze roaming the edge of the crowd—like an animal, about to flee.

"Indeed I can. There is none more qualified on this world."

"I do not expect your people to trust me, Governor. But I do expect they'll trust the word of their own archivist." Voria sketched a fire sigil, performing a detection spell. The governor began to glow. A soft white light emitted from his skin, then the light intensified—so bright that the governor was gone, eclipsed by a tangled mix of sigils wrapped around the area where his chest and head would be. "Can you tell me exactly what you're seeing, Archivist?"

"I can," Horuk called out, his clear voice echoing over the silent crowd. "The governor has been inflicted with a number of spells, the most notable a binding to shackle his will. He belongs fully to a binder, and I suspect it was he who arranged the recent attack."

The crowd burst into shouts—a mixture of shock and deep anger. They were looking for a target, and Voria needed to handle this next part delicately, or they'd quickly become a mob.

"Citizens, how you handle your own internal matters is up to you. I've nominated Archivist Horuk to serve as acting governor, until Ternus High Command can help you install another. The governor is yours to deal with as you see fit. I would argue leniency. Once the bindings are removed, he will have to live with what he did. In a way, he is blameless in all this—a victim, as all of us are."

The shouts died to dark murmurs, but at least the calls for the governor's blood had died.

"And what of you, Major?" Horuk asked. "Will you depart this world, or stay and protect it?"

"I will stay—and more," Voria yelled. She faced the crowd, clenching a fist. "Tomorrow at first light I will take the fight to the Krox. I will find Nebiat, and I will stop her from achieving whatever her aim here is."

The crowd roared their defiant approval, their collective cries drowning out the sorrow.

47

DIDN'T I MENTION THAT?

Aran finally unclenched as the crowd of locals gradually filtered away from stage. They were moving off in groups, most talking quietly. They looked thoughtful, though there was definitely an undercurrent of anger. Many glared hatefully at the governor, who stood under Marine guard.

Nara pulled her helmet off, freeing a river of dark hair. "Did you have any idea she was going to do that?"

"No. I don't think the major told anyone, and I can't blame her." Aran removed his own helmet, enjoying the cool breeze. He did not enjoy the scent of ash over everything.

"You got that right," Crewes rumbled. He walked off a short distance, into the shadows of a relatively undamaged building. "She didn't say it, but I've seen her do this sort of thing before. In the morning, we'll move out. She'll make a call to the locals to see if any militia will join us. Most won't. Then we're gonna march out into the swamp."

"I wish Bord was going with us." Nara gave a heavy sigh, kneeling to scoop up a pile of ashy dirt with her gauntlet.

"He is," Aran said, smirking. "Didn't I mention that? The major brought him back from the dead."

Kez clomped up in her heavy armor. "Did the Krox joost knock you in the head, sir?"

Aran gave a wide smile. They'd been through it, and they needed a victory. This, he realized, could be exactly that victory, exactly the morale boost that would get them all back in the game after being punched in the crotch.

"Right before the major pulled her stunt with the governor, we paid the morgue a visit," Aran explained, pausing for dramatic effect. Even Crewes was watching him with rapt attention. "When we met with the Drifters, they sold her a brew they claimed could wake someone from the dead."

"And it worked? Bord is alive?" Nara gave a musical laugh, then threw her arms around Aran. "That's incredible."

"I can't believe it myself." Aran returned the hug, but quickly disengaged since the squad was watching. "The major gave him the rest of the day off, and he's back to active tomorrow."

"Just in time to join us in the muck," Crewes rumbled cheerfully. "Perfect. Every time I think she can't surprise me, she does it again. Back from the gods-damned dead. Who'd believe that shit?"

Aran surveyed the squad, realizing that everyone's armor was at least partially damaged. Most had empty canisters, and one of Crewes's had been shattered by a hit from an enforcer.

"If we're moving out in the morning," Aran said, "we should make good use of the time. Let's get back to the barracks. Kez, can you help us run repairs on our suits while you all catch up with Bord?"

"I betcha we can get it all fixed up tight in a joost a few hours," Kez drawled in her sing-song accent. "But I have to warn you, sir. After a fight like that, I plan on drinkin'." The faceplate to her armor popped up, framing an oval face with a wicked grin. "Ya should join me sir. Discover the fine line between drunk and drunker. We certainly got cause to celebrate."

"I'll see if we can't requisition a keg from the major," Aran promised, smiling at his friends. "We'll kick back, as much as we're able. Run light repairs, then get some sleep. Tomorrow, we're heading back into it."

He put his helmet back on, still smiling. In some ways, a single soldier coming back from the dead was a small thing —not enough to turn a battle on its own. But in another way, it demonstrated the major's unfailing ability to snatch victory from the jaws of defeat.

Tomorrow, some of them were probably going to die. But they'd go willingly to that death, knowing they were following a woman worthy of that allegiance.

48

THE CIRCLE

Nebiat flapped her wings, descending slowly toward the mossy mountain below. Eight sites had been erected around it, each attuned to a different aspect, each with a large urn in the center. Those sites glowed with power. All eight aspects would be needed today, though in different proportions.

Enforcers moved the last of the urns into place, completing the outer ring. That ring, the magical repository, could be managed by lesser binders. All they needed to do was funnel power into each urn, power she would consume when she cast the ritual.

She transformed as she fell toward the mountain, and was a full human by the time she landed gracefully at the summit. Unlike many of her brethren, she usually preferred the human form. It was frail, but it also allowed the kind of manual dexterity a much larger body prohibited—the kind of manual dexterity needed to draw an immensely complex ritual circle, for example.

Nebiat knelt, drawing from the well of power in her chest. She sketched the first sigil, beginning with *void*. She prided herself in the artistry, having drawn countless such circles in her lifetime. Never had they been as important as this one.

If she succeeded, if she were able to remove the seal, then Marid would become a staging ground to conquer the Confederacy. From this world she could launch a dagger at Ternus itself, and then at Shaya. The Confederacy would fall in years, instead of the decades her father had allocated.

In the incredibly unlikely event that she failed, she'd turn that to her advantage as well—though it seemed impossible that anything could prevent her victory at this point. Voria had proven annoying, but was unlikely to even reach the ritual before it was complete, much less muster enough force to stop Nebiat.

Nebiat had husbanded her forces, sending only the weakest and least trained to assault the Confederates. Those who remained were her strongest, and were more than a match for anything a human could bring to bear.

She made the second sigil, adding *fire* next to *void*. Then came *dream*, and *air*. She took her time with *life*, the most complex sigil and the aspect she had the most trouble mastering. She continued to *water*, then *spirit*. Finally, she added *earth*, completing the circle.

Rising, she surveyed her handiwork. She would need to strengthen each sigil several more times, but the framework for the spell had been created. Now it was time to test it. She waved a hand, and a puff of spirit energy drifted into the air.

The circle seized it instantly, channeling it into the sigil she'd drawn. She smiled. All she needed to do was test the outer circle, then strengthen both. Within a few hours, she could begin casting the spell that would end the hated Confederacy—and, after that, the entire sector.

Her father would be enraged at the death of her brother,

but if she could deliver him this world he would forget about it soon enough. If she managed to bind Drakkon? Then he would barely notice the loss of a son, and she'd be showered with honors.

She smiled. There had been setbacks, but she was still very much in control of the situation. Still, it was best not to grow overconfident. The Confederates were coming, of that she had no doubt. Perhaps she needed to arrange another distraction.

"Serephala, attend me," Nebiat boomed, in a voice far louder and deeper than should have issued from a human throat.

A Wyrm near the *life* urn leapt into the air, flapping her powerful wings as she climbed toward the summit. She banked, landing on an outcrop above Nebiat. "How many I serve, elder sister?"

Nebiat did not look up from her work on the circle. "I'm giving you a chance to make up for your failure on the station. I want you to slaughter every snake, every cat, every creature in the swamp around us. Gather them, and hurl them at the Confederates. Slow them. Make their march excruciating. Make them pay for every meter."

"I will simply crush them all and remove the problem," Serephala boasted, flapping her mighty wings.

The wind tugged at Nebiat's hair, blowing it across her face. She shot her younger sister a glare, and the Wyrm dropped her gaze. "Do not be arrogant. Kheftut is *dead*. As are many others. We've never had so many of our siblings die in so short a span, not since the godswar. Do not risk yourself, sister. Harass, and fade away." Nebiat ceased her work, staring up at her sister again. "Do not engage them directly, am I clear?"

"As you wish," her sister muttered sullenly.

"Good. Then see to it." Nebiat bent back to the circle, content that there would be no more distractions.

49

DEBRIEFING

Voria closed the door behind her, pausing to breathe. The archives bore the rich fragrance of books, her very favorite perfume. Even after being introduced to Ternus datapads, she'd never lost the love for books.

Horuk sat hunched over a table, scrawling notes into a journal with a feathersteel pen. He looked up at her approach, setting the pen down with the kind of precision she envied but was far too impatient to implement in her own life.

"Welcome, Major." He rose slowly to his feet, smoothing his jacket. "You've come for the debriefing, I assume?"

"I have." She nodded, moving to sit in the chair opposite his. "I realize I've given you very little time, but I'm hoping you've put it to use."

"It was well spent." Horuk reached for his journal, flipping it to another page and sliding it across the table to her. "Take a look."

"This isn't the page you were writing," Voria mused, scanning the contents. "How old is this? It's not dated."

"Just over a decade," Horuk confirmed. "I memorize the dates, so I've little need to apply them to my personal journal."

Voria turned the page, eyes widening as she read. "You've been to the Catalyst."

"You can't be surprised." Horuk gave a dry smile. "I'd been sentenced to this backwater for four years before I finally decided to explore the mists. It took another two years to locate the Catalyst."

Voria set the journal down. She cocked her head to the side, studying the archivist with fresh eyes. "Tell me."

"The Catalyst is the body of a Great Wyrm. She wasn't a mere Void Wyrm. She was a true god, fashioned by gods even more ancient than she." Horuk picked up his journal, running a finger along a page, lost in memory. "She was killed by one of Krox's puppet gods, slain because she would not submit, and was simply too powerful to control. Her body fell from orbit, making the crater around us. Her heart, a fount of magical power, lay at the center of that crater."

"An open wound? That would have called primals from all over the sector." Voria interrupted, though she was intrigued by the tale.

"And it did. The swamp is full of giant snakes, the youngest form of the drake. As they age, each becomes more and more a true Wyrm." Horuk set the journal down, eyeing her earnestly. "At some point, the wound was covered. A mountain now stands above it, blocking the magical signature. This slowed the development of the Wyrms in the swamp, keeping them from progressing to their final forms."

"It probably also kept Nebiat from finding it. A Water Catalyst is powerful, but not powerful enough to warrant the kind of forces she's committed here. What's so special about this one?"

"I don't know. But I believe this world's import is greater than I first guessed," the archivist mused. "The part about strange skies? The original natives of this planet kept detailed star charts, painted in caves on the southern continent. I spent months studying them, and not a single one matched the current night sky."

"Stellar drift?" Voria asked.

"That was my assumption too, but drift would only partially modify constellations, not completely alter them. No, when these people say *strange skies*, I think they mean the entire sky changed." The archivist watched her closely, waiting for her reaction.

"The only way that could be possible is if the planet were moved." Voria shook her head, trying to understand the kind of magical power that would be required for such a feat.

"Yes, and you can see why I'm so troubled. Someone went to a great deal of trouble to hide this world." He shook his head. "The fact that the Krox have found it now? I believe that may be far more catastrophic than the Confederacy realizes."

"What do you think Nebiat is planning?" Voria asked, reaching again for her missing staff. Blast it, she was going to need to replace that.

"At a guess, I think she might be trying to remove the patch over the wound. If she can do that, maybe she can tap into the energy more fully." Horuk shrugged. "I don't really know."

"I don't think that's it." A chill passed through Voria, and she rose from her chair. "In fact, I think I know what Nebiat is planning. If she removes the patch, then the primals will begin coming again."

"And those already here will continue to develop."

Horuk's eyes widened in understanding. "She'll have an army of Wyrms, and a way to make more over time."

"You begin to see the problem. What about the Guardian?" Voria asked. "There's no way any Guardian would let a binder approach, and there's no way a Catalyst this powerful doesn't have a Guardian."

"Again, I don't know. During my trip I expected to meet a Guardian, to find something of immense age watching over the Catalyst. Given its scope and power, the idea that there is no Guardian is unfathomable. Something would have moved to control the Catalyst, millennia ago. Perhaps whatever erected the seal over the wound." Horuk walked over to a bookshelf, scanning for several moments then selecting a tome. "Hmm, I think this is the one. Yes, there it is. Look at this sketch."

Horuk passed the book to Voria. It showed a towering god hurling a crackling magical spear at a titanic Wyrm. The spear had impaled the beast, and the beast slammed into the world beneath it. If the depiction was accurate, it would have been apocalyptic for the people of this world.

"This is the battle, I assume. What am I supposed to be seeing?"

"The location of the wound, hopefully. It's a bit off center, but near enough."

"It will suffice." Voria sketched a quick trio of sigils, then touched the journal hanging from her belt. The image shimmered, then a copy shot into her tome. "Is there anything else you can offer, any warning about the dangers of the swamp?"

"Nothing you don't already know. The Krox will come for you, of course. The local fauna most likely will not. They'll be easy enough to frighten off with loud weaponry." Horuk frowned again. "I don't know what happened to the

Guardian, but I suspect that you, and this binder, are about to find out. Is there anything else you require before your journey?"

"Sleep," Voria muttered. She rubbed at her temples. "If you can arrange to have the citizens in the square to see us off in the morning, I'd be grateful."

"You intend to ask for volunteers." It wasn't a question. "These people have already sacrificed much."

"I will not demand they sacrifice anything further, but they have a right to choose their own fate," Voria countered. "Some may join us, and odds are good those who do will not return. If none do, so be it. We'll fight Nebiat with every resource at our disposal."

"Good night, Major. I think my people may surprise you."

50

INTO THE MIST

Voria accepted Captain Davidson's hand as he pulled her atop the tank. "Thank you, Captain."

He nodded respectfully at her, but didn't say anything. His attention remained fixed on the mist below, scanning ceaselessly as he watched for another Krox assault.

The turret of the tank met the main body in a seamless join, the kind that could only be accomplished with magic. The weapon might fire conventional ordnance, but its construction involved some of the finest sorcery the Inurans were capable of.

Voria turned to face the crowd, which was far larger than she'd have expected given the previous day's attack. Every last face—most of them dirty, and all of them weary—peered up at her.

Not with hope, which she'd seen on some worlds. Not with despair, which often crowded out hope. These faces wore anger. They'd been used, and they were eager for payback.

Eager enough to risk their own lives? She was about to find out.

"Behind me, you see an entire armor-reinforced battalion, complete with a company of tech mages," Voria yelled, her voice echoing over the square without any need for magical amplification. "In exactly one hour, we will be heading into that swamp." She pointed down the slope of the mountain, into the pool of mist covering much of the swamp. "We will be marching to the Catalyst at the center, where we will confront a Krox dreadlord—the same Krox dreadlord who killed your sons, and daughters, and fathers, and brothers. We will stop her from completing a ritual that would make your world a target for every primal in the sector—a ritual that would give her control over an army of Wyrms, to be used to conquer and destroy other worlds like this one. We go to stop her, because no one else can. I want each and every one of you to reach down deep, and decide what your homes are worth. Will you fight for them? Because we need your help. But before you decide, think carefully. It is highly unlikely anyone who goes into that swamp will return."

Voria paused. She watched them, proudly. Every citizen waged their own internal war, wondering if maybe they could spit in the eye of the enemy that had taken so much from them. She let them stew in in before speaking again.

"You will be given the finest Inuran armor and weaponry. You will be added to veteran units, fighting with men and women will look out for you. You will be fed and cared for, protected to the best of our collective ability. But make no mistake: anyone who joins us, fights. You take up arms, and you defend your world to the death. If you are with us, simply cross that line."

She pointed to Aran and Nara, who stood on either end

of a chalk line they'd drawn. Voria wasn't sure what to expect. Most worlds had a few zealots, a few people looking to take up a cause—any cause—just to have a purpose.

A woman of perhaps sixty crossed the line, moving to stand next to Sergeant Crewes in his massive armor.

A pair of lost-looking teens joined her next.

Then the flood began. Dozens of citizens crossed the line and stood proudly on the other side. When it was over, nearly a hundred militia had gathered. The rest lurked on the other side of the line, still trying to find their courage.

"Captain Davidson, please see the militia armed, equipped, and prepared to march," Voria ordered. Then she hopped down from the tank, letting Davidson take over. He immediately started barking orders, breaking the militia into more manageable chunks.

He handed off groups to his officers, who in turn integrated the militia into their own units. It was smooth, efficient. She approved.

"Sir, are we certain it wouldn't be smarter to create a separate unit for the militia?" Aran asked, guiding his spellarmor into a hover near the tank. The question was neither timid nor impertinent; it was merely a request for information, the kind she preferred officers use.

"I considered that option, but a separate militia unit would be nothing more than cannon fodder. Worse, that unit would know it. They'd break during the first engagement, and that would make the survivors useless. By mixing them with the Marines, we stiffen their morale while also making the unit look larger. I'm not naive enough to think the militia will do much in their first battle, but some of them may surprise us."

"I see. I hadn't considered the effect on morale. Thank

you for explaining, sir." Aran's tone was respectful, such a welcome change from Thalas.

"You always have the right to ask questions, so long as you do not presume that I owe you explanations." She turned a baleful eye on him, and while she couldn't see his reaction behind his helmet, she had a feeling it caused the desired effect. "Have the ground-based members of your squad protect the main troop body. Your more mobile units—"

"—should aerially scout our perimeter?" Aran interrupted, a note of amusement in his voice.

"Precisely, Lieutenant. Nothing reaches the main body without us knowing about it." Voria climbed back atop the tank. "I will be riding inside with Captain Davidson if you need me."

She turned toward the swamp. A grey mist blended the sky into the ground, making it impossible to tell where fog ended and sky began. Somewhere in that soup lay the confrontation predicted in the augury she'd received.

Perhaps she'd finally learn who sent it. If she survived.

51

OLIVE BRANCH

Aran glided out over the swamp, circling wide ahead of the convoy. The armor moved in a single column, flanked by platoons of Marines, that stretched almost a kilometer and disappeared into the mist behind them.

"We sure do make a tempting target for a foe with superior mobility," Aran muttered into the comm. "Like, say, a dragon."

"I was literally just thinking the same thing. Well, not literally, but I enjoy misusing the word." Nara gave a soft laugh. "Point is, we're exposed. Especially with the mist. How do we plan to deal with that?"

"We can't," Aran said, zooming higher into the mist. It thinned, but not much. He had perhaps a hundred meters of partial visibility up here. Clumps of trees burst out of the water here and there, and occasionally an entire island. "It will take a concerted effort, and that requires Davidson. I'll sit him down when we get to camp and see how he wants to handle deployment."

"I think you're breaking a lot of taboos doing that," Nara

replied, her breathing a little harder now. "I had to encourage a forty meter snake to move away from the convoy. Ick."

"You're right about the taboos. Thalas treated the Marines like garbage, and I gather that's a pretty common attitude among officers. That's going to take time to undo, but I think it starts with deferring to Davidson. I mean, he does outrank me. " Aran came to a halt, scanning the path ahead of them. It leveled out a bit on a long stretch of relatively dry land. They weren't likely to find a better campsite, and it would be getting dark in an hour or two. He switched to an open channel. "Major, this is Lieutenant Aran, do you copy?"

Her brisk voice came back almost instantly. "What's the situation, Lieutenant?"

"I see a potential campsite. It's a little island, maybe two feet above sea level." Aran flew closer. "It's uninhabited, besides a few local fauna. Looks large enough to accommodate all the militia, but the armor will probably have to park in the water."

"Good find, Lieutenant. We'll make for your position."

Aran guided his spellarmor to the island, giving it a more thorough aerial pass. There really wasn't anything remarkable about it. The few trees were too scraggly to use as cover, though at least the troops would have solid footing. If he had to defend the little spit, he wasn't sure how he'd do it. Hopefully the major or Davidson would have some ideas.

He glided to a halt on the far side of the island, watching as the column approached. The battalion's single troop transport arrived first, stuffed with supplies instead of men. Davidson's Marines began quickly assembling pavilions and setting up a chow line.

Aran waited for a break in the crowd around the captain,

then flew over. He landed next to Davidson, withdrawing his helmet.

"What can I do for you, Lieutenant?" Davidson asked, accepting a bowl of something resembling stew from a militiaman. He made no move to eat, instead watching Aran with undisguised suspicion.

"I was about to ask you the same thing." Aran smiled, and Davidson slowly returned it. "As I understand it, Thalas refused to accept your orders, keeping my company a separate military force. That's stupid in a battle like the one we're about to wage. We need a clear chain of command, and after counting the bars on my collar I'm pretty sure you outrank me. Sir."

"So, are you suggesting I start giving your company orders?" Davidson asked, though cautiously, as if suspecting a trap.

"Where needed, sure. I'm not saying we'll come to you for every little thing, but when the Krox attack I want you to be able to deploy your armor, knowing you can order my company in to support," Aran said. He held up a hand to forestall the captain's reply. "Ultimately the major has final say, and if she orders me elsewhere I'll take care of whatever task she assigns us. Failing that, we're at your disposal, sir."

"Wow." Davidson sat down on the bumper of a parked hover tank—his tank, Aran was pretty sure. Davidson enjoyed a spoonful of stew, then waved the empty spoon in Aran's direction. "So what you're telling me is that, for the first time, we get to run this like a real military operation? That I'm not going to be hamstrung with a noble who won't even speak to a grunt from Ternus?"

"Yeah, that's about the size of it." Aran said.

"Corporal Young, get this man a bowl of stew. ASAP." Davidson barked. The stern exterior melted, and he grinned at Aran. "I cannot even believe this. The next thing you're going to tell me, we might actually survive this excursion. I got 500 to 1 odds back on the Ternus transfer station. If we don't buy it, I'll have enough to buy...well, dinner maybe. There's a lot of men to feed."

"My memory only goes back six days," Aran said. "But from what I've seen so far I'm not sure I'd bet against the major, even going up against the Krox. She'll find a way to get us out alive." He accepted a bowl of stew from a tall smiling woman with almond-shaped eyes. "Thank you."

"I can already see it," Davidson said. "You care more about the unit than you do personal glory. That's necessary in the Marines, but damned near nonexistent among tech mages." He paused, seeming to realize he'd insulted tech mages. "Not that I mean...I'm just saying, you're different than Thalas—different than any other mage I've met."

"I'll take that as a compliment." Aran offered Davidson his hand.

The captain shook it, then patted the bench his men had erected while they were speaking. "Grab a seat. I've got a few deployment ideas I want to run by you..."

52

SPLASH

"Contact!" Crewes' voice snapped Aran to wakefulness, and he groggily checked his HUD. Sleeping in the Mark XI was far more comfortable than in a bunk, and it took a moment to rouse himself.

The last bits of sleep fell away as he saw the animated corpse of a two-hundred-meter snake rear over the southern part of the island. It lunged, and a Marine vanished with a surprised yell. The snake rolled, crushing the rest of that Marine's squad, including a handful of militia.

Davidson's people were already moving, the tanks swiveling their turrets toward the threat. Aran rose into the air, turning on a hunch to face the opposite direction.

A massive shadow passed overhead, then dove toward a tank in the back line. Aran snapped his rifle to his shoulder, hastily tracking the target as it fell through the mist. Aran stroked the trigger, grunting as the rifle tore a level three void bolt from his chest.

The dragon was about the same size as the one on the station. In fact, it was exactly the same size. Aran was fairly sure he recognized her, and even more positive when the void bolt slammed into her and she shrieked. Aran remembered that cry, and remembered it well.

The Wyrm banked suddenly, disappearing back into the mists the way she'd come. Apparently she wasn't interested in a rematch just yet.

"Bord, move to the south perimeter. Get a ward up between the Krox and those tanks." Aran zipped to the left weaving erratically through the fog as he sought his quarry. "Kez, provide Bord support, and keep the Krox from punching through the outer perimeter."

"Yes, sir." Bord said, and Aran glanced at the wiry medic as he sprinted to a cluster of soldiers near the back of the one of the tanks. Bord raised both gauntlets, and a dome of pure white energy sprang up between two of the tanks, effectively blocking that route to the center of the island.

Kez trotted up to stand next to Bord, her brilliant white spellshield held high in case a caster lobbed a spell in their direction. All around them, Marines took up firing positions behind rocks, trees, or the tanks themselves—just in time.

The stench of rot preceded a shambling mass of bodies. Many were human, but there were several many-legged cat creatures, dozens of snakes of all sizes, and something that appeared to be a cross between an alligator and a scorpion.

Chattering automatic weapon fire echoed from the Marines, focusing on the larger targets. Most went down quickly, encouraged by support fire from the tanks. The militia followed suit, emulating the Marines as best they could. Aran could see now how integrating them worked, and why it had been such a good idea. In time, the more competent militia would learn to emulate the Marines.

Several more giant snakes rushed from the mist toward the south perimeter. Kez trotted out to meet the first one, which lunged at her. The snake was large enough to swallow her armor, yet moved with blinding speed. Kez was faster. She hopped backward as the snake's head slammed into the ground where she'd been standing.

Before it could recover, she darted forward and brought her hammer down in a brutal strike. The snake's skull shattered, and its bulk crashed to the ground. Supporting fire from the tanks quickly cut down the rest of the snakes.

"That's the last of that wave, but there's more in the mist," Aran said into the comm. "We've got the southern perimeter secure, for now. Nara, Crewes, reinforce the northern perimeter. Try not to use much in the way of spell magic. They're trying to soften us up for the enforcers."

"On it, sir," Crewes Barked. In the background, Aran heard the deep *whump* of Crewes's spellcannon.

Nara's armor zipped through the fog above him, her level one void bolts picking off any target the Marine's automatic fire didn't bring down.

Davidson's voice crackled over the comm. "Lieutenant, you get the sense we're being played? This all feels a little too easy."

"You are correct, Captain," the major's smooth voice cut in. "Nebiat probably sent one of her weaker binders to corral everything she could possibly bind, then throw it all at us. It means we're under very little actual risk, but it serves her purpose. It keeps us penned here while she finishes whatever dark sorcery she is about. All this binder needs to do is avoid direct confrontation, knowing that if we leave this island we'll begin to lose people."

"What do you suggest we do, sir?" Davidson asked, a bit tentatively.

"We kill the binder. Aran, you've already tangled with her once. Take Nara and Crewes, and hunt her down. She has to remain close to command her army, and we can use that against her."

"You heard the lady. Nara, Crewes, you're with me. Bord, Kez, you're attached to Davidson's unit for the time being." Aran waited for everyone to acknowledge the order, then glided into the fog. He kept a steady pace, watching the whirling mists carefully. "Nara, fan out a hundred meters north. I'll do the same to the south. Crewes, you're walking up the middle. Let's fly a ring around the camp. If you spot movement, engage. We'll all hear the shots."

Aran lost sight of Nara, and could barely see Crewes. They flew a quick patrol, always watching for the telltale flapping of wings. Behind them, they could hear continued weapons fire, but Aran tuned it out. That wasn't their job right now.

They moved deliberately, systematically checking all areas around the camp. They'd nearly finished their sweep when Nara spoke. "Aran, I've got movement. Just a quick flash of dark scales, and maybe a tail."

"Copy that. Stay on her Nara. Crewes and I are on our way." Aran shot through the mist in Nara's direction, the clouds of white parting only long enough for him to pass, then filling in his wake just as quickly. "Major, I've still got that potion of Shaya's Grace your brother gave me. Do you think now is an appropriate time to use it?"

"Negative, Lieutenant. If no one has stressed the power contained within that potion, allow me to do so: save it for the moment you are certain you are about to die, or when you see an opportunity to end the ritual."

"Standard spells it is then," Aran muttered, coming up short in the mist when he caught a flash of black scales ahead of him. "Contact."

"I see the bitch," Crewes roared. Bright orange light

flared in the mist, then the mist boiled away, revealing the Wyrm fully.

Aran didn't hesitate. He snapped his rifle to his shoulder, sighting at her chest. He braced himself and pulled the trigger. The rifle tore power from him, loosing another level three bolt that hit the Wyrm in the chest, right under the ribs. Scales, bone, and muscle boiled away, disintegrated by the attack.

Dark scarlet blood flowed freely from the wound, and the Wyrm wrapped a clawed hand over it. She dove into the mists, gliding swiftly along the floor of the swamp.

"Don't let her get away." Aran shot after her, dodging around clumps of trees as he tried to keep pace. The dragon accelerated, and he struggled to match. He glanced behind him to find he was outpacing both Nara and Crewes.

He needed to make a choice, and he needed to do it right now. Aran decided to pursue. He willed the Mark XI to greater speed, slowly narrowing the gap between him and the Wyrm. He flipped the selector to level one, then squeezed off a quick void bolt.

The Wyrm was quick, rolling away from the spell. It blasted apart a tree trunk, sending up a spray of splinters as Aran shot by. He fired again, forcing the Wyrm to evade. Each time the gap between them narrowed.

"Ah, you prideful fool," the Wyrm roared, wheeling suddenly. She raised both titanic wings, flapping away mist as she hovered in place. "You are alone now. Your companions cannot help you."

Aran thumbed the selector back to three. He had maybe two more shots, but hopefully they would be all he needed. He eyed the spell amplification icon on his HUD. This was as good a time as any to test it. He willed the golden icon to depress.

"What makes you think I need any help?"

Warm golden energy suffused the suit, bursting brilliant out around him. Aran stroked the trigger, and the spellrifle tore loose a level three bolt. Only, the bolt was both larger, and more dense than any level three.

The ebony bolt streaked toward the Wyrm.

As expected, her hand shot up and she sketched a counterspell. The amplified spell punched through the counterspell, through the dragon, and through the trees behind her.

"Whoah." Aran willed the spell amplification to disengage. The icon had already changed, showing an 87% under it. "Looks like it doesn't last long, but man does it power up spells."

He felt a swell of pride, and knowing his victory was due more to the armor than to anything he'd done. "Major, this is Lieutenant Aran. Target has been eliminated. We should be clear to proceed."

53

TRUST

Voria surveyed the battlefield, stepping over the rotting corpse of a snake as she walked the perimeter. She reached out into the fog with the awareness that she'd gained when she touched the mind of the god Kaji. She'd journeyed to the Catalyst hoping for fire magic, but magically sensitive vision was an excellent consolation prize.

There was nothing—or rather, nothing magical. After Aran had radioed his success Voria had searched for other binders, but if they were out there they weren't casting any spells. The battle was over, far more quickly and efficiently than she could have hoped.

"Captain Davidson," Voria called as she approached his tank. She waited until she'd closed the distance before speaking. "Casualty report."

"We had nineteen fatalities, seventeen of them militia. Seventy-one wounded, only a few badly enough that travel will be an issue. I've spread out the wounded among the tank crews. There's room inside for two people in each. The troop carrier is already a tempting enough target, so I was reluctant to use that."

"Excellent thinking, Captain. You've been showing a lot of initiative of late." Voria gave the man a crisp salute, and he returned it.

"I have to be honest, sir. That's a whole lot easier to do without...certain other officers around," Davidson said, a little sheepishly. "I'm sorry you had to do it, but it was the right call, sir."

"I know," she said, though privately she'd questioned the decision many times since making it. Executing Thalas would have dire consequences—assuming any of them survived their confrontation with Nebiat. Had she been a prudent politician, she'd have used the brew on Thalas, not Bord. Augury or no. "The incident was regrettable, but he gave me little choice. The proof that the decision was correct is clear. You and Aran work well together, and that bodes well for our survival."

"I've never seen a battle run like this. Well, not outside Ternus anyway," Davidson said, smiling now. He rested a large chrome wrench on his shoulder. "The battalion took almost no damage, and downed a full Krox binder. Even when we were ambushed back at the starport, we pulled it out. By all rights the Krox should have wiped us out, but we turned it around."

"I'm pleased by your confidence, Captain, but I have to temper it." Voria folded her arms, staring up at the captain. He was so young. They all were. "What we've faced thus far has been nothing but a preamble. Nebiat sent her weakest remaining binder to slow us, a contemptuous move. The fact that we brushed it aside is impressive, but only the first test. We must find Nebiat, and we must do it quickly. We do not sleep until we locate her. Get your men ready to move out."

"Yes, sir. Thank you for taking the time to speak to me like an equal, sir. It means a great deal." Davidson offered her a hand.

"I understand why you hated Thalas, Captain. He left you little choice. I do not hate you, nor do I consider you *zeros*. We are all soldiers, fighting the same war." Voria took his hand and shook it firmly.

A symphony of light and power burst into existence deep in the fog. Multicolored lights played in the distance, painting the fog into a purplish haze. Power pulsed in a steady rhythm, just beyond hearing. *Whum, whum. Whum, Whum.*

"Sir?" Davidson asked, staring out into the fog.

"Get your people moving right now, Captain. We are out of time." Voria turned from him, striding quickly toward where Aran had gathered his squad.

All four stood around a small fire Crewes had set with a cantrip. The flames pushed the mist into a corona of light around the fire.

Nara spotted Voria first, and rose quickly to her feet. She picked up her helmet from a log beside her. "Are we moving out, sir?"

"In a moment, Private," Voria said, moving to stand next to the fire. The warmth thinned the chill, but didn't banish it. "Davidson is moving the column. We're pushing ahead toward the ritual, as we cannot afford to wait for the infantry." Voria nodded at the purplish fog. "All of you felt that?"

"I think people on the other side of the sector felt that," Aran said, his attention on the mist. "What kind of spell is she casting?"

"Most spells are quick. You pour in some power, scribe the correct sigils, and you get a specific effect. Nebiat is performing a ritual, which is magic on a whole other level." Voria blew into her hands, then splayed her fingers before the fire. "A ritual usually involves many mages working together, pouring power to achieve a specific effect. The difference is the scope of that effect. Ripping the patch off a god's wound requires immense magical strength. The ritual will serve as a sort of cup, holding all the energy Nebiat and her mages unleash. Filling that cup can take days."

"So if we can reach her before the cup is full we can disrupt the spell then?" Aran asked.

"That's more difficult than you might think," Bord said, speaking up for the first time since Voria's arrival. "A ritual can survive the removal of any specific mage, so long as there are other mages to take up the slack. Mages will be let out to sleep, then relieve other mages when they wake up. With enough mages doing that, you can accomplish almost anything. Some rituals last months."

"So how do we disrupt the ritual?" Kez asked. "Especially if we're assuming she's got an army of binders around her."

"We break the metaphorical cup," Nara said, rising from the log. She brushed a lock of damp hair from her cheek. "Rituals are delicate, and can be damaged. If we can remove the receptacles they're using to store the magic, we can deny the spell the energy it needs to complete."

"Precisely, and that is exactly what we will attempt." Voria turned reluctantly from the fire, touching each of them in turn with her gaze. "Davidson can provide a little support, and can keep their minions off us. But we're going to have to deal with the binders ourselves, and we have no way of knowing how many they have."

"Nara can fly a lot faster than the caravan. Why not have her scout the ritual?" Aran suggested. "Depending on what she finds, it might even make sense to break away from the infantry. At the very least, we'll know more than we do now."

"Do it," Voria said, nodding to Nara. "But take no chances. If you are detected, flee instantly."

Nara nodded soberly, putting her helmet back on. Voria watched the woman fly off into the mist, considering her retreating form. She turned to Aran, lowering her voice. "Do you trust her?"

"If you'd asked me a week ago, I would have sworn that woman couldn't be trusted," Aran said, watching Nara's retreating form. "Now? Yeah, I trust her. She's committed in a way I don't think the old Nara could ever have managed."

Behind them, the tanks whirred to life. The column started into the swamp, moving toward the light.

54

SCOUT

Nara zipped over the tops of another cluster of trees—the only way she'd found to navigate the thick soup she'd been forced to fly through. Scouting was damned difficult when you couldn't see anything. She flipped her armor in midair, swinging her pistol around...at nothing. Only more mist. But the sense that something watched her didn't diminish; it only increased.

Panicking, Nara closed her eyes and triggered a pulse of power into her armor. It shimmered, then faded from sight. She hovered there, weightless, waiting. Moments passed, with the only change the pulsing *whum, whum* coming from the purple mists ahead.

An overpowering urge to flee rammed a cold dagger into her resolve. There was so much power in those mists, the kind of power that reshaped worlds. The kind of power smart mages avoided. She could feel the old Nara thrashing about like a caged cat.

"No. I'm not you any more." Nara willed her armor to accelerate, pushing toward the purple light. She gained another fifty meters of altitude, which put her higher than even the tallest trees. It might make her visible to anything that could see in the mist, but theoretically her invisibility spell would still prevent them from seeing her. For a few minutes at least.

Ideally she'd have waited to cast it until she was closer, but it wasn't like she could un-cast it. She simply had to make the best use of the time. Nara accelerated again, and again gained fifty meters in altitude. The mist whipped around her, and she thought if she found the one mountain in this swamp it would probably end badly.

She burst suddenly from the mist, into an overcast twilight, and quickly surveyed her surroundings. "Major, I've found the edge of the mist."

Before her stretched a large moss covered mountain, with a bright purple glow coming from the peak. There were camps set up at even intervals around the base of the mountain, each camp centered around a bright multi-colored bonfire inside of a golden urn. She could feel the power coming from those fires.

"Those must be the receptacles for the power they're gathering," she muttered to herself. She studied the camps, counting six enforcers and one full-sized Wyrm at each bonfire.

There was something familiar about the pattern they'd established. Her invisibility would last for several more minutes. Perhaps it was worth risking a closer look.

Nara flew straight up several hundred meters, then glided over one of the camps. There were eight in total, and each fire burned a different color. The side she'd discovered contained blue, green, and purple.

"It's the Circle of Eight." She couldn't remember precisely how, but Nara knew that symbology. Knew it to her core. She remembered—only a flash—participating in a ritual, but there was nothing she could hold onto.

Nara shook herself out of the reverie, gliding over the peak of the mountain. Most of the slopes were covered in moss, over what she assumed must be granite—perhaps the same granite as the walls of the crater.

Six enforcers guarded a ring of sigils, forming an enormous ritual circle. This too was familiar, and Nara had a flash of drawing a circle around herself with a flourish. This magic, this thing they were doing...it was so familiar.

A pale-haired woman danced inside the circle, leaving sigils wherever she passed. The sigils formed chains, each chain stretching back to the circle. The complexity of the magic exceeded anything Nara had ever seen, and the spell had yet to reach its crescendo.

The woman looked up suddenly, eyes narrowing as they landed on Nara. "You fools, there is a mage among us. She fooled you with a simple invisibility spell. Find her, and kill her. Now!"

Nara fled, pouring everything into the suit. She shot back toward the mist, panting desperately into the comm, "I've mapped their encampment, but they saw me. I'm coming in hot. I've got three medium-sized Wyrms on my tail."

Aran's confident voice spilled onto the comm. "Copy that. Crewes and I are inbound. See if you can shake them."

"Can do," she replied, cutting into a steep dive. "Let's see how smart you guys are."

All three wyrms dove after her, narrowing the gap. They were almost in breath range...but not quite. Nara laughed, then suddenly reversed course. The Wyrms shot past her, continuing on toward the ground. Only one was fast enough to breathe, but Nara dodged the cone of white.

Nara accelerated upward at an angle, away from the Wyrms. They righted their course, but paused as she neared the mists and then hovered there, watching, as she plunged out of sight.

"They stopped pursuit when I reached the mists. I think I'm clear, but I definitely blew it. They know we're coming, and I'm sure they're going to be ready."

"It can't be all bad. Did you get a look at their camp?" Aran asked.

"Yeah, I can describe it in detail. I'll see what I can sketch up to show the major," Nara said. "I don't know how much time we have, but I suspect not much."

55

NOW

Voria peered through the hovertank's narrow viewport, out into the fog. Nara's report was sparse, and she wished she'd seen the ritual with her own eyes. But she had to work with what she'd been given.

"Captain Davidson, please order the Marines and militia to make best speed toward the coordinates Nara provided. Have the tanks accelerate to full speed in the same direction." Adrenaline made her hands shake.

"Sir, we'll outpace the infantry. By the time they arrive this will all be decided, one way or the other. Besides, leaving the Marines unsupported is an open invitation to pick them off." Davidson didn't look up from the tank's central monitor. It was Inuran make, with a black-bordered screen displaying the area outside the tank.

"I realize that, Captain. It's unfortunate, and I understand how callous this makes me sound. But, given Nara's description, the ritual will reach its crescendo soon. If that happens before we arrive, then our arrival will no longer matter. Nebiat will have removed the seal, and will be free to turn her whole attention on the battalion." Voria planted her hands firmly on her knees, forcing herself to stop fidgeting. "It's better to hit her with what we can, even if that means abandoning the infantry. I sincerely hope the Marines survive this encounter, but if the Krox are forced to react to them, then they are helping us win this in their own way."

"By dying as a distraction?" Davidson snapped. But he tapped away at his keyboard, sending out orders to his men.

Voria hated making decisions like this, hated weighing a planet full of lives versus the men and women conscripted to serve. It wasn't fair, but someone had to make these choices. She tapped the comm again. "Lieutenant Aran, do you copy?"

"Yes, sir."

"We're moving at best speed toward the coordinates Nara provided. I'll need your company to take up position behind the tanks. Let us come out of the mist first, and let the enemy engage. Once they've done so, I want you to counterattack." The tank rumbled over another tiny island, then splashed back into the water. "Limit your spell usage until we've assessed the situation."

"Yes, sir. We're moving into position now. We'll wait right behind the tanks." Aran paused. "Sir...if I may, they know we're coming."

"Which means they'll be waiting for us, yes. Our only option is to hit hard and hit fast."

"But sir, if we use the same coordinates Nara gave us it will mean coming out of the mist right where she went in," Aran ventured. "Won't that be where their ambush is concentrated?"

"He's got a point," Davidson called over his shoulder.

"That's exactly where the bulk of Nebiat's defenses will

be concentrated, but she'll keep the rest mobile," Voria explained, watching the mist impatiently. "She'll expect us to launch a sortie from another direction, perhaps as a feint. Then, she'll expect us to launch whatever our real assault is. She will expect both assaults to be aimed at opposite sides of the ritual, and she'll expect that neither target will be the place Nara went into the mists. By assaulting her with everything we have all at once, we'll face only the portion of her forces allocated to that spot. The mobile group will take time to reach us, and if we are quick we can dispatch the defenders before reinforcements arrive."

"Copy that, sir." Aran's voice crackled back.

"Once the battle begins, I will not have time to answer questions. If I give orders—to you, or Davidson, or directly to a subordinate—they will need to be obeyed instantly." Voria had given Aran far more latitude than she had Thalas, and that choice was already paying dividends. Yet establishing boundaries was also necessary.

"Yes, sir," Aran replied. "Of course. What's your ETA?"

"Davidson?" Voria asked.

"We're about two kilometers out, so maybe three minutes?" Davidson guessed. The tank rumbled over a large tree trunk, the right side lurching a meter into the air. Davidson seemed unfazed, quickly righting it.

"Excellent. Get into position, Lieutenant. We'll be coming out of the mist in a few minutes."

Voria fingered her bracelet. She rubbed the sapphire, and the spell within swirling in response. The power was immense, far beyond what Voria could safely cast. It was the kind of power Nebiat would wield casually. Voria could match it once, and only once. Once the bracelet was empty, she'd be helpless. It wasn't a comforting thought.

The splashing receded, and the tank moved onto a

stretch of muddy land. It picked up speed, and the engine howled as the mist parted. It didn't thin, like normal fog; it simply ended, and the tank burst into the clearing Nara had described.

A squat mountain stood before them, magical power flowing around it in quantities Voria had never seen before —not even on Shaya itself.

But she didn't have time to study it, or the ritual. As expected, the Krox were waiting.

Several dozen human corpses in Ternus armor raised their rifles and opened fire. The rounds pinged harmlessly off the tanks, but Voria slammed the viewport shut anyway. She moved behind Davidson, observing the battle over his shoulder.

"Roll right on over 'em, kids," Davidson barked, pushing the tank's accelerator. The tank shot forward, bullets ringing off the hull like hail, and bowled over the corpses, crushing them under the pulsors as the tank rumbled over their lines.

A line of Krox enforcers stepped forward from behind the corpses, raising their spellcannons. They unleashed a barrage of acid bolts, peppering the tanks as they approached. Each time a bolt hit, Voria heard sizzling as armor boiled away into nothing.

"Oh, man," Davidson whispered in a low tone. "I thought we were dead for sure."

"Inuran tech uses dense iron in all armor," Voria explained, watching as the tank's turret took a bead on one of the enforcers. "Dense iron is both incredibly resistant to kinetic force, and highly resistant to magic—like that enforcer's hide."

"Good thing their hide isn't gauss resistant." Davidson laughed, tapping the fire button on his console. A high-pitched whine built, then the entire tank kicked back two meters as it fired. A knot of white streaked into the enforcer, and it simply ceased to exist.

Another enforcer stepped into its place, and another behind that. A shadow passed over their ranks. A large shadow.

"They've committed their dragons. Now, Lieutenant."

56

CREATIVE SOLUTIONS

"Bord, Kez, support the armor. The Wyrms are going to come at them fast and hard," Aran roared. He exploded out of the mist into the clear sky, already taking aim at the closest dragon. There were four, all hovering above the tanks.

Below, Bord sprinted out of the mist. A dragon moved into a dive, its head rearing back to suck in a breath. It expelled a cloud of pallid, white, death. This was the first time Aran had seen it in the full light of day, and he noticed writhing faces within that fog.

Bord leapt into the air, landing in a crouch atop the lead tank—the major's tank. He raised both hands, and a latticework of white sigils burst out of both gauntlets. They spread like spiderwebs, quickly weaving a dome over the major's tank and the area immediately around it. The dragon's breath washed over the ward, flowing around it.

"Sir, if we could avoid a repeat of last time, when the Krox played *gank the healer*, I'd appreciate it," Bord panted into the comm.

"Sit tight, Bord. We'll take care of the Wyrms. Kez, watch

those enforcers coming around the south side. They've switched to melee weapons. Spellblades, it looks like." Aran unleashed a level two void bolt, tagging a wyrm in the right side of his face. Scales exploded outward, and when the Wyrm turned its hateful expression on Aran only one eye remained.

The Wyrm banked, swooping up over Aran...right into Nara's sights. Her spellpistol kicked twice in rapid succession, both shots hitting the exact same spot Aran had already wounded. The Wyrm jerked with each shot, and after the second its body went limp, and it fell from the sky. The body slammed into several Krox enforcers, crushing them into the ankle deep water. One didn't rise, though the rest wriggled out from under the dead Wyrm.

One of the remaining Wyrms sketched a sigil, and a bolt of lightning crackled toward Aran faster than he could react. The energy arced over his spellarmor, crackling through his entire body. He went rigid, gritting his teeth as his body resisted being electrocuted.

"Aran," Nara yelled. He was dimly aware of falling, then his flight being arrested as Nara's arms wrapped around him. "It's okay, I've got you."

"Sssokay," he slurred. The suit was already pumping his system full of healing potion. "Just need a sec."

"You want a piece, you scaly piece of space bacon?" Crewes roared from below. His spellcannon boomed, and a fat hunk of magma shot from the barrel. It arced into the Wyrm from below, catching it squarely between the legs.

The Wyrm screeched, flapping frantically to gain altitude as flaming rock splashed across its legs and groin.

Aran raised a shaking arm, centering the barrel over the dragon. He squeezed the trigger. A level two bolt caught the bone connecting the wing to the back. The bone shattered, and the wing fluttered loose.

"Nice shot," Nara said.

"I was aiming for its face," Aran admitted.

The dragon clawed futilely at the air with both arms, launching a desperate cone of breath at Aran and Nara. Nara dodged smoothly to the right, carrying them both to safety as the Wyrm fell. It slammed into one of the rear tanks, driving the hovertank deep into the earth.

The tank recovered a moment later, delivering a gauss cannon round from the turret into the dragon's broken body. It flung the beast away, allowing the tank to crawl out from underneath.

"Same side, Lieutenant," Davidson called over the comm.

"Yeah, uh, my bad." Aran pushed away from Nara, switching to external speaker. "Thanks for the save. I owe you."

"Good, I like having you owe me." Nara laughed. "Uh, sir."

Aran scanned the combat, and liked what he saw. The enforcers and the corpses they commanded had been put down. Three out of the four dragons were down, and Bord was easily keeping the remaining one at bay with his wards.

"Well done, Lieutenant." The major's voice crackled over the comm. "We can move on to the next phase of the plan. The *spirit* urn is the closest, and the most important. If we break only a single urn, that's your target. Captain Davidson and the surviving tanks will assault the *water* urn, the secondary target. If we can disrupt both, I don't think Nebiat will be able to complete the ritual."

"You heard the lady, tech mages." Aran glided lower, Nara trailing in his wake. Crewes had caught up to Bord and

Kez, and the trio stood near one of the dead Wyrms. "All right guys, this isn't going to be like what we've dealt with so far. We're rushing an entrenched position, and every Krox between here and that urn is going to light us up."

"You're right about that," Kez said, popping up her faceplate. She was panting, her platinum hair plastered to her face from sweat. "There's a whole lot of enforcers between us and that thing. They're going to come at us with a vengeance."

"This isn't doable, sir," Crewes admitted. He trotted over to Aran, resting his spellcannon on his shoulder. "Those enforcers are going to gun us down before we reach them. Do you remember fighting that pair on the station? These things don't go down easy, and we don't have enough spells to take them all down."

"So let's cheat. Bord, how long can you sustain a ward?" Aran asked.

"Hmm. Three minutes, maybe? But they're immobile. I need to focus to keep the ward up," Bord said.

"Kez, I want you to carry Bord on your shoulders, so he can focus on the ward," Aran explained. He pointed toward the spirit urn. "Run full-tilt for that thing. Bord will hold up his ward around you. The rest of the company will stay inside, theoretically safe from dragons. We'll concentrate fire on anything that gets inside the ward. That will be critical. Make sure you focus the same targets. Sergeant, we'll assist off you. Knock 'em down, and Nara and I will make sure they stay down."

"That's the craziest gods-damned plan I have ever heard," Crewes rumbled. He sounded impressed. "All right, wipes—let's move out. You heard the Lieutenant."

"I don't like this plan," Bord said, forlornly.

"You joost don't like being carried around like a sack of

potatoes, because you know I'm recording this to send to your mum," Kez teased. She scooped up Bord's much smaller armor, and deposited him behind her neck. "Now hold on. If you have to go the bathroom do it now, because once this trip starts, it ain't stopping."

"If we're going to do this, I guess we may as well do it." Bord sighed, hanging his head in embarrassment. "Someday I'm going to get a dignified role in one of these fights."

"One more thing," Aran said, eyeing the golden sigil on his HUD. "I'm going to use the spell amplification thing the armor came with. I'll do what I can to—."

"You've had spell amplification this entire time?" Kez interrupted. "Seriously? My gods you have no idea what it does, do you?"

"I have a pretty good idea," Aran said, maybe a touch defensively. "I used it to kill that binder back in the swamp."

"Sir, what Kezia means," Crewes growled. "Is that spell amplification is designed to help an entire unit. If you use it, we'll all get the benefits. Basically, it will up all our spells by one level. It usually don't last long, but it should be long enough for us to run and gun some enforcers."

"Well all right then." Aran laughed. "Let's do this. Kez, start your run."

Kez broke into a run, and Aran glided after her. Bord raised both hands, and the protective latticework sprung up around them. They started across the distance to the urn, where the Krox had gathered their forces.

Aran triggered the spell amplification, and the golden light once again burst from his armor. It washed over the rest of the company, covering the area around him for about thirty meters.

"Nara, you've got the best eyes. How many enforcers are we looking at?" Aran asked.

"I count eleven, but other than the binder I don't see any other Wyrms," she said, zooming at little past Aran but making sure to say within the protection of the ward.

"Sounds like good news to me," Crewes said, laughing.

They charged across the field, and a Wyrm shimmered into existence above them long enough to launch a cone of breath. It washed harmlessly off the ward, and the dragon began circling them, evidently confused.

"This one's a bit slow, innit?" Kez said, chuckling. She ate up the distance to the urn, crossing the gap in huge leaps.

The enforcers moved up to engage them, several drawing long, wickedly curved spellblades. They charged Kez, and a knot of them reached the ward and plunged right through. The Krox fanned out, attempting to encircle Kez.

She didn't slow, punching the closest enforcer with a massive metal gauntlet. The blow knocked the creature from her path in a spray of dark blood and scales, and she vaulted her opponent.

Aran took aim at the next closest enforcer, coring it through the back with a level two bolt right between the wings. With the spell amplification, the bolt left a two meter hole in its wake. Crewes lobbed another magma mortar. The usually destructive explosion had been greatly amplified, and blasted a pair of enforcers into a pair of smoking piles.

"Didn't the major say to conserve spells?" Nara chastened him.

"Are you kidding? We downed three enforcers with two spells. They don't do us any good if we're dead," Aran countered, zipping closer to Kez. "We've almost reached the binder. Get ready for the real fight."

Kez crashed into an Enforcer, grabbing its head in both hands.

Above her, Bord yelled in a high-pitched voice. "Seriously? Trying to maintain a spell here."

Kez squeezed, and the Enforcer's skull cracked. It still didn't go down. She brought down her armored head, slamming it into the enforcers face. The creature went limp. "Sorry about the bumpy ride. Sit tight."

They picked off more Enforcers, pushing a wedge through the Krox forces. Their ferocity combined with the spell amplification forced the enemy back, and finally they burst through, into the outer edge of the ritual circle. Before them stood a wide golden urn, its surface covered in tiny sigils. A sickly white glow came from the top, and Aran could feel the immense power gathered within.

Next to the urn stood an unassuming man, not much taller than Kez.

"He's a drifta, I think," Kez said. "Don't matter none, though. Gonna have to do for him."

"That's a real interesting ward ya got there, mate," the Binder said, taking a few steps closer. "Seems to have gotten ya this far. Mighty inventive, that. But you ain't getting any closer. I can promise you that."

"End him," Aran ordered.

The squad lit up the binder, a flurry of spells converging on his rough location. Every last one halted in midair, four meters before reaching him. Iridescent ripples flowed through the air where the spells impacted, then dissipated.

"See?" he said. "Mine's better'n yours. Unless you've got a true mage you're hiding, there's no way you're getting trew that ward." He laughed, giving them a playful grin. "Time is very much on my side. My mates will be here shortly. Joost sit tight."

57

FEAR

"Eddings, move to support the right flank," Davidson ordered. "Concentrate your fire on that Wyrm with the torn wing. It's slower than the others."

The tank bounced over another rock, sending Voria tumbling into the wall. She caught herself, seizing the back of Davidson's seat.

"You'd be safer if you buckled in, sir," Davidson said without turning in her direction. He guided them behind two of the other tanks, adding a shot from his gauss cannon that finished the wounded Wyrm the tanks had been focusing on.

"I need to be unrestricted, in case I need to counter a spell." Voria watched his screen intently. It showed such a narrow view of the battle, and she wished she'd thought to ask her mother for a scry-falcon that could have transmitted an aerial view. She was all but blind in here, but couldn't risk leaving the vehicle.

A shadow passed over them, and one of the largest remaining Wyrms breathed on Eddings. There was no final cry or death scream. The tank simply slowed…then stopped moving entirely.

Voria clenched a fist. In a few moments, if the Wyrm were willing to expend the energy for the spell, Eddings would be bound and his tank turned back on the Confederate line.

"We've almost reached the binder, sir," Davidson called, unnecessarily.

"I can see the screen as well as you, Captain." Voria studied it, reaching out with her senses. "Pull the tanks up short. There is a barrier around the urn."

Davidson quickly turned the tank, and the other tanks did the same. They zoomed around the urn, swinging their turrets into position.

"Don't bother with the barrier. Focus your fire on the approaching Wyrms," Voria ordered. She moved back to the viewport she'd closed earlier, slamming it back open. She needed line of sight to cast.

Voria quickly sketched a counterspell, then flung it at the invisible barrier around the urn. The barrier exploded silently, flinging a cloud of iridescent mana shards in all directions. The shards quickly dissipated as the last of the spell dissolved.

"It's exposed, Captain. Fire."

The tanks let loose with a staccato of gauss rifle rounds, each streaking toward the urn. To Voria's immense surprise, the rounds impacted against a shimmering blue barrier, centimeters from the urn. This ward had been hastily erected, but reinforced with considerable strength—an alarming level of strength.

Voria tried to peer upward, but the narrow slit prevented her from seeing. "Davidson, open the turret."

Davidson didn't ask why, fortunately. He opened the

turret, and Voria quickly scaled the ladder. She popped her head and shoulders out, and her mouth went dry when she saw the titanic Wyrm looming in the shadows of the mountain, hovering right above the urn they'd come to destroy.

Nebiat's midnight scales glistened in the light of the ritual, saliva trickling from jaws that could easily swallow their tank whole. But it wasn't the physical body that filled Voria with terror. It was the volume of magical power. If Voria's magic was a bonfire, then she was seeing a sun, in all its terrible brilliance.

Nebiat's tail swished languidly beneath her, casually knocking a transport-sized boulder down the mountain slope. She flapped her wings, and the wind forced Voria to cling to the tank's ladder.

"Ahh, Major Voria. I've heard so very much about you. Some of my colleagues believe you to be a skilled mage—a few have even said *archmage*. Is there any truth to that?" Nebiat began lazily sketching sigils, a flood of them, with a long black claw. The latticework of the spell was too complex for Voria to follow.

Nebiat assembled the spell faster than Voria would have believed, then flung it outward. It expanded into a ball of swirling grey energy, then burst in a wave that washed over everyone for hundreds of meters. The tanks afforded no protection, and the magic washed over Voria as it did everyone else. Immense, towering panic filled her mind—overwhelming, teeth-chattering terror, born of the certainty that she was about to die.

Davidson clawed frantically at his safety harness as he tried to unbuckle himself. "We're going to die. We need to run. Now." The magic had him, and no doubt had the rest of her forces as well. It would not have her, too.

"Noooo!" Voria screamed, slamming her fist into the wall

of the tank hard enough to bloody her knuckles. She fought off the magically induced terror, using her anger to tear apart the sigils trying to wrap around her spirit.

Voria seized her bracelet, pulling it off her wrist, and climbed back up the ladder to glare out at Nebiat. Then Voria slammed her bracelet into the tank, cracking the gem.

Intense sapphire light burst out, and Voria used the bracelet's latent magic to guide the counterspell toward the spell Nebiat had cast. A bubble of blue swirling energy rose, mimicking the original spell. Then, as the terror spell had, it burst outward. Everywhere it touched the fear spell dissolved, and her people stopped running.

"I'm no archmage, but if you think you can dismiss me as some apprentice, you're about to find out otherwise. You want a fight, you come and get me!" Voria ducked down the ladder, leaning down to peer at Davidson. "There's no way we're taking out that urn. She's going to come for us fast and hard. Make for the fog, and don't be shy about the evasive action."

An eardrum-splitting howl of draconic rage echoed off the mountains. "I. Will. Kill. *You.*"

58

RUNNING ON EMPTY

Aran swooped back down to the ward around the binder. Nara landed next to him. Crewes trotted up with Bord and Kez in tow. The spell amplification sigil flashed red, then ticked down to 0%. At least the enforcers had all been killed.

"Now that was damned impressive," the binder said, giving them a genuine smile. "Your major joost counterspelled Nebiat herself. Ain't never seen that happen before. Looks like she's a mite miffed about it though." The drifter nodded at Nebiat's gigantic form, flapping after a fleeing tank.

"Man, I wish I'd saved one of those counterspell potions," Aran groused, hovering outside the ward.

"Oh I don't know," Nara protested. "I kind of liked how both those counterspells were used. Especially the one where the Wyrm was about to nuke us, until you kicked her legs out from under her."

"Crewes, do you have any suggestions on how we can reach this smug little bastard?" Aran asked, hopeful. "You've got more experience than the rest of us put together."

"We need a true mage, and that means the major." Crewes said, turning to face the hovertanks. They were all fleeing from Nebiat, scattering in different directions as they made for the wall of fog. "Guess that isn't going to happen, though."

"We're pretty well fooked." Kez said, slamming her hammer into the barrier. It rebounded off, sending her flying backward.

"Yeah, ya are fooked. And not the good kind of fooked neither," the Binder taunted, spinning around and shaking his rear in their direction.

"So I joost don't understand. How did you come to be serving the Krox?" Kez demanded, looming in her ivory armor.

"Yer just tryin to distract me, which is fine by me. I got nowhere to be until the ritual is done. Not long now, by the way." The drifter winked up at Kez's spellarmor. "Yer not getting trew, and in a little bit yer all gonna be dead anyway."

"Everybody stand back," Nara said, her voice colder than Aran had heard since...since before she'd been mind-wiped. He could feel the anger smoldering in her, could feel it bank inside of her as she summoned her magic.

Nara raised a single gauntleted hand, sketching a bright, purple sigil. She added a white, then a green. The binder watched curiously, then his eyes widened as he studied the spell. "Oh fook."

Nara finished, and a pulse of multicolored light shot into the ward. It rippled for several moments, then flickered out of existence. Aran wasn't familiar with the magic she'd used. It wasn't a counterspell. Some sort of nullification?

The binder turned to run, but Aran was already moving. He sighted down his scope, lining it up with the binder's back, right behind the heart. Aran thumbed the selector to level three and fired. The bolt took the binder from behind, knocking his body to the mud and blowing a ragged, smoking crater in his back.

"Eww," Bord said. "Guess the mortal binders aren't nearly as tough as the Wyrms."

"Nara, that was incredible," Aran said, though privately he admitted to being the tiniest bit afraid at even that little bit of the old Nara suddenly surfacing.

"I don't even know how I did it." She held up her own hand, examining it with wonder. She looked up at Aran and grinned. "Let's finish this."

Aran eyed the urn. "The major was nonspecific about exactly how to destroy this, so I'm going with brute force. Kez, will you do the honors?"

"Sure, but it might be good to stand a few meters back." Kez trotted to the urn, giving her hammer an experimental swing.

Aran zoomed backward a good fifty meters, as did the rest of the squad. "All right. Do it."

Kez raised her hammer and brought it down on the urn. A wave of thick grey light exploded outward, washing over everything in an irresistible wave. The magic flung Aran backward, and he rolled across the ground, bouncing along for fifty or sixty more meters before finally coming to a complete stop.

Several areas of red had appeared on the paper doll in his HUD, but the armor still seemed functional.

"Oww. Maybe we should have stood further back." He rose shakily to his feet.

"Sir, you might want to look west," Crewes cautioned, also struggling to his feet.

Aran pivoted to find a mass of approaching figures. Most

—at least a few dozen—were Krox enforcers. Reinforcing them were hundreds of infantry—infantry Aran recognized.

"Oh no." A wave of numbness knocked Aran back a step. "Major, this is Aran, do you copy?"

"I'm a little busy just now," the major snapped. "What do you need?"

"The Krox have wiped out our Marines. They're being deployed against us."

"Have you destroyed the spirit urn?" she demanded.

"Yes, sir."

"We were unable to destroy the water urn. Take your company and make an attempt. The ward is already down. Nebiat summoned a secondary one, but I imagine that's very temporary and will expire as soon as she stops concentrating on it." Her voice was tight and hard, as controlled as ever. "I'm going to get her to follow me. See if you can make it to the water urn. Perhaps we can salvage this."

Aran spun around to face the approaching Krox army—not only the corpses of the Marines, but the dozens of enforcers. How in the depths was he going to deal with them, much less make it to another well-defended urn? His people were tired, and almost out of magic.

59

PRETTY WELL FOOKED

Aran rolled under an Enforcer's blade, then leapt up into the air over the Krox. He yanked his blade from a void pocket, ramming the weapon through the Enforcer's neck. The thick hide resisted, but Aran thrust forward with a yell, slicing deep into its throat. Thick, black blood poured out, first from the throat and then the creature's mouth. The spellblade vibrated in a way that somehow conveyed satisfaction.

His chest heaved, and a sheen of sweat had dampened his hair. He glanced around quickly, assessing the situation. Their line—if it could be called a line—was collapsing. Somehow Bord had kept the ward up, and Crewes and Kez had moved to protect him, but there was nothing to stop the Krox from walking through the ward, and they were coming in by the dozen.

"Anyone got any bright ideas?" Aran asked, backpedaling then delivering a hasty parry to knock away another sword.

"Nope. This is pretty much as bad as things can get,"

Crewes called, laughing. "Woo! That's right. Get some, scaly."

Aran risked a glance at the major's position, regretting it immediately. "Oh you can't be serious."

"What is it?" Nara asked.

Aran pointed. "Three more Wyrms just moved to help Nebiat catch the major. They're herding her."

Nebiat's utterly massive form glided after the tanks, a bird of prey swooping down on rodents. Aran knew they'd never make it.

"Wait," Nara said, darting several meters higher to avoid an acid bolt. "I'm such an idiot. Nebiat left the summoning circle."

"Is that good or bad?" A kick from behind knocked Aran to one knee, but Kez darted forward and batted the Krox's into the air. It sailed out of the ward, crashing to the ground forty meters outside. The creature rose, and started trotting back in their direction.

"Thanks." He accepted Kez's hand, and she pulled him back to her feet. "What do you have, Nara? I'll take anything."

"The ritual isn't complete. If Nebiat's left the circle, then anyone can step inside." Nara paused to deliver a roundhouse kick to another Enforcer. The creature was flung back, and Nara peppered it with a trio of void bolts as it started to rise. The creature dropped back to one knee, and Nara finished it with a final bolt. "A true mage could take control of the ritual and either terminate it or mangle it so badly it doesn't work."

"You'll never be able to reach the circle," Bord said, his voice thick with weariness. He'd recast the ward two more times, and had to be close to empty. "There are still half a dozen Wyrms patrolling that island, and who knows what kind of defensive force at the top. That's assuming you could even break loose from this combat."

"If we go for the circle," Aran pointed out, "their binders will see it. They have to understand the danger, right? So they'll probably pursue us with everything they have." He grinned. "That might work out nicely."

"Nicely?" Nara snapped. "What's nice about any of this?"

"Remember that potion of Shaya's Grace?" Aran asked. "The major said I should use it when it looked like everything was over. I don't know exactly how it works, but if anything can get us up to the top of that mountain, it will be that potion."

"I see where you're going with this." Nara's voice shifted to excited. "If we fly in that direction, they'll have to pursue. That means they'll probably leave the rest of the company alone."

"It also means Nebiat will probably turn right around and come after you," Crewes pointed out. "I know you're only wipes, but you can't be that stupid. Ain't no way you can pull this off."

"What's the alternative?" Aran demanded. He slashed through an Enforcer's wing, then reversed the blade and decapitated it.

Crewes cocked his head to the side, then crushed an Enforcer's skull with his elbow. He smiled. "Good point, LT. It's been good knowing you. You're not nearly as pathetic as I assumed."

"Likewise, Sarge. Nara, can you climb on the back of my armor?" Aran didn't know what the potion would do, but even without it his Mark XI was faster than her spellarmor.

"If we pull this off, I want a raise," Nara said, climbing on.

"If we pull this off, I want a vacation." Aran laughed. "All right guys, here goes."

He willed the suit to administer the potion, and watched as the glowing liquid flowed out of the canister. The golden motes swirled eagerly as they disappeared.

Power thrummed through his armor, resonating with something deep inside of him. Time expanded, slowing to a mere crawl. Infinity stretched in all directions, every possibility layered on top of the next. The experience was new—but it wasn't. He remembered a similar sensation, when he'd been inside the mind of Xal. Was he seeing as a god saw?

Aran could see his death, a hundred times over. A thousand times. A million. There were so many ways to die.

But he also saw a course of events where he did *not* die. There was a path through the chaos, a way around the madness of battle. If he flew perfectly, and circled the Krox line in exactly the right way, there was a hole in those defenses.

He just needed to exploit it.

Aran leapt into the air, and his Mark XI flew like never before. He darted around a Wyrm, dodging its breath weapon even as he rolled past a lightning bolt cast by another dragon. He laughed as he twisted around another spell. Acid bolts streaked up from Enforcers all over the battlefield, especially from the ritual circle itself. In every case, Aran found a possibility where the bolt did not hit. He flowed from possibility to possibility, seeing every movement he made a split second before he made it.

More Wyrms were aware of him now, moving swiftly in his direction. Aran increased speed, shooting straight up. He cut suddenly to the right, and a beam of blue-white flame streaked through the area he'd just vacated.

Aran dove, flying an erratic corkscrew pattern that

flowed through the Krox ranks. He dodged spell after spell, effortlessly flowing around each.

The power went deeper than that, though. The energy he'd expended throughout the fight had returned, and more. A deep reservoir of power flowed through him, far more than he'd ever held. Enough to cast a dozen level three spells—perhaps more.

"Wait, do you see that?" Aran asked, pointing at the mountain.

"See what?" Nara called back.

"It almost looks like a face in the rock there, right below the peak. Right above the summoning circle." Aran made for that circle, which was as empty as they'd hoped. Nearly a dozen Enforcers stood around it, but there was no sign of any binders or Wyrms.

"We can sightsee later. Just get me down there." Nara tightened her grip around his shoulders, and Aran leaned into the dive. They fell like a star, slowing suddenly at the last second. The suit's gravity magic bled away their inertia, leaving them hovering a few meters above the circle. "Hop off and get started. I'll deal with these bastards."

Aran flipped the selector to level one, and began to move through the Krox ranks. He flowed from shot to shot, unloading a continuous stream of level one bolts. Each was empowered by the potion, tinged with golden motes. The shots—every shot—found their targets. Each hit the Krox in the most vital area: the face or the heart. It made spell amplification look like a parlor trick.

Twelve Krox fell in four seconds, leaving Aran and Nara alone in the circle. The Krox outside the circle swiftly dove for cover, taking up defensive positions as they prepared a counterattack.

"That was incredible." Nara whispered.

"Yeah well, it's probably also short-lived. You'd better get to work." Aran scanned the sky above. Wyrms were already gathering, and several were swooping in their direction. "We're about to have company. A lot of it."

60

NOT ON MY WATCH

"Sir I don't want to state the obvious, but I think we're in trouble." Davidson said, as calmly as he'd have delivered the munitions report.

"Why would you think that?" Voria wielded her sarcasm like a club, clinging to the ladder as they roared their way toward the wall of mist in the distance. She stared up at the flight of Wyrms, most of whom were pulling off pursuit to return to the mountain. Most, but not all.

"Well, that uh...that Nebiat Wyrm lady, she seems to have taken a particular dislike to us. Maybe because you taunted her," Davidson pointed out.

"Just keep moving, Captain," Voria ordered. She watched Nebiat glide closer, flapping those titanic wings to narrow the gap between them. "We're at the extreme edge of casting range, even for a binder of her skill."

Nebiat disappeared. Voria scanned frantically in all directions, trying to locate her. She was about to sketch a *pierce invisibility* spell when Nebiat reappeared directly above them.

"Goodbye, little mage." Nebiat breathed, and the all-too-familiar cone came down at the tank with inevitable finality.

Voria quickly sketched three symbols, drawing deeply from void magic. She bent space around her, around the entire tank. When it snapped back, the tank was forty meters west, right outside the area affected by the breath. The grass where they'd been sickened and died, a grim reminder of their own potential fate.

"Whoah. A little warning next time. I think I'm going to up my lunch." Davidson struggled with the controls, slamming into a tree. They rolled over it and continued toward the mists. "Just keep her off me for a little bit longer. We're almost there."

Voria didn't have the heart to tell him they were being toyed with. The mist would provide no safety. She looked up at Nebiat, wondering... Was there something she could have done differently? Something she'd missed, or some choice she had or hadn't made? Should she have kept her staff instead of trading it to the drifters?

But that would have meant not having the potions—neither the healing nor the one that had brought Bord back to life. There was simply no right answer.

She wondered again at the augury she'd received. Who had sent it? Had they planned for this very moment, and if so what did they gain from Voria's death? It was maddening, and it irked her that she'd die without answers.

Nebiat swooped lower, her face splitting into a draconic grin. Acidic saliva dripped from her fangs, each droplet hissing into the swamp below.

"I will genuinely miss you, Voria. On any other battlefield, I might even take the time to bind you. You'd make an excellent servant." The Wyrm laughed, swooping closer.

"Not on my watch, scaly," the sergeant's gritty voice

boomed out over the battlefield. A hunk of red-and-black magma arced onto her wing, exploding spectacularly. The tiny patch of flame only served to underscore Nebiat's relative size, but even she had to feel it.

The sergeant leapt into the air, fire pouring from the thruster on the back of his suit. He roared wordlessly, flying directly at Nebiat, who began sketching another spell—one Voria recognized.

Voria licked her lips, feeling her reservoir of magic. "If I can pull this off, you are going to be one pissed-off dragon."

A streak of black wider than a tank shot from Nebiat's claw, streaking toward the sergeant. He twisted to avoid it, but the spell adjusted course to pursue. His fate was sealed, unless Voria did something.

So she sketched the most complex counterspell she could. She'd been called gifted with counterspells, but she knew Nebiat was on a whole other level.

Her counterspell shot after the homing void bolt, slamming into it with a soundless explosion of light. Voria snarled when she saw the bolt had survived, but eased when she realized it was firing up and away from Crewes. She'd deflected it.

"Your antics are no longer amusing," Nebiat roared, turning back toward Voria. Her eyes narrowed to slits. "Your resourcefulness is impressive, but I can feel you weakening. How many more counterspells can you cast, I wonder?"

Nebiat sketched the same spell again, and another void bolt shot after Crewes. The sergeant fired another hunk of magma, hitting the same wing, in the same place. Nebiat roared her fury, but it turned to laughter when the void bolt caught Crewes. The energy blasted into the sergeant, enveloping his entire armor.

Crewes's smoking body tumbled from the sky, slamming into a bog in an explosion of muck.

Voria longed to help him, but knew she couldn't reach him. And even if she did, she'd only draw Nebiat's attention to him. "Davidson, cut forty-five degrees to your left, then angle around and look for Bord and Kez. They've almost reached us."

Nebiat swooped after her. "Oh, you are cruel. You have to realize that if you go to your tech mages for help, I will only dismember them in front of you. Do their lives matter that little to you?"

Voria didn't answer. She didn't say she treasured their lives, each and every one. Even Thalas.

Nebiat breathed. The cone angled at Bord and Kezia.

Bord's arms shot up, trembling, but still held high. A small latticework flowed out around him, the tiny ward reaching completion just as the breath hit them. It was barely big enough to cover him and Kezia, but they were knocked sprawling by the breath. The ward flickered and died, and Bord slumped to the ground. Kezia moved to stand defensively over him, screaming her wordless rage at Nebiat.

"Hear me, Wyrm," Voria roared. "If we are going to die, then we are going to do it defiantly. We are going to do it fighting, proving to you that the Krox will never break us. The Confederacy will oppose you wherever your forces appear."

"Really? Like they opposed us on Starn? Or Vakera? And now Marid?" Nebiat taunted, flapping her titanic wings, her shadow darkening the world to twilight. "You have fought bravely, Voria, but you have lost. Die with honor, little mage. Know that you have impressed the spawn of a god."

But death didn't come.

Nebiat's head shot up, and she turned back toward the mountain. A heartbeat later, Voria realized why.

The ritual's resonance had changed. Someone was manipulating the spell.

Voria spun, facing the bog where Crewes had gone down. She relaxed her death grip on the ladder, smiling grimly as the sergeant climbed back to his feet.

Apparently not even Nebiat could drop the Sergeant.

61

FINISH THE SPELL

Nara stepped slowly to the center of the ritual circle, raising her hands. Vast currents of magic pulsed around her, strong enough that they nearly lifted her into the air. Each flow was pulled from one of the urns, and all were delivered to this precise spot.

She could feel a vast reservoir of power, each flow corresponding to an aspect—save for *spirit*, which they'd destroyed.

"Any time, Nara," Aran yelled, decapitating an Enforcer with his spellblade, then yanking its body up to shield him from several acid bolts. He hurled the smoking corpse back at the Krox, gunning down another pair as if they were corpses, and not full Enforcers.

"This isn't like casting a cantrip," Nara snapped, trying to tune out both Aran and his conflict with the Krox. Doing so left her vulnerable, but if Aran couldn't keep them alive then none of this mattered anyway.

Nara examined the latticework of sigils Nebiat had been crafting. Already its complexity exceeded Nara's ability to understand, but she saw things she thought she recognized. That light blueish area was designed to unravel a sleep spell, though a sleep spell far beyond anything any mortal mage could cast. This kind of power must have belonged to the gods.

She walked around the spell, studying another part. This one wove into the spirit of a creature, binding its will. It was familiar, a type of magic she sensed she was already proficient with. This too was far more complex than she'd seen before, the kind of trap one might set for an incredibly powerful archmage, or some sort of demigod. But what was it doing here? There was nothing to trap.

Nara understood Nebiat trying to remove the seal, but not how the sleep spell and the binding accomplished that. There was something she was missing. Something of massive importance.

"The potion is starting to wear off," Aran roared, his words punctuated by the whine of his spellrifle. "You've got a few more seconds. Make them count."

"Okay. Well, then, I'm about to do something stupid," Nara said, biting her lip as she studied the spell.

"What kind of stupid?" Aran called, rolling between an enforcer's legs. A Wyrm dove from above, breathing a cone of white at Nara. She flinched, but before she could dive out of the way Aran was already moving. He leapt skyward, faster than she could track. He raised his tiny spellshield, which somehow deflected the entire cone. The forced knocked Aran to the ground near her, but he rolled quickly to his feet.

"I don't fully understand what the ritual does, but part of that ritual is a binding, for a really powerful creature." Nara inspected that part of the spell again, looking for a way to sever it. "I'm thinking I could remove that part, then complete the spell."

"I very much doubt that Nebiat would like that." Aran laughed. He landed, spinning to impale an Enforcer. This time he was too slow, and the Enforcer backhanded him. He went flying, tumbling across the broken ground until he'd nearly reached the edge of the circle, and rose shakily to his feet. Clearly, the grace provided by the potion was gone. "Do it! We're out of time."

Nara turned back to the spell, dissolving the sigils connecting the binding to the rest of the spell. There were dozens of tiny connections, but she meticulously severed them one after another. She ignored the sounds of combat, though she winced when Aran gave a pained yell.

Finally, she'd severed the last one. This was the moment of truth. A spell, especially a ritual, needed an enormous amount of power to sustain itself. By destroying the urn, they'd deprived the ritual of some of the power it needed. Normally, that would mean the spell couldn't finish—but, by removing the binding, Nara had lowered the power requirements of the spell.

She sketched the final sigil, closing the ritual. A sharp hum began, just past the edge of hearing, thrumming through her entire body. The ground trembled, then bucked wildly. She was tossed from her feet and rolled across the ground.

The flows of magic thickened, and power surged from every urn at once. The ritual circle drank it eagerly, feeding the magic into the spell Nara had created. The hum deepened until it rattled Nara's teeth, until she could feel it in her eyes.

Brilliant, multicolored light exploded outward from the

circle—not in a single pulse, but in a continuous torrent. The power washed over the entire mountain, clinging to the mossy slopes. That magic accumulated in drifts, almost like snow. Then, ever so slowly, the magic sank into the mountain.

The stone began to glow, and a wave of dark heat boiled outward. Had Nara not been in her spellarmor, she doubted she'd have survived.

The moss burst into flame, burning away from the mountain, and gave the rock definition, particularly around the face Aran had pointed out earlier. The "mountain peak" was a pair of spiraling horns topping a draconic head. The slopes of the mountain revealed themselves as two colossal wings wrapped around the Wyrm.

Rocks and burning trees tumbled away as the island trembled. A pair of starport-sized eyes blinked slowly open, and the wings slowly unfolded. The Wyrm raised its head and looked around.

Its gaze settled on Nara. She floated there in her spellarmor, paralyzed. Perhaps, if she kept very still, the creature wouldn't notice her.

One of those eyes moved to within a few meters of her, the golden slit narrowing as it studied her. "If you believe remaining still will protect you from my wrath, you are very much mistaken. I see you, tiny mage. I hear your thoughts, and that of many others. There is much that concerns me."

The Wyrm's voice thrummed through Nara's entire body, and she was thankful for the suit's protection.

"You should be concerned," Aran yelled, zipping into view over Nara's head. The eye moved away from Nara. She could have kissed him. "She stopped a ritual designed to enslave you."

The Wyrm rose to its full height, shook itself, then

scratched behind an ear with a leg that could have flattened most towns. "Yes, I am unsurprised. I see Krox's damnable children are here. They were always fond of such tricks. I will see them...punished, for their transgression. Then we will speak of yours."

62

FLEE

Nebiat couldn't remember a finer moment, not in all her centuries. Those able to vex her rarely survived long enough to present a challenge, but in her short time this pitiful human had managed to wreak incalculable damage on the Krox invasion timeline.

Now, she'd have her moment of vengeance. Major Voria's infernal interference would finally be at an end. Then she could return to—

Nebiat's head shot up, facing the mountain. Someone was manipulating her spell, making significant alterations. She flapped her wings, gaining enough altitude to see the ritual circle.

A human in spellarmor stood in the center, manipulating the ritual. A second human, this one a tech mage, battled her followers outside the circle. He moved in a way that could only be achieved with immense magic, but that magic was already fading. Soon, her followers would overwhelm him—but not soon enough.

The spell reached a crescendo, which should not have

been possible with the amount of power available. Not unless significant parts of the spell had been removed.

The mountain rumbled, and the great Guardian Drakkon stood up for the first time in dozens of millennia. His gleaming blue scales were magnificent, many times older and thicker than Nebiat's, covering a body brimming with power far greater than even her father could muster.

The magical slumber imprisoning Drakkon had dissolved, as planned. But where the binding should lay—the part that would allow her to control his mind—there was nothing.

The Guardian was awake, and free-willed.

Nebiat considered her course for a single heartbeat. Then she fled. Voria could be killed at her leisure, but if she didn't leave right now Drakkon would turn his attention to her. She very much doubted she'd enjoy the results.

Fortunately, enough of her followers had survived to serve as a distraction—a distraction she intended to use, immediately.

Nebiat banked toward the mist, quickly sketching a short range teleportation. She used it three more times in rapid succession, blinking a thousand meters each time. Then she flapped her wings furiously, fleeing for orbit. She glanced down at the battle, at the retreating forms of her followers, only once.

Nebiat had spent seven centuries building this army—seven centuries slowly recruiting and manipulating. And now, that army was gone. Not a single Krox would escape, of that Nebiat was sure. Her surviving brothers and sisters were about to meet their end.

She'd no doubt be punished for this failure, but at least she'd be alive to be punished.

Once she reached the upper atmosphere, Nebiat

stopped flapping and took over with her gravity magic. She shot up into orbit, away from the hated world below. She could still feel Drakkon's strength, and knew merely reaching orbit wasn't enough to keep her safe.

Nebiat plunged into the void, fleeing for the planet's umbral shadow. She wouldn't stop fleeing until she reached the Erkadi Rift, where her father could offer his protection.

63

MARID

The torrent of emotions threatened to swamp Voria. She could do nothing but stare—first as the mountain stood up, then as Nebiat fled. She'd reconciled herself to death, and it remained unclear whether that was still about to happen.

"Lieutenant, do you copy?" Voria said into the comm. She could see a pair of tiny figures hovering in the air near the Guardian, and prayed those figures were her people.

"Affirmative, sir," Aran whispered—only a breath, really.

"Status report."

"Well, uh, you can pretty much see the status," Aran protested. "I'm not sure what to report. Nara woke it up, and it looks pissed. She said something about removing a binding from the spell."

Voria grinned, then she began to laugh. She laughed so hard tears streamed down her cheeks.

"Sir?" Captain Davidson called from the tank's interior.

"It's nothing, Captain." Voria struggled to catch her breath, still chuckling. "I understand what happened now. There was no seal over the wound—or rather, the Guardian *is* the seal. Nebiat wanted to enslave him, to take control of this place. Can you imagine unleashing that thing on Ternus?"

"Uh. That would be a very short, very messy battle." Davidson gave a low whistle. "But Nebiat doesn't control this thing, so now what?"

"That's the question, isn't it?" Voria said, still watching the Wyrm.

It raised a single claw, sketching a sigil. That sigil grew into two, then twenty, then countless sigils. They burst out from the Wyrm in an endless wave, growing in all directions. Wherever the sigils touched, death followed. The flows moved unerringly toward the Krox, singling out Enforcers and corpses alike. They even wove into the sky, catching the several remaining Wyrms. Every last dragon died in just a few heartbeats.

Voria's mouth went dry. She'd always considered herself a quick thinker, but in the sight of something of this... magnitude, she simply didn't know what to do. For the first time in her life, Voria had no idea which course of action to take. Should she flee? Would it even matter?

The dragon took a step, and a blast of blue-green light flooded out of the place where the Wyrm had been standing.

"Oh, no," she whispered.

"What is it?" Davidson asked.

"The Guardian was covering the heart wound. Now that it's gone, there's nothing between us and the strongest Catalyst I have ever seen." Voria braced herself.

Blue-green light exploded outward in all directions, blinding her. She had only a moment to fear for Davidson's safety, and then Voria was sucked into the mind of a dreaming god.

She'd catalized before, but each time had been different. Each god saw the universe in a unique way. Some had been violent and filled with rage, others peaceful and content.

This mind, she could tell immediately, was ordered. Logical.

Yes. You see into my mind. I am called Marid, the same name your people use for this world.

Her consciousness was plucked up like an insect, and dropped a hundred hundred centuries in the past. She appeared in an unfamiliar star system, a blue star floating alone save for a tightly packed cluster of asteroids, shaped roughly into a sphere.

You see the world Ephera—or its remains. My children used their magic to keep the planet from final destruction, and even managed to preserve an atmosphere.

Ships flitted back and forth between fragments, dozens of them. Her perspective zoomed closer, and she saw entire settlements on the larger asteroids. A thriving culture dwelt there, thriving among the ruins of their planet.

"Why are you showing me this?" Voria asked. "And how is it you can show me anything? I thought you were dead."

You are speaking with an echo, one I created at the moment of my death. Even now your young companion experiences that death, trapped in the memory of my final confrontation with Shivan. I was created to speak to you, and when our conversation is done I will cease to exist.

"You knew I'd come, back during the godswar?" Voria asked, staggered by the implications.

Yes, but only if I made it so. I created a possibility where you might reach this world in time to stop Nebiat.

"You sent the augury, didn't you?" Voria asked, finally understanding.

Indirectly. At the moment of my death I created a living spell, one designed to carry out the billions of specific actions necessary to create this exact moment. That spell sent you the augury, and will send others in the days to come.

"Why me?" Voria asked.

You are not the only tool I have chosen. Each of you was chosen because you possess the abilities to accomplish part of a greater plan—a plan you are not yet ready to know in its entirety.

For this part of the plan, you were not the most important variable. In every possibility where you were used to stop the ritual the Wyrm Nebiat slew you. So I sought another possibility. I arranged for you to have a true mage, and a war mage. Both had no memory, making their threads very difficult to predict.

"You're talking about Aran and Nara. You've jerked us about like a puppets." Voria's words were cold. Speaking angrily to a god might not be the best idea, but from the sound of it this thing needed her. "The least you can do is explain to me why you did it, and what you're after."

For now, be content knowing that I oppose Krox. If he rises, your galaxy will be reshaped to fit his whims. Krox, like me, is one of the eldest gods. He possesses both the power and will to enslave your species. If allowed to rise, Krox will raise other gods. And he will enslave them, forcing them to help reshape the galaxy. There is no end to his lust for control.

I release you now, to leave this world and continue to fulfill your purpose. The days ahead will be difficult, and you will make many sacrifices. If you succeed, you will die, but the galaxy will survive.

If you fail, you will become that which you fear most. Be ever vigilant, mortal.

64

ANSWERS

A well of infinite power burst up underneath Aran, blinding him even as the power swept over his armor. It suffused his being, the unfamiliar energy resonating with every cell in his body. Then, as it had been with Xal, he was elsewhere—in the memory of a god.

He—she—stretched out vast, leathery wings. There was no need, as her magic propelled her through the vastness of the void. Her shadow covered the entire planet, a blue-green world rotating around a bright orange sun. That world bore the same name she did: Marid.

This world had potential; it was the first to be worthy of her name. The life she had seeded flowered across all its continents, expressing itself in a variety of ways. The species were as of yet primitive and superstitious. They believed their world the only one in the cosmos, the center of the infinite they were so ignorant of. Yet, in time, they would progress much.

Marid raised her head ponderously, looking back the way she had come. Something twinkled there, too bright to be a star, too bright even to be a planet. Too large to be one of the crude spell-

ships the younger gods were constructing. There was only one thing it could be: a god. An old one.

She hovered in space over her world, preparing a litany of magical defenses. Yet, as the deity approached, Marid knew all those preparations were useless.

"Why have you come, Shivan?" Marid demanded, floating a bit further away from the world so it would not be caught in a stray spell, should this turn to battle.

"I have come with grave news," the destroyer said. He cradled an immense golden spear in his right hand. Marid recognized Worldender, though she'd never thought to be its target. "Draco Matrem has fallen. Her mind has been ensnared, her body left where it can draw out her children. When they approach, Krox seizes them. He plants his own children within hers. It was a masterful stroke."

Marid recoiled, the implications rippling outward. She contemplated sixteen trillion possibilities, quickly reaching an equilibrium. "Then only I remain, of the eldest. Should Krox take me, all the Wyrms will serve that monster. The galaxy will never recover."

"Yes," Shivan said, hanging his head.

"Yet Krox will not face me himself. Instead, he sends you. When did he seize you, Shivan?" Marid asked, sadly inspecting her cousin's aura.

"Countless millennia ago. His hooks were buried deep—so deep I didn't even recognize them, until he pulled them for the first time." Shivan raised Worldender. "I am sorry, cousin. It shames me to be an instrument in this."

Marid sketched a defensive ward, even as the spear left Shivan's hand. The weapon twisted in the void, growing closer at an alarming rate. Marid considered three trillion possibilities. Only two might result in the eventual defeat of Krox, and neither allowed her survival.

Marid abandoned her ward, instead sketching a complex spell. She breathed upon it, giving the spell life. "Go now. Go to the world I have shown you. Take up residence, and wait for her to come. When she does, aid her against Krox and his foul children."

The spell swam through the void. Thankfully, Shivan did nothing to stop it. Perhaps it was a final sign of defiance, a shred of his will maintained in the face of Krox's binding. Whatever the reason, the spell escaped, even as Worldender punched through Marid's chest. The weapon carried her into the world below.

Her coming doomed her children on this world, filling the sky with endless dust and ash that would blot out the sun for full cycles. How pathetic that her last thought was for her children. How fitting. That compassion was the reason they were losing, the reason their children were being overcome.

Marid stared up into orbit, watching as Shivan flew from the shattered world. Already her mind fragmented, thoughts breaking apart as she crumbled.

Aran came to with choking gasps, looking around frantically as he tried to understand who and where he was, to understand what he'd seen in Marid's mind.

"Yes, you begin to understand," the Guardian rumbled, its slitted eye moved within a few meters. Aran could only gawk. "I see my mother has gifted you with water magic, to aid you in your war against Krox and his children."

Aran realized the beast was speaking to him. He looked around, not seeing any of the others. As the beast had indicated, he felt a new source of power in his chest. It was cool, and fluid, ready to be called upon.

Nor was it the only thing changed. Aran's armor was whole, the battle damage completely repaired. His spellrifle had grown longer, and now bore a primitive intelligence just as his spellblade had. This one seemed more curious, and less aggressive.

"You are the first to return. In a few moments, we will see if they too have survived a brush with my mother's mind."

"So, uh, this is your mother's grave?" Aran asked. How did one make small talk with a demigod dragon Guardian mountain thing?

"Indeed, and I am the Guardian of that grave. Though I have tended poorly to my responsibility. In my grief at my mother's death, I sought magical slumber. I hid from the truth, and hid my mother as well. First, I moved the world to a distant system, planting it in orbit around a similar sun. Then I created the ward to hide my mother's signature. I hoped the other young gods would come together to kill Krox, and I can see from your memories that they seem to have succeeded."

"What will you do now?" Aran asked, feeling a swell of pity for the poor creature, even if it did scare him enough that he wanted to wet himself.

"In breaking the ward, your companion has left me little choice." The Wyrm flapped its wings, turning in midair to face the night sky. "The primals will come now, a vast swarm of them. They will seek my mother's light. If I do not stay and protect them, then Krox's children will enslave them. They will be sent to scourge your worlds, and the carnage will be terrible for both sides."

"You paint a pretty grim picture. But you're going to stay here and raise these primals?" Aran asked.

"I will shepherd them, and I will watch over this world. When the time comes, I will lead them into battle against the children of Krox. I do not yet know who leads them, though I am thankful Krox himself is dead. If he were not, all of us would be nothing more than mindless husks." The

Wyrm glided gracefully, landing silently despite weighing as much as a small mountain. "Ahh, your companions emerge from mother's mind. I will return you to your vessel, where you may rejoice in your shared survival."

"What if we need to contact you?" Aran asked, knowing the major would want him to ask.

"You have not seen the last of me, war mage. One day, we will ride to battle together, against an unbeatable foe."

"Uh, okay," Aran allowed. "See you around?"

There was a blinding flash of light, and Aran was standing back in the *Wyrm Hunter's* hangar.

65

CONSEQUENCES

Aran stared down at the blue-white planet through the hangar's airlock membrane. It looked so peaceful from up here, so untroubled by all the suffering and death that had taken place over the last few days. He rested a hand against the bulkhead, thankful that —for now at least—the dying was over.

He didn't really understand everything that had happened, or what he'd seen inside Marid's mind. They were embroiled in something larger than them, a war between gods that had died dozens of millennia ago. Longer, maybe. But somehow, they had a role to play in that war.

Aran could feel Marid down there, the power echoed inside of him. He'd gained something there. Water magic, if Drakkon were correct. Maybe he'd even have enough time to learn what that meant now that he wasn't being shot at.

"I feel naked without my armor." Nara's voice came from behind Aran, startling him out of his reverie. He shifted to face her, smiling.

"All I heard was naked," Bord said, sprinting up. "I'll play the pity card if I have to. I mean, I did die..." He grinned at Nara hopefully, and Nara rolled her eyes.

Aran couldn't help but laugh. As crass and crude as Bord was, the bastard was growing on him.

"Just go wait in the airlock, Bord," Nara said sweetly. "I'll be right in."

"You can't jettison me into space. You need me. I'm the healer. And I'm a water mage now." He pointed both of his thumbs back toward his chest. He did start walking away, though, back toward the stall where his armor sat. "Also I'm pretty. Don't forget that. If you change your mind, I'll be right over here, watching."

"Yeah, watching creepily," Kez said, hopping down from her armor. She put a hand on the small of her back, stretching. "I know what you mean, Nara. After so many days in that armor, I feel weird outside of it. Like I'm going to get picked off by a sniper."

Bord started walking back over to the drifter. "You're right, Kez. Being in that armor was murder on my back, too. I bet you could use a massage—"

"That you'd be happy to give her?" The major's voice came from the edge of the hangar. She walked swiftly in their direction, Captain Davidson in tow. He'd been almost mute since they'd returned from the swamp, and hadn't spoken about whatever ability he'd gained from the Catalyst.

Aran couldn't really blame him. His Marines had been wiped out nearly to a man, and from what Aran gathered that outcome was all too common at the end of most battles involving the Krox. It was a sobering reminder of the price they paid every time they fought.

"Uh, hello, Major." Bord hurried away from Kez, back to

his own armor. "I wasn't doing anything improper, just, uh trying to fulfill my duties as medic."

"At ease, Specialist." The major gave a rare smile. It softened her face so much Aran barely recognized her. "I've come to talk about what happens next."

"Already?" Crewes said, clanking up in his armor. The surface had been scorched black during the battle, and it amazed Aran that it still functioned. He lit a cigar with a small torch, then used an armored hand to put it between his lips. "Come on sir, how about a day off?"

"Sergeant, we delivered a crippling blow to the Krox here. These Wyrms cannot simply be replaced. But that will only make the Krox more desperate, and desperate enemies make bold moves," the major explained. She clasped her hands behind her back, pursing her lips. "I didn't come to put you to work, though. You'll have plenty of time to relax over the next week, while we're in the Umbral Depths. Now that the battle is decided, I need to report to Shaya, to answer for my actions here. There is every likelihood I will be stripped of command."

Everyone protested at once, but fell silent when she raised a hand.

Aran spoke up. "Sir, they can't do that. If you hadn't done everything exactly as you did, this planet would belong to the Krox. They'd have had an unstoppable army in another year or two."

"Ternus will speak up for you, at the very least," Davidson pointed out. "Admiral Kerr thinks the world of you, and the people think the world of the admiral. You've got a strong ally there."

"Isn't your mother an important part of the consortium?" Bord asked, blinking.

"Enough," the major snapped, the smile gone. She

raised a hand when Crewes moved to speak. "I appreciate what you're doing. Anything could happen when we reach Shaya. I do have allies, and our success here gives us some leverage as well. Depths, they could even decorate us. But I want you to be prepared for the very real possibility I will have to answer for my decisions here. My career could be over. We'll fight that battle soon enough."

"You've got our full support," Aran said, "for whatever that's worth."

The rest of the company nodded their agreement.

Crewes awkwardly patted the major's back. "You might catch some flak for what happened here, sir. Especially to Thalas. But in my book? You did something no one else could. We're proud of you, sir."

"Today's victory wouldn't have been possible without all of us working together. That said, there's one person I think needs to be thanked publicly." The major looked uncomfortable in a way Aran had never seen. "I'm sorry, Aran, about forcing you to enlist. Technically, my actions were legal, but they are against the spirit of the law. My brother gave you a way out, and no one would have blamed you for taking it. I wouldn't have blamed you. Thank you for choosing to fight."

"I understand why you did what you did, sir." Aran smiled, releasing a tension he hadn't even realized he'd been holding onto. "You did the right thing. At first I wanted to run. I thought this wasn't my fight, but after peering into the mind of Marid...after seeing what Krox did, and what Nebiat and the other Void Wyrms are doing in his name? They have to be stopped. I'm committed to that now. This is bigger than us."

"I couldn't agree more," Nara said, offering a hand to the major. After a moment the major took it. "I don't know who

I was before, but I know who I am now. I'm a Confederate Mage, sir. And I'm with you."

"And I'll be right behind her, staring at her backside," Bord said, framing his hands over Nara's butt. He gave her an exaggerated wink, which she ignored.

"All right then," Voria said, sliding her hands into her pockets. "You've got the day off. Tomorrow, we start training in water magic. That includes you, Captain Davidson."

"Sir?" Davidson said. "I'm a Marine. I need to rebuild my unit, not prance around as a tech mage."

"There's nothing to say the head of the Marines can't be a tech mage. And you've now got an unfair advantage, Captain. One you can use to protect your men." The major pointed across the hangar at the three surviving tanks.

Aran hadn't noticed them, but now that he looked he realized one of the tanks was larger and sleeker than the others.

"Inuran technology is a blend of magic and tech, Captain. Every tank is designed to benefit from a Catalyst, and yours is now both more powerful and bonded to you," Voria explained. She smiled, patting him on the shoulder. "I know we've sacrificed a lot—but not everything. In some ways, we emerged stronger, better able to protect our people in the next battle with the Krox."

Davidson stared dumbly at the tank. Then he started to smile. It was the first crack in the depression they'd seen since Davidson had learned the fate of his men. "Well, all right then. Let's get back to Shaya, get the major cleared, and then get back in the action."

Aran stared at the lot of them, from Nara and Kez laughing, to the grin on Davidson's normally too serious face. Somehow, these people had become family. He might not have a past, but he damned sure had a future.

EPILOGUE

Nebiat halted her flight, sketching the first sigil in her Fissure spell. It brought light to a lightless plane, a beacon for the denizens of this place. Even she feared the worst of what lurked in the depths, though the odds of anything threatening reaching her before she completed the Fissure were slim.

She sketched the next sigil, and the next. The process look longer than it would have if cast through a starship, and she knew her father would chide her for her growing dependence upon such technology.

A heavy crack split reality, fissuring outward around the break. The cracks widened, their blazing purple glow illuminating the depths behind her. Nebiat saw something slithering through the void in the distance, growing slowly larger.

She plunged through the Fissure, releasing the magic behind her. It snapped shut, walling her off from the depths. If she had needed to breathe, she'd have sighed in relief. As old as her kind were, they were children compared to the things that lurked in that place.

Nebiat focused on the system she'd arrived in. A large red dwarf smoldered near the center, orbited by dozens of worlds. Each world belonged to a Void Wyrm, but she didn't make for her own world, the fourth in the system.

Instead Nebiat flew toward the second system, the world belonging to her father. It was a tiny ball of magma, a pool of superheated rock kept together by the star's still considerable gravity. She made for the planet's light side, scanning seas of magma as she sought her father.

An enormous black spot lay right under the surface of the southernmost magma sea, the hottest part of the planet. She glided closer, hovering over the world but keeping to high orbit, ready to flee if she had to.

The magma around the black spot roiled and bubbled, ejecting a Wyrm many times larger than herself—larger even than Drakkon had been. Her father's scales were covered in scalding magma, which quickly cooled to a thick rocky crust as he glided up into orbit.

"Tell me everything." He raised both wings, basking in the glow of the nearby sun.

"Kheftut is dead. Drakkon is awake, but not bound." Nebiat left out the part about every other Wyrm she'd been sent with also being dead. It was trivial, next to the other two facts.

"So, you've managed to free one of our most powerful enemies, while ensuring he has cause to focus solely on opposing us," her father roared, the magic surging up within him.

Nebiat cringed, but resisted the urge to flee. She couldn't outrun her father.

"In the process, you lost your elder brother—and, I suspect, all your younger siblings?"

"Yes, father," she said, as meek as she'd ever been.

Her father flipped over, exposing his back to the sun. He basked for several seconds before speaking again. "I do not believe you are entirely at fault in this."

"Father?" she asked, blinking. "I don't understand."

"I've long suspected the intervention of a third party," her father mused, "a god or gods bent on opposing Krox." He looked at her, flames flaring in his eye sockets. "This time I have a much simpler task for you. Find this god. Destroy their tools. Lay waste to their plans. Can you do this for me, daughter? Or should I consume you now and hope my next spawning proves more fruitful?"

"I will not fail you again, father. I know exactly who our enemies are using as their principle agent, and I look forward to picking apart Major Voria's mind to find out who she serves."

Nebiat smiled cruelly, already envisioning Voria's adoring smile after her will was broken.

Want to know when **Void Wyrm: Magitech Chronicles Book 2** goes live?

Sign up to the mailing list!

Check out MagitechChronicles.com for book releases, lore, artwork, and more!